FOREVER *and* FOREVER

OTHER PROPER ROMANCE NOVELS

Lord Fenton's Folly by Josi S. Kilpack

A Heart Revealed by Josi S. Kilpack

My Fair Gentleman by Nancy Campbell Allen

Edenbrooke by Julianne Donaldson

Blackmoore by Julianne Donaldson

Longing for Home by Sarah M. Eden

Longing for Home, vol. 2: Hope Springs by Sarah M. Eden

OTHER BOOKS BY JOSI S. KILPACK

The Sadie Hoffmiller Culinary Mystery Series:
Lemon Tart, English Trifle, Devil's Food Cake, Key Lime Pie, Blackberry Crumble, Pumpkin Roll, Banana Split, Tres Leches Cupcakes, Baked Alaska, Rocky Road, Fortune Cookie, Wedding Cake, Sadie's Little Black Recipe Book

FOREVER *and* FOREVER

The Courtship of HENRY LONGFELLOW
and FANNY APPLETON

JOSI S. KILPACK

Visit us at ShadowMountain.com

Library of Congress Cataloging-in-Publication Data

Kilpack, Josi S., author.

Forever and forever : the courtship of Henry Longfellow and Fanny Appleton / Josi S. Kilpack.

pages cm

Summary: "Based on the true love story of poet Henry Wadsworth Longfellow and Boston socialite Fanny Appleton, this novel chronicles their seven-year courtship through Europe and Boston" —Provided by publisher.

ISBN 978-1-62972-142-2 (paperbound)

1. Longfellow, Henry Wadsworth, 1807–1882—Fiction. 2. Courtship—United States—History—19th century—Fiction. 3. Longfellow, Fanny Appleton, 1817–1861—Fiction. 4. Boston (Mass.), setting. I. Title.

PS3561.I412F667 2016

813'.54—dc23 2015030576

Printed in the United States of America

Edwards Brothers Malloy, Ann Arbor, MI

10 9 8 7 6 5 4 3 2 1

Author's Note

Listen, my children, and you shall hear
Of the midnight ride of Paul Revere,
On the eighteenth of April, in Seventy-five;
Hardly a man is now alive
Who remembers that famous day and year.

In 1861, Henry Wadsworth Longfellow wrote "Paul Revere's Ride," which has since become many people's reference point to an event that ushered in the Revolutionary War and resulted in America's freedom from British rule. Longfellow was the grandson of Revolutionary soldiers from both sides of his family tree and a great patriot in his own right.

He knew that Revere was not the only rider who set off to warn the colonist troops and that Revere himself was captured at Lexington on his way to Concord. Longfellow's goal in his narrative poem was not to give a perfectly accurate historical account of the event, but rather to keep the story from becoming myth. He also wanted to remind readers of the importance of patriotism, even as the United States faced events that would shortly lead to the Civil War.

AUTHOR'S NOTE

In writing the love story between Henry and Fanny Longfellow, I have used the same license as Longfellow. The public details regarding their courtship—as relayed through biographers, letters, and journals—are minimal, and I have attempted to flesh out the facts enough to bring Henry and Fanny to life again.

It is my hope that you will read this novel knowing it is a creation based on impressions made upon me through my study of fact and crafted through possibility. This story is not meant to be a biography or detailed accounting, but rather a sketch of two people who lived, and struggled, and ultimately loved one another enough to find great happiness together.

If, after reading this novel, you feel drawn to see a broader scope of Mr. and Mrs. Longfellow, please consult the bibliography, which lists the nonfiction resources I explored in creating the framework for this story. There are also Chapter Notes at the end of the book that outline specific details of fact and fiction.

Lives of great men all remind us
We can make our lives sublime,
And, departing, leave behind us
Footprints on the sands of time;

—From Henry Wadsworth Longfellow,
"A Psalm of Life," 1839

1836

Europe

One

Thun, Switzerland

The increasing rain made Frances Gold Appleton—Fanny, to her friends and family—quicken her step. She looked up from beneath the brim of her bonnet long enough to measure the distance left between her feet and the door of the chalet where her family had been staying for the last five days. Fifteen yards. Ten. Six. Four. Two.

She burst through the door and shut it behind her quickly, leaving the rain to wash the already clean Swiss streets and clear the already clear Swiss air. With her back against the heavy wooden door, Fanny took a breath and smiled. Her exertion had left her skin tingling and her heart racing.

Fanny's older sister, Mary—though everyone called her Molly—stepped out from the parlor. "How was your walk?" she asked. "You were longer than I expected."

Fanny untied the ribbons of her bonnet, now soaked through, and smiled at her sister. "I watched the most impressive storm roll in," she said. "And simply could not tear myself away." The storm had swallowed the Bernese Alps as the clouds descended into the Thun valley and then crawled upon the silvery lake toward the red-roofed village as though it were a cat creeping toward its prey. That Fanny had waited too long to turn toward the chalet, however—not wanting to miss a moment of nature's show upon the most excellent of canvases—was her responsibility. "I'm sorry if I worried you, Molly."

Molly nodded her forgiveness and then glanced through the parlor doorway, causing Fanny to realize her lateness was not all that had raised Molly's anxiety.

"Is William no better, then?" Fanny lowered her voice even though she could see that their cousin William—he was like a brother to them all—was asleep on the lounge. His face was gray, and his increasing frailness was reflected in his thin face and hands.

At first, the demands of traveling seemed to be well with him—just as the family had hoped when they had invited him to join their Grand Tour. Such European trips were once reserved for young men just like William, but now they were accessible for any family wealthy enough to spare the expense. Fanny's father, Nathan Appleton, had generously included William in the hope that Europe would be kinder to his frail health than Boston had been these last years. William had done well on the sea voyage, and he'd enjoyed France and Italy with almost the same energy as any of the rest of them. But he'd caught an influenza in Florence that left him with a cough that triggered the Appletons' anxiety. Consumption, the doctor said a few weeks later. The diagnosis had felt like bullets.

The family went to Switzerland in hopes that the mountain air would bring William relief. They had been in Switzerland several days, however, and little improvement had followed.

"He says he feels better, but he has eaten little."

"Perhaps he will take some broth when he awakens," Fanny said.

"Perhaps," Molly said, but her fear hung unspoken between them. What would they do if William's condition worsened? What if he died as their brother Charles had not quite a year ago, and their own mother a year and a half before that, when Fanny was just fifteen? For a brief moment Fanny wondered how any of them could still have hope of recovery when one after another of their loved ones fell prey to the dreadful disease. What was the point of hope at all?

"You must get out of those wet things," Molly interrupted, saving Fanny from the dark road of her thoughts. "I shall order some broth for William and see that tea is ready by four o'clock. I do not think I will join you, however. I fear my headache has not improved."

"I am sorry you were worried for me *and* in such discomfort," Fanny said, frowning. She should have been more compassionate for her sister who suffered while she had allowed the rapture of the Thun valley to carry her away, if only for a few minutes. She vowed to be better.

"It is no matter now," Molly said, though she raised a hand to her head. "I shall rest awhile and hope to join you all for dinner. Father said he and Tom would be back in time for tea. I shall leave you to explain my absence."

"You are very good," Fanny said, giving her sister a grateful smile before casting one more glance toward their sleeping cousin.

Perhaps hope of recovery is *a foolish thing,* she thought as she climbed the stairs in search of a dry dress and a more optimistic perspective, but did not a hopeful countenance comfort those who were afflicted? Did it not allow their failing days to progress more peaceably when those about them seemed unaware of the impending doom? Would it not do anything but increase William's pain if his family mourned him already?

And he might not *die,* Fanny reminded herself. They were in Switzerland, where the air was cleaner than any other in the world and the water more pure. *If ever there has been reason for hope, it is here, and I shan't deny William such a thing.*

At a quarter to four o'clock, Fanny returned to the main level of the chateau dressed in her favorite London day dress of pink linen; it would be the envy of all her friends once she returned to Boston. The Appleton girls had loved Paris, making themselves drunk on the art, shopping, and opera. From there they traveled to Italy and the more classical style Fanny adored. By now, nine months into their journey, most of the clothing Fanny had brought with her for the tour had been sent back to Boston. She had a European wardrobe and a broader view of the world than ever before.

If Father had not enjoyed indulging his daughters, Fanny would feel badly for allowing him such generosity, but a new light had entered their father's eyes during this trip. Removed from the loss of his wife and son, Father had indulged his mind in culture, theater, art, and the company of people he admired. His energy had returned, his mind had quickened, and he approached each new portion of their journey with renewed enthusiasm. He seemed alive once again. Spoiling his daughters was simply another way he was returning to the man Fanny remembered from her youth.

If not for William's recent decline, this trip would have been a dream, and Fanny was reminded of her hope as she entered the parlor. William was sitting on the settee, but had a rug over his lap and seemed to be leaning against the piece of furniture to better support himself. He smiled when he saw her, as he always did, and waved her into the room. On the table beside him was a mug Fanny assumed had held broth. She was relieved to see it empty. He needed nourishment to get his strength back.

"Ah, dear cousin," he said, patting the cushion beside him. "It is about time you came to keep me company. Tell me what you saw today. Paint it for me in such rich color that it is though I were there too."

The request stung Fanny's chest—it was not fair that he should be in such a beautiful place as this and confined to the views from the windows—but she remembered her earlier determination to not add to his burden and so she ignored the sting and did as he asked, using every beautiful word she could think of to let him see through her eyes and feel through her skin the impressions of the day. William was two years older than Fanny—the same age as her brother Charles, now buried in Boston. Would William live to turn twenty-one? She pushed the thought from her mind and focused on her telling.

At some point William closed his eyes, and Fanny feared he had fallen asleep until she paused in her narrative and he lifted a thin hand to wave her to continue. She was finishing an exaggerated version of her run to the chalet when the front door of the house opened and she heard the boisterous voices of Tom—her older brother by nearly six years—and Father. William opened his eyes, and Fanny rose from her place.

"What bulls they are," she said with a smile to her cousin before moving forward to greet the men.

William laughed at Fanny's joke, but his mirth turned to a cough, and he was soon pressing his handkerchief to his mouth. Fanny returned to the settee, took his free hand in both of hers, and blinked back the tears building up behind her eyes. He was in such pain, his body was wracked with it, and yet there was nothing they could do other than administer the laudanum that allowed him rest and hold his hand to provide a measure of comfort.

By the time William recovered from the fit—his body spent—Tom and Father had entered the parlor, sharing worried glances between them. An uncomfortable silence greeted them. William opened red and pained eyes. He attempted a smile even as he slumped back against the settee.

Fanny tried to think of some way to distract them all from what had happened but worry prevented her from finding a topic.

"A card, Uncle Nathan," William said between ragged breaths, providing the distraction himself. Perhaps too well as Fanny had no idea what he was talking about.

"A card?" Father repeated, as confused as his daughter.

"By the door," William said, then paused to catch his breath. "A man called while you were out. . . . Burns took his card. It's on the table, just there."

Tom crossed to the small table near the doorway and picked up the card.

"Henry Wadsworth Longfellow of Portland, Maine," Tom read out loud as he returned to his chair and handed the calling card to Father.

Father took it and held it at arm's length; he often commented on the burden of old eyes. "Longfellow," Father mused. "How do I know that name?"

"He wrote *Outré Mer,*" Fanny said with a frown. "I hope he does not call on us, he sounds like very dull company." In every city they visited, they had been called on by any number of politicians, distant acquaintances, or friends of friends. For the most part it was enjoyable to meet new people and have women willing to chaperone her and Molly through the cities. But a venerable writer—for Mr. Longfellow was certainly an old man—sounded not the least bit diverting. Fanny much preferred dancing, music, and adventurous stories that would lift her from the ever-increasing doom that licked at her heels. Not old men and pipe smoke.

"Not even a year in Europe and look at what a snob you have become," Tom said, raising his eyebrows. "Did you not like the book?"

The maid brought the tea tray in and placed it on the table set in the center of the room.

"I liked it well enough," Fanny admitted, almost despite herself. She had read *Outré Mer* in preparation for this very trip as the book was a collection of prose sketches from a European tour the author had taken some years earlier. Mr. Longfellow's name had not been listed on the work, but there were not so many Americans publishing books for their identities to remain a secret.

Mr. Longfellow was a professor of some kind with an apparent appreciation of Spanish women Fanny did not find impressive. Beyond that and his writing she knew nothing of the man, which meant he was not part of the same social circles as her family—Maine or otherwise. She would already be acquainted with him if he were of their same level. It was her experience that people within her own social class were far more respectful of her father, whereas those with something to gain by being known by him put great effort into being noticed.

Fanny poured the tea while she justified her feelings regarding the visit of Mr. Longfellow, or anyone else for that matter. "I have simply enjoyed the peace of Switzerland and am not eager to entertain a stranger." She imagined an old man wanting to pontificate on literature with her father, who did not know that topic as well as he liked to think he did. And moreover, why would a professor of literature seek out her father's attention in the first place? The literary types were not usually so determined to connect with the wealthy industrialist. In fact, did they not see wealth and society as beneath the notice of their more *sophisticated* minds?

"Why are you smiling?" Tom said, accepting the cup and saucer she handed him.

"No matter," Fanny said, embarrassed by her private thoughts. She dropped the smile and refocused on her duties.

"I am not opposed to a visit," Father said after replacing his cup on the saucer. "Did he say where he is staying, William?"

"I don't believe so," William said. He had taken a sip of tea when Fanny first handed him the cup, but now the saucer rested in his lap, and Fanny worried he lacked the strength to hold it up.

"It would not be hard to find him in a village as small as this," Tom said. "I shall undertake the task if you would like, Father."

Fanny let out a sigh, then felt caught when she realized her response had drawn her brother and father's attention. "I'm sorry," Fanny said, sincerely sorry for being petulant. "I should not have complained. Molly and I would be most happy to welcome Mr. Longfellow if you would like to make his acquaintance."

Father sipped his tea, then lowered the cup and shook his head. "Upon greater thought, we leave for Interlaken soon, and it would be difficult to accommodate him before we go. But I thank you for the offer to find him, Tom. Besides, if this Mr. Longfellow is on a tour then our paths shall cross again. Fanny has the right of it, I think."

Tom snorted and Fanny looked sharply at him. "What?" she said, not wanting his censure even as she realized she likely deserved it.

"Oh nothing, *Lady Frances,*" Tom said with a lilting voice. "Only that I am *so* very glad that *your* comforts shall come before everyone else's."

Fanny felt her neck heat up. "I did not ask that my comfort should—"

Tom cut her off with a laugh, followed by a wink. It seemed she had been on the losing end of his joking nature all her life. She narrowed her eyes at him and then turned pointedly to her father and asked what they had done while they were out.

The conversation swirled around the room until William leaned forward and attempted to put his nearly full cup of tea on the table. There was not have enough table beneath the saucer when he released it and the cup tumbled to the floor, spilling tea all over his lap rug as well as the carpet.

"Oh, I am sorry," he said as Fanny hurried to retrieve the cup.

"It is no matter," she said, giving him a reassuring smile. "The cup did not break, and tea is easy enough to clean up." She turned toward the door. "Burns!" she called. A moment later the hired man appeared in the doorway, and she asked him to send the maid with a cloth.

The reminder of William's frailty ushered awkward silence into the room. Fanny set about clearing the tea tray to spare her from the halting attempts at conversation between Tom and Father. Once the maid had cleaned up the spilled tea and left, William cleared his throat.

"Uncle Nathan."

Fanny could hear the gravity in William's voice. He lifted his chin and fixed his eyes on the patriarch in a display of confidence. "I should like to speak with you in private, please."

Fanny's heart caught in her chest, and she met Tom's eyes only to see her own fear reflected there. When they had asked—fairly begged—William to come on this trip, he had agreed only under the condition that, should he become a burden on the rest of the party,

Father would support an early return for himself alone. As William's health had continued to fail these last weeks, Fanny had worried about him asking for such a council. He was not a burden. He was family. Fanny could not keep her tears at bay but tried to hide them from the others.

No one spoke for several seconds, until Father nodded. "If you wish to speak to me in private, William, I would accommodate it."

"Thank you, Uncle," William said, staring at the tea stain on the carpet.

Tom stood from his chair. "Let's remove to the upstairs sitting room, Fanny. You can tell me your thoughts of *Outré Mer*."

Unable to speak, Fanny nodded, left the tea tray, and walked from the room. Once the door was closed, and she was alone with Tom in the foyer, she covered her face with her hands and began to cry. Tom came up behind her and put a hand on her arm, then embraced her trembling shoulders. Fanny turned, muffling the sounds of her sobs in his coat. For all his teasing, Tom *was* her older brother, and he had a tender heart.

"We have known this was coming," Tom said, patting her back and attempting to sound soothing.

Fanny shook her head against his shoulder. Fearing such a turn and having it arrive were two very different things.

"He deserves our respect of his wishes, Fanny."

Does Tom still have hope for William? Fanny wondered. Did he feel William could survive the voyage home? And then what? They were not quite halfway through their Grand Tour and would not return to Boston for another year at least. Even if William made it to Boston Harbor, would he survive long enough for them to be reunited? Or would they see only his headstone, set beside the other Appleton graves of those who died too soon?

"How can we bear to lose another?" Fanny said when she could finally contain herself and pull away from Tom's coat. Was the only protection from this kind of pain not to let people inside one's heart? It was a vain thought, since she already loved her family so dearly, but surviving another loss seemed impossible. "What is the point of having a heart if it is only to be broken again and again?"

"I wish I knew the answer, Fanny," Tom said sadly, his face drawn. "I wish I knew."

Two

Interlaken, Switzerland

Henry Wadsworth Longfellow stood on the dock in Interlaken and watched the steam-powered boat—a relatively new addition for Lake Thun—move toward him and the other bystanders. He would not have guessed the ship would be in operation on a Sunday, but obviously he was mistaken. He looked from the crystal-clear, sea-green water to the majestic mountains holding the valley in its embrace and tried to find deep and profound words that would capture the timeless beauty of the Alps juxtaposed against the modern miracle of steam power. After struggling for some time, he sighed in defeat. Though he was a master of languages and a writer with a poet's soul, he could not describe the scene before him adequately.

So then, why am I here? he asked himself as he turned away from the lake. *What do I hope to gain from finishing this trip? What a solitary man I have become.*

Henry walked away from the dock, heading for his hotel, and reminded himself that he had not come to Europe simply to admire the place and wax poetic of the vistas. He'd come to shore up his qualifications for the position of Smith Professor at Harvard

College by returning to the places he had first seen ten years earlier. Remembering his reasons for being there, however, did not lessen the frustration he felt regarding the wall that seemed built up around the creative portions of his mind.

Henry's first European tour had lasted three years and cemented in him a love of Europe. He was an American to his bones and embraced the values and virtues of the young country with his whole heart, but being immersed in European culture and literature showed him the portions of American society that could be better. Stronger. More.

Now, he was here again to strengthen his European credential—only the trip had been nothing as he'd expected. When he had set out with his wife, Mary, more than a year ago, she had brought two traveling companions. Attending to three women had required considerable changes to the expectations of his trip. When Mary announced she was expecting a child, he'd been overjoyed, and yet concerned as well. Both for Mary, who had always been fragile, and for how he would get the education he needed while caring for a family.

That worry felt foolish now, vain and recriminating. Mary lost the baby several months into her pregnancy, and a month later, Henry lost her, too. Her body had been sent back to Boston in a lead-lined casket where she waited for a proper burial. That Henry had not returned with her filled him with guilt, yet he had to complete his tour; he could not afford to come again.

Clara Crowninshield, one of Mary's traveling companions, had wanted to stay as well. And so they did. He had tried to make the most of his months, closeting himself in university basements and sitting in the back corner of lecture halls, but his effort was halfhearted, and at times he worried he was too broken to ever be fit for Harvard, no matter how many languages he learned or books he added to his personal library.

Henry stopped in the middle of the sidewalk and tried once more to allow the scenery to overpower his heavy thoughts. The red rooftops rising above the white plaster walls, the cobbled streets with bright flowerpots that stood out like small, multicolored suns, and the whole of it framed by the green fields and splendor of the magnificent mountains. It should be the perfect distraction, and for a moment Henry *did* get lost in the beauty, then the horn of the boat sounded and his familiar melancholy muted his senses once again.

Perhaps his sorrow would forever be a part of him, like a curtain he must peer through all the days of his life. Mary had told him to live a full life, she had wished him to find a good woman and have a family, yet Henry could not imagine such a thing. To wish it, much less want it, felt wrong, but a life alone seemed worthless. Mary had been gone nine months, and he could not yet see his future without her.

Henry moved forward again, his legs burning from days spent trudging the alpine footpaths in hopes of outrunning his depression. The Hotel Beausite, the newest and most modern hotel in Interlaken, appeared ahead of him, and he longed for a hearty meal, a glass of wine, and a good book. He had indulged himself in the extravagant lodging in Interlaken in hopes it would restore his spirit. So far the grand lodgings had not done so, but the well-appointed room had not further lowered him as decrepit lodging had in the past. He had already shipped a trunk of books back to his parents' house in Portland, but he had several other works he was eager to read beside the fire. Books had become his closest friends these last months and his only escape.

In the hotel lobby Henry nodded a greeting to two men who seemed to be on their way out before he turned toward the hallway that would take him to his room.

The sound of his name being called in a thick accent caused Henry to turn around. The clerk at the front desk waved Henry over. He had written down the address of a man in town with a book collection—Mr. Gurmand would welcome Henry to peruse his books the following day. Henry took the paper and thanked the clerk in German before turning to see that the two men he'd passed a minute earlier were standing, waiting for his attention. He could see they were American and felt a twinge of disappointment that they might have noticed he was as well—if that were the case then his attempt to dress and sound like a European was poor indeed.

"Pardon our attention, sir," the older of the two men said. His companion looked enough like him to declare them father and son. "But did the clerk address you as Longfellow?"

"Not very clearly," Henry said with a polite smile, folding the paper and putting it in his pocket. "But, yes, I am Henry Wadsworth Longfellow."

The man extended his hand, which Henry accepted cordially. "You left a card at my chateau in Thun some days ago, but we were soon departing for Interlaken. I am Mr. Nathan Appleton of Boston." He turned to the younger man, who also put out his hand, which Henry shook in turn. "This is my son, Thomas Gold Appleton."

Henry smiled more sincerely. "I am pleased to meet you both," he said, looking between them. "I made the acquaintance of some relation of yours, John James Appleton, in Stockholm nearly a year ago. He told me that I might encounter you and asked that I share his well wishes should our paths cross. When I learned you were in Thun, I stopped to pay such respects, but then moved on to Berne shortly thereafter." Henry did not admit that he hadn't felt fit for company enough to pursue the acquaintance with much vigor.

Mr. Appleton smiled. "What a kindness to hear such things when we are so far from home. Thank you for seeking us out."

"I am glad to have had the opportunity," Henry said with a nod of his head.

"My sister has told me of your book," Thomas said, taking Henry off guard. The American edition of *Outré Mer* had been published almost three years earlier. But with all that had happened since, it was painful to reflect on the work he had written while Mary sewed or read beside him in the parlor of their Portland house. Mr. Appleton must have seen Henry's smile fall, as his eyebrows came together in confusion. "Mr. Longfellow?"

"I am sorry," Henry said, attempting to repair his expression. "I am unsure what I should say, I suppose. The last encounter I had with a reader was rather awkward; he was not much impressed with the work."

Tom Appleton's smile returned and his brow softened. "Rest assured that my sister was complimentary."

"I am relieved to hear it," Henry said, and indeed he was. Though he had published some poems and essays in his earlier years, *Outré Mer* was his first attempt at publishing prose, and his first foray into earning an income through his writing. The attention made him feel uncomfortable, so he turned to the older Mr. Appleton. "Have you enjoyed your tour so far?"

"We have found it a remarkable experience," Mr. Appleton said. "My daughters, Molly and Frances—Frances is the one who has read your book—accompany us, as does my nephew William, though he is rather ill."

"I am sorry to hear of your nephew's poor health," Henry said, feeling the regret keenly. He wished there was some way he could help the Appleton family, but he was no doctor—as Mary's situation had proved only too well. On the night she had lost their child, Henry had been the only one to attend her. He had felt so inept, awkward, and frightened. If they'd had a doctor attend her, would things have turned out different?

"Thank you," Mr. Appleton said graciously. "I see that you have just arrived back to the hotel, and perhaps you'd like to rest, but we would invite you to join us for supper in our rooms if you feel up to it."

Henry had not expected such an offer. Even when he presented his card at their chalet in Thun it had been purely out of courtesy to John James Appleton. The Appletons were well-known in New England and far above Henry's station. But the invitation was sincere, and Henry felt humbled by the offer. "I would be pleased to join you if you are sure it would not be an inconvenience. I don't wish to intrude."

"It would be a pleasure for us all," Mr. Appleton said. He paused, then lowered his voice. "William's health has been a difficult thing for my family of late, especially for my daughters, who love him as a brother. A new voice at the table might be the very thing we all need to lift our poor spirits."

Henry felt the pressure immediately. He was not equal to the task of providing entertainment to a family fearing for one of their own. Yet refusing their invitation would be insulting. And it was not beyond his notice that a friendship with the Appletons could only be to his advantage once he returned to Cambridge. He also knew what it was to feel as though grief had driven your heart to the soles of your feet. If somehow his company could distract them from any amount of pain they were feeling, he would not regret it. He even felt a flutter of hope that new voices at the table might do *him* some good as well.

"I must warn you that I have spent the last several months cloistered in libraries and classrooms. My skills at conversation might be rather dismal." Both men smiled, softening his anxiety even more. "But if your expectations are not too high, I would be honored to join you and meet the rest of your family."

Three

Tom Appleton

Henry was grateful for Mr. Appleton's invitation, even excited at the invigoration of such esteemed company, but as the hours drew closer to the event, his anxiety increased. In the months since Mary's death, he had, of course, had to tell his tale to people he met. He kept the details scarce and accepted their condolences before turning the attention to the reason he was there—to study and learn. Since the majority of his associations were professional, his personal tragedy did not regularly take center stage. But now he was dining with a *family*. He could not distract them with questions regarding the semantics of a verse or phrase. They would ask after his situation, and he would add to the despair they were already feeling for their cousin. By the time the hour of dinner had arrived, Henry was pacing the floor of his room and sweating beneath his starched collar.

There was a knock at the door. He stopped, took a breath, and answered it, expecting a servant—surely the Appletons had brought several with them—but instead Thomas Appleton stood in the doorway with a well-humored smile on his face. Based on what Henry had seen of his disposition, and that of his father's, it was difficult to believe that a sense of grief and mourning was afflicting the family.

"Are you ready, Longfellow? I stepped out to enjoy my pipe before dinner and told my father I would collect you on the way back to our rooms. We are on the third floor."

"Thank you for collecting me," Henry said with a nod.

The two men continued to the staircase, speaking lightly of the weather, which had been fine that day, until Henry found that he could not continue until his conscience was cleared. He stopped at the base of the stairs. "Mr. Appleton," he said quickly, "there is something I must confess before I meet the rest of your family."

"Confess?" Mr. Appleton said, raising his eyebrows without dropping his smile. "Why, Mr. Longfellow, we have just met. I'm not sure I'm prepared to carry whatever sin you might feel the need to unburden."

He was making a joke, but Henry felt his face pale.

Mr. Appleton noticed, and his smile fell. "I have misspoken," he said quickly. "I did not mean—"

"I am recently widowed," Henry blurted out with all the tact of a pugilist. "I feel that, in light of your cousin's illness, I might not be good company for your family. I worry my situation will only add to the sorrow."

Mr. Appleton blinked at him, then his face softened into sympathy. "How recent was your loss, Mr. Longfellow?"

Henry looked away so as not to be embarrassed by the other man's pity. "Nine months," he said, and then, sensing Mr. Appleton's sincerity, Henry told him the whole of it, attempting to keep his sorrow at bay long enough to relate the story. "So you see, my feelings might be so tender that I am the wrong choice for your dinner party tonight. I am sorry."

"You are not the wrong choice for our party," Mr. Appleton said with a shake of his head. "I am truly sorry for your loss. We have lost my mother and older brother these past few years; I believe that is why William's decline has struck us all so deeply. Europe has been a good diversion from our grief until these last weeks when his illness has advanced. There is nothing you could do or say that would deepen the burden we carry." He paused as though considering his words. "Just a few days ago, in Thun, William and my father discussed his situation. William agreed to this trip only if we promised to let him return to Boston if his health turned. He believes—and I cannot help but agree with him, though I hate to do so—that he is not well enough to sustain the return voyage. He has asked that we allow him to stay so that he might die within the great adventure of his young life. My father has agreed to his wishes, and though we will be slowing our journey to spare him too much travel, he hopes to reach Schaffhausen where he might be close to his Protestant roots."

Henry blinked and swallowed the lump in his throat. "I am sorry, Mr. Appleton."

"As am I for you," Mr. Appleton said with a nod. "I do not wish to burden you with our struggles, but my father was perfectly sincere when he said another voice at the table would be a welcome diversion. I have no wish to rekindle your pain, or cast a pall over the evening, so if you are agreeable, I will help keep the conversation from such things that would be painful. In exchange, I would appreciate your help on keeping up the conversation. You could tell us about your book, perhaps, and your first tour if this one is too difficult to mention. There is no need for any of us to delve into painful memories—for one night at least. Is that acceptable to you or would you rather I give your regrets?"

Though a part of Henry felt guilty essentially ignoring the hole in his heart for an evening, there was enough relief at not having to explore the pain with strangers that Henry had little hesitation. "I would be pleased to attend such an evening as you have described, Mr. Appleton. Thank you for your compassion and kindness."

The grin returned to Mr. Appleton's face. "Perhaps wait until the end of the evening to thank me. Our plan might not work, but I shall give it my very best."

"As will I," Henry confirmed.

Tom turned to the stairs and Henry followed him up. When they reached the landing, Tom stopped. "I have one more favor to ask."

Henry raised his eyebrows in expectation.

"Will you please call me Tom? I prefer to be called Tom in most situations—it suits me—and with so many Appletons in the company, I shall have a headache if you attempt to address all of us properly."

It was unconventional to address another man by his Christian name, but it hardly seemed something to argue. "You may call me . . . Henry, then, I suppose."

Tom cocked his head to the side and smiled. "I shall call you Longfellow. I would not want to make you uncomfortable. And, as you are a writer and professor, I should refer to you as due your situation."

"Thank you," Henry said, glad for Tom's respect.

"As I said, don't thank me yet," Tom said. "I must warn you that my sisters are a spoiled pair and wish to be dancing tonight, even though there is no such entertainment available as it's Sunday. I hope they won't take their disappointment out on us."

Four

First Impressions

Fanny regarded the man at the other end of the table and wondered what it was exactly that was bothering her. There was a nervousness about him that caused Fanny to feel unsettled in his company. In an attempt to discover the source of his discomfort, she'd watched him all through dinner—which she worried was increasing his anxiety. Tom and Father had already informed her that Mr. Longfellow was not an old man, as she'd first expected, but she had not considered that he would be handsome. Though he was rather too thin for the bold features of his face—a firm jaw, bright blue eyes, distinguished nose, full lips, and strong chin—it was not his physical attributes that had her on edge. She was well-acquainted with many handsome men and confident in their presence. It was something else. Something she could not quite identify.

Perhaps the fact that they had been talking about *Outré Mer* all evening was part of her mood—she had hoped for more energetic entertainment—but the discussion *was* interesting. She had given her review of the book and asked him questions, which he answered with ease. He was not arrogant about the attention given to his work, in fact at times he seemed almost embarrassed by it, but Tom was intent to stay on the topic.

Maybe *that* was the true cause of her discomfort. *Tom* was not acting like himself, and Fanny didn't understand why. William had joined them for a brief time, but had already retired to his room. Molly seemed to be trying hard to hide her boredom.

"What of your *current* tour, Mr. Longfellow?" Fanny asked, interrupting what felt like a needlessly long description of his impression of Germany ten years ago. "How long have you been in Europe for *this* tour?"

When Mr. Longfellow did not answer right away, Fanny looked to Tom, who was uncomfortable, and then to her father, who was as expectant of the answer as she was.

"He has been touring for just over a year, have you not, Longfellow?" Tom said, turning his full attention to Mr. Longfellow, who looked as though he'd forgotten his own name.

"Can he not answer for himself?" Fanny asked, spurred forward by the reaction of both men, though she kept her smile polite. She did not want to appear cross. "And why does he call you Tom? Did not the two of you only meet today?"

"I asked him to call me Tom—you know how I hate being called 'Mr. Appleton' in informal settings. Don't be peevish."

She held her brother's eyes a moment, then turned her gaze to Mr. Longfellow, undeterred. How could his tour a decade earlier be more interesting than what he'd seen and done in the more recent past? "How long *have* you been on this tour, Mr. Longfellow? When did you leave Maine?"

Mr. Longfellow blinked before he spoke. "I have been in Europe for fifteen months," he said in a slow, calculated tone. "I shall be returning to Cambridge in a few months to accept a position at Harvard College as the Smith Professor."

"And how have you enjoyed *this* tour?" Fanny pressed, though there was some niggling within her, warning her to retreat from this line of questioning. She argued with herself but did not give up. "Has it been so dreadful that it is not worth speaking of? Is there nothing of this trip you would like to tell us? Were you in Paris already? Did you enjoy the opera?"

"Oh, Fanny, leave him be," Tom said, attempting to keep his tone light but not succeeding entirely. There was a warning in his voice. "I am interested in his *first* tour, and in his book."

Tom's defense only drew out her curiosity. "Which we have had a very interesting discussion about already—so much so that I would love to hear how Europe has changed in the last decade. Did you not invite Mr. Longfellow here for conversation, and should not that conversation be—"

"Fanny," Father said, cutting her off. "You are being rude to our guest."

Fanny turned her attention to her plate, embarrassed at having been called out by her father—something that happened rarely, even when she deserved it. The room was silent long enough for her to take a breath and remember her manners. "I'm sorry, Father. I did not mean to be rude."

An awkward silence descended as Fanny's cheeks burned.

"To answer your question, Miss Frances," Mr. Longfellow said after a few miserable seconds had passed. "Yes, much of my tour this time has been quite dreadful. I told your brother the whole of my situation prior to dinner because I feared I would not be good company. He offered to help avoid difficult topics. I am sorry for the discomfort the avoidance has caused, however, and that the conversation is not so diverting."

Fanny closed her eyes as the humiliation in her face and stomach burned hotter. Knowing what had been irritating her—he *had* been hiding something and was therefore being careful—did not make her feel better. She had embarrassed him, her father, and herself by being so intent. Why could she not keep her thoughts to herself as a young lady was taught to do? Why did she take it upon herself to fix everything and, in the process, not fix anything at all? Not William. Not this awkward dinner.

The room was still quiet, and she sensed everyone was waiting for her. She met Mr. Longfellow's eyes from across the long table. She noted again that he was a handsome man, yet now she could see the pain in his eyes and the shadows beneath them. For a moment she wanted to know the cause of his pain—and then she stopped such wondering.

Fanny did not know precisely what Father and William had discussed in the parlor in Thun. She had asked for details, and her father had refused her—which may have added to her surly mood when she felt left out of another conversation tonight—but she could sense the heaviness of whatever the discussion had been, and her heart felt bruised within her chest. There was no room for her to bear anyone else's pain, and so as quickly as she wondered what dreadful things had befallen Mr. Longfellow, she wanted to hear nothing at all.

Her inability to bear her own misery had driven her to seek out dancing and music in which to pass the time. She could forget the troubles that nipped at her when the energy was high. Evenings like this, calm and conversational, were not nearly as distracting. But that was not Mr. Longfellow's fault, and she hated to know that she'd added to the difficulty he'd already experienced on this trip. Should she not be lifting the burdens of the people she met rather than adding to them?

"I am sorry, Mr. Longfellow, for pressing you, and for the difficulties you have faced. I was out of place to be so direct, and I pray your forgiveness." She meant every word and hoped he would know it.

"You owe me no apology, Miss Frances." For a moment the softness of his words held her like a cord, and she found she could not take her gaze from his. In some way she could not understand, she felt . . . *seen* as she had never been seen before. It was strangely flattering, but also made her feel vulnerable—something she could ill afford to feel. She forced her gaze to her father, who regarded her with concern.

"Father, might I be excused? I fear I am too fatigued to be good company tonight."

"Of course, my dear," he said with a nod.

"I certainly wish you the best, Mr. Longfellow," Fanny said formally as she stood from the table and put her napkin on her chair.

"As I do for you, Miss Frances."

She curtsied slightly but did not meet his eyes again as she left the room and hurried for the chamber she shared with Molly. She hated how she had behaved this evening. She hated even more the idea that Mr. Longfellow might depart as quickly as possible in light of her treatment of him and then she would never have the chance to redeem herself. She could not stand the thought that he would return to Boston, where their paths may likely cross again, and he would remember her as a sharp-tongued harpy who would not allow a man an evening's peace.

Fanny closed the bedroom door and leaned against it, playing through their conversation in her mind again. What she would not give to start the evening over and be better than she'd been. *Oh, why couldn't there have been music and dancing tonight?* She was not to be trusted in company that did not distract her from the ache in her heart. She raised her hands to her face in hopes to keep the tears at bay. They would not change anything, after all.

Five

Confessions

The evening did not improve much after Miss Frances's departure, and Henry regretted again accepting the dinner invitation. After a polite period of time, Mr. Appleton invited his other daughter to leave the men to their brandy. She seemed eager to follow her sister from the room. The maid entered and began clearing the dishes.

Mr. Appleton turned to Henry. "I am very sorry for this evening, Mr. Longfellow, and especially for Fanny hounding you. I assure you she possesses better manners than you saw on display, and I can only think that the strain of William's illness is taking a toll."

"You owe me no apology," Henry said, shaking his head. "And neither does she. I should have been forthcoming."

"It was my fault," Tom said, accepting the glass of brandy from the footman. "If Fanny were simply a silly girl with flippant thoughts and thin attention we would have been successful, but I should have known better. Despite her petulance this evening, the girl is far too smart for her own good."

Henry did not know what to say. To agree with them would insult the young woman, and he didn't fault her for noticing the choppy attempts at avoidance—rather, the fact that she noticed was to her credit. She was young and energetic, but well-spoken and self-possessed too.

"I am also very sorry for your struggles," Mr. Appleton said with enough curiosity in his voice that it would be rude for Henry not to explain. For the second time that evening, Henry recalled the painful events of the last year and accepted a stranger's condolences. It was exhausting to revisit the pain—not that he was ever away from it completely. They had invited him in hopes of lifting the mood, and he had done exactly the opposite.

"I think," Mr. Appleton said after Henry finished, "that the lot of us make quite a group. All of us touched by sorrow, each of us trying to lose ourselves, or perhaps heal ourselves, in the diversion of Europe. I find it odd that we might meet with one another at all, don't you, Mr. Longfellow?"

"It is rather strange," Henry said, though he had little energy to sustain his wonder.

"My dear wife was a God-fearing woman," Mr. Appleton continued. "And she would say that it is not mere coincidence, but that our paths were meant to cross exactly like this. What do you think of that, Mr. Longfellow?"

"If I am to be completely honest," Henry said, "I do not put much stock into theories such as fate and Karma. I believe in God, and I believe there is purpose to our existence, but I am unsure of how much attention He might give to such things as people meeting in a foreign land." He looked at his host. "I do not mean to argue your point, nor take away from your wife's faith, I only mean to say that if such things as *this* happen for a purpose, then I must say that *all* things happen for a purpose, and I see no purpose in the suffering we have experienced—not yours, not mine. Not your children's."

Yet another silence followed his words, and Henry mentally chastised himself for his honesty.

"Perhaps you are right," Mr. Appleton said. "Perhaps things happen for no particular reason and we are left to make of them what we will. To our betterment or our detriment, depending on our choice in the matter."

"I mean no offense, sir, but who would choose to make something work toward their detriment?"

"Those who punish themselves unnecessarily." He spoke so fast and with such certainty that Henry's muscles tightened and released almost in the same instant. Mr. Appleton spoke as though he knew Henry blamed himself for Mary's death, but how could he? Henry could barely articulate such thoughts to himself, and he certainly would never tell anyone for fear they would offer hollow platitudes and weak justifications. Or worse, agree that if he had not brought her to Europe she would still be alive and well.

"Mr. Longfellow, would you join us for tea tomorrow?" Mr. Appleton asked.

Henry was shocked. Why on earth would they want him to come back? Was not one ruined evening enough to convince them that his company was to be avoided? He was prepared to make a quick retreat. The idea of making another attempt of friendship with these people—Miss Frances Appleton especially—only spurred him to want an escape that much more. And yet Mr. Appleton had issued the invitation and, as had been the case earlier, Henry felt unable to refuse it.

"If you should like me to attend, I shall attend." It was the most feeble answer Henry had ever made to anything in his life.

"Tomorrow, then," Mr. Appleton said with a nod and a smile. "Come to our rooms at four o'clock."

After a restless night, Henry spent the morning and early afternoon with Mr. Gurmand and his fabulously diverting collection of Swiss and German literature. Henry purchased a few volumes he had learned of in Heidelberg and made plans to come back the next day. Once he left Mr. Gurmand's company, though, his mind returned to the Appletons.

Henry had accepted Mr. Appleton's invitation to tea out of politeness, but the more he thought on it, the more grateful he felt for the second chance to make a new impression. The green of the mountain meadows and the grandness of the rocky cliffs above him seemed to empower him so that, when he returned to his rooms, he chose his dress carefully to shore up his confidence: the claret long coat—nipped in at the waist in the European style—and gray trousers tucked into knee-high boots.

At precisely four o'clock, he knocked at the door of the Appleton's apartments. But a moment later, when the servant showed him into the parlor where only Miss Frances Appleton was in attendance, his confidence fled.

"Good day to you, Mr. Longfellow," she said, giving him a quick curtsy. "Do come in." Then she smiled, softening her face into an expression that renewed his hope in redemption.

Her dark hair was curled beside her face and pulled up in the back. She wore a light blue dress featuring the European style of a lowered waistline and a fuller skirt. He noted how the modern style defined a woman's figure better than the higher waist of previous decades before he felt the horror of having noticed a woman's figure at all.

She held his eyes, and he feared she could see the heat creeping up his neck. He tried to think of something appropriate to say.

Tom's voice from behind spared them both. "Mr. Longfellow, good to see you."

Relieved, Henry turned immediately from Miss Frances's intent look and greeted Tom, who had that jovial grin on his face that Henry suspected was part of the man's wardrobe. "I do hope Fanny took this chance of private conference to apologize for her boorish behavior last night."

Both Henry and Miss Frances were silent, which was answer enough for Tom. He laughed and then shook his head at his sister. "I swear, Fanny, you are a trial."

"And you are a brute," she said, her tone thick with irritation and embarrassment.

"As I said last night, she owes me no apology," Henry said, smiling at her so she might know the sincerity of his words. Her grateful smile caused a rush of energy to course through him. "I am the one who brought such discomfort, so it is her forgiveness I should be seeking."

"That is not necessary," she said, looking down demurely. "I expect that all shall be well between us from now on."

"As I would hope." Henry feared that between last night and this afternoon, she had been told of his misfortune and pitied him for it.

She met his eye, and they held one another's gaze for a breath, then she stepped forward. "We are having tea in the back parlor as it provides a better view of the lake," she said over her shoulder, obviously expecting the men to follow her.

Henry fell in step beside Tom and pulled at his coat nervously, hoping he did not look like too much of a dandy. That hadn't been his intent, but he felt out of place next to Tom, who dressed as an elite Bostonian would—long black coat, navy trousers beneath which peeked the top of well-polished shoes.

"Fanny has promised to be on her best behavior," Tom said quietly enough that Henry expected his sister could not hear. "She was rather mortified when she learned the whole of it last night."

So Henry was right in that she knew. Would he have an entire room full of pity when they reached the back sitting area? "Does the whole family know?"

"They do," Tom said apologetically. "I felt it only fair after my poor attempts to avoid it ended so badly."

"And what do they think?" Henry said, trying not to sound vulnerable. "Do they think me a bear for not returning with Mary's casket?"

Tom stopped in the middle of the hallway and held Henry back as Miss Frances passed through the doorway ahead of them.

Henry met the other man's eye, braced for his judgment. When he felt his own recrimination so severely, it was not difficult to assume everyone else felt the same.

"Goodness no," Tom said, sounding surprised that Henry should consider such a thing. "We have heard of such situations before. After investing so much into a tour of this scale, one cannot so easily turn back. We are sorry for your pain, that is all. You are in good company, Longfellow, I assure you of that."

It took a moment for the sincerity of his words to seep into Henry's mind and heart but when they did he was deeply touched. He had Miss Crowninshield's support, which he appreciated, but to be among people so determined to include him and put his mind at ease was the greatest charity he could imagine receiving.

"Thank you," Henry said, wishing he knew what else to say. For a man who loved words, he had a difficult time finding the right ones sometimes.

Tom grinned. "Don't thank me too much just yet," he said, leaning close and putting his hand beside his mouth in an exaggerated attempt to block their conversation from exactly no one—they were alone in the hall. "William is hoping you might be willing to talk poetry with him. He is a great lover of verse written in the Romantic languages, and when I told him what an accomplished linguist you were and of the focus of your study these last months, well, his eyes lit up as they haven't in many weeks. He is hoping you might have some translations to share with him."

"Much of my tour has been concentrated on the translation of such works," Henry said, invigorated to have someone interested in his current work. "I would be pleased to speak with him. I have been quite fascinated with Novalis and Uhland of late—though perhaps they are too sorrowful."

"Isn't all poetry sorrowful?" Tom gave an exaggerated shake of his head. "If it shall entertain William, and you don't mind, it shall be very welcome."

Henry smiled. Oh, but Tom's lighthearted manner was refreshing after so many dismal months stuck in his own mind. Henry followed Tom through the doorway to where the rest of the Appleton family waited.

Mr. Appleton rose from his seat beside William and crossed the room to shake hands in greeting. Miss Molly was pouring the tea while Miss Frances placed a selection of sweets and savories on the small plates.

Miss Frances looked up at him and, though he could not call her a great beauty, she was very striking—to the point he felt sure he could draw her when he was alone. He noted the graceful lines of her neck and collarbone and the way she moved with confident elegance. He noticed too much. Too soon.

"Do sit down," Mr. Appleton said, reclaiming his chair.

"How do you take your tea, Mr. Longfellow?" Miss Molly asked.

"Cream only, please," he said. Tom had taken the seat on the far end, leaving Henry no choice but to take the only other empty chair—directly beside Miss Frances. It was the last place he felt he should be sitting as unwelcome notice and unrestrained thoughts cycled through his barbaric mind.

He tried not to watch Miss Frances's elegant fingers as she prepared the plates. Perhaps his notice of so many details about this woman was another sign of his weak and fractured mind. He was going mad, that was it, mad and devilish.

"Well, cousin William," Tom said as he crossed one foot over his other knee, "Mr. Longfellow has just now told me that he is as equally besotted as you with the Romantic poems of Germany. Now how is that for a stroke of luck, I ask you?"

Henry appreciated the permission to turn his attention to William. Mournful poetry in a foreign tongue was precisely the distraction he needed. It would remind him of his purpose and his pain, and help him push aside what he feared was an outright attraction for the young woman beside him.

"Liest du Deutsch?" William asked, surprising a smile out of Henry. The young man looked better today than he had the night before

"Yes, I read German," Henry said. *"Du auch?"*

"Ich spreche es nur schlecht."

"Your grasp of the language does not sound poor to me," Henry said.

William shrugged good-naturedly. "I can make my tongue and ear use it, but I cannot seem to train my eye."

"Which is often the case for my students," Henry said, grateful for a new topic that would take his thoughts in a more comfortable direction. "Even when they can say the words, once you ask them what they've said or expect them to understand what you say in reply, they blink at you like cattle. Your grasp is much better than I am used to."

"Father says you teach modern languages at Bowdoin College," Miss Molly said, drawing Henry's attention. Though her features were a bit finer than her sister's, they did not invigorate him the way Miss Frances's did. Blast his eyes for the whole of this notice! She handed him his cup.

"Modern languages," Miss Frances said, causing him to tense. Why she should strike him with such intensity he could not understand. "As opposed to classic languages, I assume, such as Greek and Latin?"

"Exactly," Henry said, only daring a glance in her direction. "When I move on to Harvard, I shall be teaching Spanish, French, Italian, and German."

"You *speak* all of these languages?" Miss Molly asked.

"I seem to have an ability with language," Henry said, not wanting to sound arrogant.

Miss Frances spoke again. "I have heard it said that the purpose behind learning foreign languages is to expand one's capacity to learn all manner of things, a kind of exercise for the brain that strengthens the intellect."

"That is the prevailing theory," Henry said. "Though I feel there is greater benefit than merely the preparation for other education. I believe that language—and the literature produced through it—is of intrinsic benefit for its own merit. The purpose of my tour has been to explore the literature of the European nations."

"More than just the four languages you teach?" Miss Molly asked.

"I find language of any kind a fascinating study," Henry explained. "I have embraced every one I've encountered and have certainly found great benefit in each."

"How many different languages do you speak, Mr. Longfellow?" Mr. Appleton asked.

Henry shifted his attention to the patriarch. "I am only fluent in those I will teach, but I can get along well enough with Portuguese, Danish, Finnish, Russian, and of course Greek and Latin. I have thus far collected books written in twelve different languages, and I hope to soon be able to read every one of them."

"You *enjoy* reading and speaking in other languages?" Miss Molly asked, her tone doubtful.

"Very much so," Henry said, unable to suppress a smile at the joy he found in language. "I find other nations and cultures fascinating. Understanding their language—where the words come from and how they play on a native ear—is like transporting oneself through time and place."

"My word, that is an impressive list," William said. "I hereby relinquish my title as the most linguistic of the company. I took inordinate pride in my ability with German and French. That's the real reason they brought me, you know. I speak French better than the lot of them." He waved a thin hand at the company seated around the room.

"We did not bring you to serve as an interpreter," Miss Frances said, folding her hands in her lap and looking at her cousin with wide eyes. "For you to suggest such a thing is very wrong, William."

"Exactly right," Tom broke in. "We brought you so that you could share in the tending of my silly sisters, of course. Besides, Father and I can get by on our French, so I do not thank you for the insult."

"You are quite terrible, Tom," Miss Frances said, but her eyes were merry. "In both your teasing of William and your French."

"I agree," Miss Molly cut in. "You'll make William feel sad and, besides, Fanny and I speak some French."

"I think you mean that you and Fanny remember your early lessons enough to pepper your letters with a French word here and there, but it is hardly considered *speaking.*"

William stopped the conversation with another sentence only Henry could understand. *"Ehrlich gesagt, sie sind wunderbare Leute und haben seit einer langen Zeit nicht so gelacht. Du bist genau in dem perfekten moment angekommen."* Essentially he relayed the goodness of his family and thanked Henry for being the cause for their good humor.

Henry was humbled by the cousin's compliment and inclined his head in gratitude.

"You had better not talk behind our backs right in front of us," Miss Frances said, turning her playful scowl to her cousin. "That would be bad manners of you indeed."

"I would *never* do such a thing," William said, winking at his cousin.

Her scowl turned to a smile, and she turned to hand Henry his plate.

When he took it from her hand, his thumb brushed the underside of her fingers and the warmth he felt in response had nothing to do with the tea. She met his eye for a moment, but not long enough for him to know if she had felt the same sensation.

It is simply because you have been around so few women these months, he told himself as he faced forward again. Perhaps it was best to be seated beside her so that he would not catch her eye so often. It was the Natural Man in him, that was all, nothing more. Nothing that should cause him undue anxiety. Rather, he should focus on the group as a whole, and the men more specifically, and not give primitive reactions to the fairer sex more notice than such reflexes deserved.

Firm in his resolve, when Mr. Appleton asked about the German universities Henry had visited during the winter, Henry was quick to delve into the great writers of that country. With an audience willing, if not eager, for the distraction offered by his studies, how could anything else compete for his attention?

Six

Zurich, Switzerland

Fanny gripped the handrail separating her from Lake Zurich and leaned forward until the sound of voices behind them competed with the lapping of the water on the shore. "I miss Interlaken," she said to Molly, who stood beside her.

"You do not like Zurich?" Molly said in surprise. "But you commented on all the fine shops and entertainment."

"And I do enjoy those things. It is different, though. That is all I mean." She looked over her shoulder at the bustling streets behind them. Zurich was near enough to the German border that it attracted a great deal of travelers, to say nothing of the city's own population.

Fanny thought of the trees and the mountains and the clear air of Interlaken. She also thought of the walks she'd taken with Mr. Longfellow, and the discussions of literature and poetry that had opened her mind to so many new writers and ideas. She turned back to Molly. "Did you not love the respite of the Alps?"

Molly shrugged. "I like the shops here in Zurich. And the art."

"Yes, the art is splendid." Tomorrow the sisters would take a class with a renowned painter who would help them with their own oil painting of the Alps.

It *was* beautiful in Zurich, and there *was* something satisfying about having greater society. It wasn't until they had left the smaller villages that Fanny had realized how much she enjoyed the mountain passes. Her sketchbook was filled with the things she'd seen, but she wished she could go back, hold to the comfort of that time—and William's health, which had been better there—and enjoy the feeling of isolation she'd found walking the foothill paths. It had been a different kind of freedom and independence than she had known before, one where she set her own schedule and spent as much time reading and thinking as she wanted. It was also cooler there, while the heat of Zurich in August caused her dress to stick to her skin.

"I think what you mean is that you miss the attention of Mr. Longfellow," Molly said with a teasing grin as she bumped her shoulder into her sister's. "He is not sharing *every* meal with us *every* day here in Zurich."

"He has his studies," Fanny said in an even tone, though she did not meet her sister's eye. Her feelings regarding Mr. Longfellow were complex, and she was of no mind to attempt to explain them to Molly. That Molly had mentioned any undue notice on Fanny's part, however, spurred her to further defend herself. "And besides, I do not miss his company in the least. He does not even dance."

It *was* disappointing that Mr. Longfellow seemed only to enjoy long talks or walks. He was steady and comforting to be sure, but a girl of eighteen years enjoyed music and parties now and again. Mr. Longfellow did not, and he would sit with the old men in the corner rather than join in the frivolity of the young people.

Sometimes she felt him watching her, and it would wash over her like warm honey—if he would dance with her, be frivolous and free, perhaps she could feel a different kind of connection. By the end of an evening where he spent the time in discussions with other men, she would be irritated and peevish, but then they would have a conversation about some detail he'd noted regarding Coleridge or Milton and her opinion of Mr. Longfellow would rise again.

Molly laughed. "I think you fancy him."

Fanny shook her head, refusing to let such an idea stay long in her sister's mind even if she herself had wondered at it. "I do not."

"'Oh, do translate this poem for me, Mr. Longfellow,'" Molly said in a high-pitched voice, blinking her eyes quickly. "'And, pray, share with me your thoughts on the context of this verse.'"

Fanny laughed at the ridiculous exaggeration. "If I ever spoke like that, I'd have thrown myself in Lake Thun." She turned back to Lake Zurich, much bigger than Thun had been and not nearly as clear and pristine. "Besides, it is was William's company he sought out more than mine."

Mention of their cousin put an end to Molly's light mood, and the sisters stared across the lake together, lost in their own thoughts. Fanny wished she'd brought her sketchpad for their walk today. She wished she had something to busy her hands and mind so her thoughts would not run so wild.

"Is William going to die here in Zurich, do you think?" Molly asked. "He is so very ill." By now the truth was known: William would die in Europe; no one doubted it. The Zurich doctor who attended him two days ago felt that William's passing could take place at any time, but certainly within the month.

William was skin on bones, and his voice was a whisper when he dared speak at all. Too often conversation left him in coughing fits that bloodied his handkerchief and exhausted his body for hours afterward.

His days consisted of rest—often with the help of opium draughts—and attempts to eat a little more than he did the day before.

Yesterday, Mr. Longfellow had taken a break from his studies to row the lake with Fanny, William, and Tom. He'd shared the translation of Uhland's poem "Das Schloss am Meer," and William had basked in the sunshine and splendid words. It had been a delightful afternoon, the type that could lull people into believing that all was well with the world. Tom and Mr. Longfellow nearly had to carry William back to the family's rooms, however, and realizing that the day on the lake was likely to be William's last outing left a pall over the memory.

When William was alert, his eyes were bright and his spirit was strong. They would miss him when he was gone, and yet Fanny was feeling an increasing acceptance of the way of things. Consumption was often called a kind death as it allowed its victims time to put their affairs in order. William did seem at peace—as Fanny's mother and Charles had both been in the end—and Fanny envied the acceptance. Comfort and rest awaited William, whereas those left behind in mortality had toil to endure. Their time in Switzerland seemed to represent life as a whole: a time filled with sorrow amid beautiful vistas that now and again dulled the pain.

"I hope we shall make it to Schaffhausen since he feels he will be most comfortable there," Fanny said in belated answer to Molly's question. Her voice wavered to think of burying William in a graveyard alongside a Protestant church they would never see again.

After his burial the Appletons would continue the second half of their tour. It felt so wrong, and yet, what could they do to make it right? Fanny wished her father would send William's body back to Boston as Mr. Longfellow had his wife, but William had refused. "I care not for my body," he'd said a few days ago. "And my soul is at peace. Better that I am laid to rest soon so that my spirit may be free. The mountains shall embrace me here." How could they not respect his wishes for such a thing? But how could they leave him behind? How had Mr. Longfellow made peace with his wife's death? Could he help them all find acceptance when William's time came?

"It is a lovely view of the mountains here. I am glad we could stay for a few days at least," Molly said, attempting to boost her sister's spirits.

"Yes," Fanny said, not entirely pacified but glad for the lightened topic. "We should buy some new cheeses at the market, don't you think? We could include them with today's tea."

The sisters made their way through the streets to a market not far from their hotel. Because their stay in Zurich would be short, Father had not rented a house. There was a sense of urgency about this stop. With William failing, they wanted to stay only long enough for him to restore his strength before they went on to Schaffhausen. Mr. Longfellow had given up his own itinerary to accompany them, but was using his time in Zurich to take advantage of the educational opportunities. There had been little of that available in Interlaken, and he had spent nearly every afternoon reading to William and then discussing what he studied or translating the words into English as he read. He'd purchased several books on his journey and seemed as eager to have an audience as William was to have the attention. It was very kind of Mr. Longfellow, and Fanny enjoyed sitting in on their discussions. He had an agile mind, and as she was not very familiar with intellectuals back in Boston, she found the depth of knowledge Mr. Longfellow possessed on so many topics quite fascinating.

"Miss Fanny. Miss Molly."

The girls turned, and Fanny's heart skipped a beat to see Mr. Longfellow himself hurrying toward them, one hand holding his hat to his head. He had begun calling her Miss Fanny in Lucerne, and no one had corrected him. They waited for him to catch up and then nodded in greeting when he reached them. Fanny could not suppress a smile; she had not expected to see him today.

"I was just coming back from the university and thought I recognized your fine bonnets." His cheeks were flushed with color, and as he smiled, Fanny realized how much better he looked from when they had first met a few weeks earlier.

Tom believed Mr. Longfellow had been quite depressed before their paths had crossed. To see him now, one would not guess he'd suffered, and yet he had never spoken of his wife's death to Fanny. Whether that was a reflection of the tragic circumstances, his unwillingness to discuss his wife with Fanny in particular, or a flaw in his character, she did not know, but she felt guilty for pondering on aspects of such a private nature.

"You make it a point to remember young ladies' bonnets?" Fanny asked.

"I make it a point to remember *your* bonnet," he said, rather bold enough to cause Fanny's smile to fade. He immediately turned to Molly. "And yours, Miss Molly. Green is a very good shade for your eyes, I daresay."

Molly smiled while Fanny regarded Mr. Longfellow, who was rarely so attentive to them directly. Then again, they were not often alone in his company. The few times Fanny had walked with him alone, he had read to her or shared a translation. He was not the type to fall into vain flattery.

"We were on our way to purchase some cheese for this afternoon's tea," Fanny said. "Would you like to join us?"

"Certainly," he said, falling into step with the sisters. "I sent word to your rooms that I would be able to join your family this afternoon. I'm lucky to have encountered you while I was making my way there."

"You are not spending the afternoon at the university?" Fanny asked.

"Not today. I spent the morning in the most fascinating lecture regarding the German writings of the twelfth century. I knew William would love to hear of it, so I postponed my afternoon's visit to their library until tomorrow." He held up a notebook. "I took detailed notes so William would not miss any of the information."

"That is very kind of you," Fanny said. She wondered how many other men would forgo their own ambitions to talk with a young man in his final days.

"I might go on ahead," Molly said, causing both Fanny and Mr. Longfellow to look at her. "With Mr. Longfellow to accompany you, Fanny, I could see that the rest of the tea is ready when you return. I am quite famished today—perhaps from all the walking."

"Of course," Mr. Longfellow said before Fanny could answer, bold again. "Tell your father and brother that we will be but twenty minutes behind you."

"I shall," she said. As she increased her pace she turned back long enough to catch Fanny's eye and flash a mischievous grin.

There was no remedy for the situation Molly had created. Fanny could not beg out of Mr. Longfellow's company, but found that she did not want to now that she had an opportunity to talk with him alone.

Mr. Longfellow asked what she thought of Zurich, and she expressed the same feeling she had told Molly earlier regarding how she missed Interlaken.

"Yes, I have felt the same nostalgia for that place," Mr. Longfellow agreed. He was walking with his hands clasped behind his back, holding the notebook. "It was like heaven on earth. I will forever remember Interlaken with great fondness."

"But it is not your favorite place in Europe," Fanny said, glad to know they shared such a liking for Interlaken. "Do you not like Italy best?"

"I adore Italy to be sure, especially Florence," he said with a nod, then glanced at her. "But Interlaken awakened me in ways that Italy never did."

He couldn't mean that *Fanny* had awakened him. It was far too brazen a comment for a man of such humble nature. She kept her gaze straight ahead, embarrassed to have considered such an interpretation of his words.

"I look forward to seeing Germany," she said. "Father says we will spend several weeks there before we go on to Paris."

"Yes, I told him of Basel, and he was quite eager to visit. You will enjoy Germany, Miss Fanny. It is a great place for art, and the food is incomparable, to say nothing of the people. They are among the best I have ever met. I have a good many friends in Germany."

"It is lucky for us to have a guide such as yourself," she said, feeling her cheeks warm at her own boldness. She only meant what she said—as a man who spoke German fluently he would be an asset—but she could feel the potential interpretation of her own words, and it made her feel awkward.

"I am pleased to be included," Mr. Longfellow said. "Your father is generous to cover some of my expenses in return."

Why did she feel a stab of disappointment at the reminder of their different situations? "He is a very generous man."

They reached the market, and Mr. Longfellow helped in the transaction with the German-speaking clerk. Watching him interact with a stranger, speaking words she did not understand, showed his skill. He was confident and laughed at something the clerk said.

Fanny knew humor was especially hard to grasp within language. She had been in Europe for a year, and other than a few key phrases, mostly regarding directions or greetings, she had learned very little of the languages she'd encountered. The French she had learned as a child had come back enough to make her feel a bit confident, but her ability was not such that she ever took charge of a conversation.

Mr. Longfellow finished the transaction and took the paper-wrapped parcel of cheeses.

"Danke," Mr. Longfellow said—one of the few German words Fanny understood. What would it be like to converse easily in a language so different than the one you were taught from birth?

Mr. Longfellow held the door of the shop for Fanny, and they continued their journey back to the Appletons' rooms. Mr. Longfellow was staying at another inn that he said was not very comfortable.

"What is your favorite language to speak, Mr. Longfellow?" Fanny asked when the silence between them felt too long.

"Ah, that is a difficult question to answer," he said, but she could tell he was thinking hard about the answer. "I do love German. Their literature is reflective of great depth and imagery. I have likely gained the most through my ability with that language, but perhaps the one I enjoy speaking the most is Italian. There is something lyrical about it, especially the Venetian dialect. A musical quality that quite renews my spirit."

"I enjoy listening to Italian. It is not so surprising that it is the language of the opera."

"Precisely," he said, turning a bright smile toward her that made her breath catch. Just a little bit. And likely because he tended to be more subdued with his expressions. The openness of his face was unexpected. "The language sounds like a song even in speech, like a stream moving through grassy hills."

"But you did not visit Italy for this trip?" Fanny asked.

His brow grew heavy, and Fanny regretted the reminder of how many ways this trip had not lived up to his expectations.

"My focus was on Scandinavia," he said after a few moments. "I'm afraid it did not allow for such a visit, though I very much wish it would have."

The sharp drop in his energy made her wish they could recapture the brighter mood. "Perhaps you will return again to see Italy, especially if you love it so very much."

"Perhaps," he said, smiling again but in a way that seemed to say he did not expect such a thing. European tours were expensive—for him to have made a second one was likely beyond his expectations. The hope for a third must feel very vain.

Fanny searched for a different topic. "And do you look forward to joining the faculty at Harvard College? Are you eager to teach again?"

He seemed to ponder the question for some time. "I am hopeful that I will get to *teach.*"

Fanny looked at him. "Why would you not teach? Are you not to be a professor?"

"Well, yes," Mr. Longfellow said. "But I fear my idea of teaching is not always in keeping with that of the administration. Such was the case at Bowdoin College, but I am hopeful for greater latitude with Harvard."

"Latitude? I'm not sure I understand what you mean. Is not Harvard College the best education available in America? Why would you need more *latitude*?"

"I believe Harvard College *is* among the best our fine country has to offer," Mr. Longfellow said. "But therein lies the problem.

Measuring our educational opportunity against what we ourselves offer gives us a very narrow field for comparison. Our nation has done a great deal in establishing itself in a relatively short amount of time, but there is growth left to be had within our institutions of higher learning if we ever hope to offer anything near what Europe takes for granted. For example . . ."

He went on to express his wish for his students to understand the roots of the languages they studied, learn where the adaptations came from, and appreciate the cultural influences in their literature and poetry. He described the current American education in language as lacking in depth, scope, and availability and talked about having written his own textbooks in an attempt to better teach his students—an effort that went all but unnoticed by the Bowdoin administration. Rather than seeing education as something for the wealthy, he felt all children should be educated for a minimum period of time, specifically focusing on literacy, and that higher education should be an option for all classes who should want it *and* for women.

"You believe women should go to college as men do?" Fanny said, almost with a laugh. His ideas were not unheard of, but the other voices advocating the same idea were from extreme women who Fanny found to be crass and overly independent in their ways of thinking. Their assertions of being dominated by men did not settle well in Fanny's Protestant heart. As though men and women should be the same, rather than fulfill their own God-given roles.

"Certainly," Mr. Longfellow said with a nod. "If they wish to. There are a few institutions being established that offer women the opportunity to better themselves with education, but I fear they have not received the governmental support they need to truly flourish."

"Forgive my impertinence," Fanny said, feeling a bit of a devil's advocate, "but for what end should women pursue college? Why should a woman need a greater education than what is required for running her home and managing her family—tasks she learns at home?"

Mr. Longfellow considered that a moment, then gave her a sly grin that took her off guard. "Perhaps you can answer that better than I, Miss Fanny. Why should a young woman tour Europe? In what way would that influence her life for good? How should a European education of culture and art benefit her in the running of her home and the caring of her family?"

He was being so casual with her, speaking to her as he would a man—a contemporary or a peer. Fanny found it both flattering and strange. Certainly no other man had ever spoken to her this way.

She contemplated Mr. Longfellow's question and could not keep from smiling. "I see your point, but we both know my situation is different than that of the majority of American women. I have the luxury of indulging in such things that most women do not—but I do not *need* such education. It is purely for enjoyment that I get to explore the world and the ideas it presents. Such things will have little to do with daily living, though I do expect them to be the foundation of conversation at dinner parties."

Mr. Longfellow cocked his head to the side, causing Fanny to feel as though she'd disappointed him with her answer. "If you don't mind my saying so, Miss Fanny, if all this journey gives you is dinner conversation, it would be a sad waste."

Fanny was instantly offended and opened her mouth to say so, but he spoke before she could get a word out.

"Particularly for a woman of your mind and intellect."

Fanny's offence died upon her lips. "*My* mind and intellect? I may live in a different social class than other women, but surely my intellect is average as a common sparrow."

"Oh no," Mr. Longfellow said softly, shaking his head. "You are a woman of far greater depth than most."

The compliment left Fanny speechless. She certainly had never thought of herself as dull-witted, but neither had she felt she excelled in matters of scholastic pursuit. To hear someone else, especially someone she had grown to respect so much, say such a thing was rather exciting.

"To back up a few steps, however," Mr. Longfellow said, finally breaking eye contact with her. "You said that your indulgence in educational pursuits is a luxury. But should not women have as much opportunity as men to expand their minds, and would that not expand their lives and influence just as it does for men?"

Fanny wanted to explore his comment regarding *her* mind, but did not want to appear arrogant. Or overly surprised. She focused on his last question and resumed her role as devil's advocate. "Again I would ask, to what end should women's minds be so expanded? Most women in the world shall be focused on the daily tasks of household maintenance for all of their lives. What need have they to read a travel book, for example, if they will never travel?"

"I would submit that every human would benefit from reading about the world, whether they will ever see it or not. Do we not believe that we have much to learn from history and scripture? What more could we learn from the history of other countries? And when I say 'we,' I mean our fellow Americans.

"If for no other cause than to remind us of how our founding principles differ from other nations, we should know how the world operates. Without such knowledge, we run great risk of future generations not understanding the distinction between America and the British government, for instance. If the American population had a greater percentage of educated minds, how might the influence and advancement of our culture increase? And for what reason should we base that advancement only on the male mind?

"England is educating more and more women all the time, and with a new queen taking the throne in coming years, I expect there will be even greater emphasis on equal opportunity between the sexes. America could do as much without a queen and truly put into place our ideals of allowing men and women to rise above circumstances of birth through effort."

He paused to glance her way. "I shall agree that your situation is unique when compared to the countless women toiling day-to-day in America, but I see a great future ahead of us all if we will give women the equal chance to seek the potential of their minds as you have been able to—and allow minds such as yours to expand themselves even more through higher education. The future generations that would be benefited by educated women raising children is, in and of itself, impossible to measure."

Fanny stared at him, only vaguely realizing that at some point they had stopped walking and stood facing one another on the sidewalk. She was shocked at his passion for this topic while also being invigorated by it. Not only did he see great potential in women, but he saw it specifically in *her.* "You do not agree with Mr. Jefferson that a woman lacks the mental ability to learn as men do?"

Mr. Longfellow chuckled and shook his head. "Not in the least. Do you feel that your mental ability is less than, for instance, Tom's?"

She was silenced again. *Did* she agree that Tom was superior to her in intellect? He was more educated, having studied law at Harvard. But Mr. Longfellow knew that. He was not asking after formal education but mental ability. Having never considered such a thing made it impossible for Fanny to answer with only a moment's notice.

She *was* reminded of some facts, however. Tom did not read as Fanny did, and they often had conversations regarding history and philosophy where she felt she could best him—despite that fact that her formal education had ended years earlier than his. Did that not speak to equal ability to learn?

Tom would never agree to such a thing—she was certain of that—nor any man of her acquaintance. Except, perhaps, Mr. Longfellow, who was watching her as though he could read her thoughts.

Before she could form an appropriate answer, Mr. Longfellow asked another question. "Might I ask you, Miss Fanny, who taught you to read?"

"I attended school," Fanny said. "As any other girl of my station is able."

"Yes, until the age of ten or twelve, I expect." He raised his eyebrows expectantly.

Fanny nodded, slightly embarrassed since he obviously saw that as lacking, but she did not take offense. How could she when he was paying her, and her sex as a whole, such a compliment of potential?

"And before that, who taught you your letters? Who taught you to read those first words?"

"My mother," Fanny said, feeling the warm prick of her heart that she always felt when she thought of her mother who had loved her family and spent so many years ill. Fanny had clear memories of lying beside Mama in bed and listening to her mother's voice say the letters and sounds of a word then waiting for Fanny to repeat it. The memory was so vivid that she could smell the lavender of her mother's perfume and feel the softness of the sheets and blankets tangled around her restless feet.

"As did mine," Mr. Longfellow said with a nod. "I had schooling beginning when I was three years old, but it was on my mother's lap that I was first read to, and it was to my mother's ear that I first sounded out the words she wrote down on the slate for me to learn. My mother took the Protestant principles of educating one's children quite seriously and was herself a well-read woman. I am not surprised that you learned from your mother just as I did mine because they both understood the power of ideas and the importance the written word. However, how could our mothers have taught us if they themselves had not been taught by their own mothers?"

He scarcely waited for a reply before moving forward, caught up in his excitement. "How many women right now are raising children in upper New York or in the wilds of the American frontier and are unable to teach their children to read and write? How can children of such mothers know enough to even hope for more opportunity than what their mothers have received? Boy or girl."

"Not every occupation requires reading and writing," Fanny said, engaged in the debate though she wasn't truly trying to argue. "A farmer, for instance, or a blacksmith. The frontier is being harnessed by men and women who work with their hands, not with their minds."

"Ah," Mr. Longfellow said, raising his finger and pointing at the sky. "Does not everyone use their mind? Should not every man and woman be able to read the Bible, regardless of his or her occupation? Was that not Martin Luther's very aim? I think of the understanding and insight I gained from reading *Paradise Lost.*"

Fanny nodded; they had indeed shared resounding discussions of Milton's epic poem.

Mr. Longfellow continued, "Should not every man and woman be able to access such perspective so that they too might be edified regarding the formation of the world and humanity? Should not every man and woman be able to record their thoughts and impressions of the world in a journal for future generations to learn from? Should not every child be able to print their own name and read the printing of their parents?"

His eyes were nearly dancing, and Fanny found his energy rather intoxicating. "The frontier will always be the frontier—wild and without order—until lawyers and doctors and people of political minds join those farmers and blacksmiths in forming communities. There must be law and expectations of conduct. It will take education for such things to be enacted and understood for the good of us all." He shook his head. "I must adamantly propose that all of society would improve if each member could read and write and learn for himself. Once such abilities are in place, the individuals can ponder on cultures and history, look for the pattern of things and plan so as to avoid the pitfalls that have caused such tragedies in the world.

"With basic education comes the ability to think, and a mind that thinks is a mind that improves upon itself. I would suggest that a farmer would be a better one if he could read the latest literature on soil and botany. I would say that a blacksmith will make a better kettle if he can read up on the science between the different metals he works in his forge. Everyone would have greater potential if they had the ability to learn—man or woman, black or white."

Oh dear, is Mr. Longfellow an abolitionist? Fanny's father had been an advocate for the fair treatment of slaves during his time in Congress, and Fanny herself had opinions regarding the dark-skinned men and women upon whom much of America's economy depended, but being an abolitionist was not a position to be taken lightly. Her father was a pioneer in the textile industry, which profited directly from the free labor of the cotton plantations in the south. Because of her family's relationship to the institution she did not often let her mind follow the sympathies of her heart. She hoped Mr. Longfellow would be equally tactful around her father, but she did not know how to broach the subject.

"You are a very singular man," Fanny finally said, smiling to let him know she did not mean it as an insult. "I have never heard such a vision. I am quite unsure what to make of it."

He looked away as though embarrassed by his fiery speech. "Indeed my opinions are quite singular far too often. Forgive my preaching."

"Not at all," Fanny said as they resumed walking. "You have given me a great deal to think about. To be labeled a bluestocking is a fear of many young women who enjoy literature, you know. Your ideas would make bluestockings of my entire sex."

"Using one's mind should not come with a disparaging label," Mr. Longfellow said. "Rather it should be something to be commended, something a woman should take pride in. A woman such as yourself is a shining example of the potential women have within our society. I feel our country would improve by leaps and bounds incomprehensible to our current expectations if we would give women the same opportunities now available to men and encourage them to see their value both individually and to our country as a whole."

"And yet the beginning of this discussion was sparked by your disappointment in what men are currently offered in our American colleges."

"I would say that at present a diploma from an American university is not much more than a reflection of a man's status in society and a tribute to the discipline he showed in attending to his studies. While those studies certainly expand a man's mind and vision, for the majority of those who graduate, the greatest benefit will be the connections they have made to other students."

"Oh, but you *are* severe," Fanny said, shaking her head at his candor. At the same time, she knew that the connections Tom had made while attending Harvard were the part of his education he valued most.

"I am honest," Mr. Longfellow said, shrugging. "Having spent a great deal of time in classrooms—both as a student and a teacher—I can honestly attribute the majority of my learning to that which I have sought out on my own, much of it done at university campuses in Europe. I should very much like to bring greater opportunities to Harvard and structure teaching in a way that the students truly *learn* the subjects, not just recite lessons. I feel a great many women—like yourself—would benefit from such study. Perhaps they would even appreciate it more than some of these spoiled young men who simply see their collegiate years as a time of independence rather than edification."

They reached the hotel where the Appletons were staying, and Mr. Longfellow hurried the last few steps to open the door for Fanny. She thanked him, feeling a bit shy as she passed him to enter the foyer. They walked in silence to the base of the stairs that led to the Appleton rooms.

"Thank you for such a fascinating discussion, Mr. Longfellow," Fanny said as they began climbing the stairs side by side. She wanted to ask him what made him see her as above women in general but could not form the question in a way that she felt reflected the very intelligence he had spoken of.

Mr. Longfellow smiled, and she noted what a handsome man he was, especially when his features softened. He would have no difficulty in finding another wife if he chose to. The flash of envy and regret she felt took Fanny off guard. And worried her. Mr. Longfellow was too old for her and, besides, Fanny was devoted to her father.

Without her mother to care for the household, it was Molly's and Fanny's responsibility.

Mr. Longfellow interrupted her thoughts. "Thank you for letting me bend your ear, Miss Fanny, and I hope I did not come across *too* strongly. I'm afraid that when I feel passion for something I am quite difficult to dissuade."

For the second time, Fanny felt a twinge of envy for the possible future Mrs. Longfellow, but the topic of *this* jealousy caused her cheeks to heat up. It was one thing to admire the fact that he would treat his wife with equality, quite another to ponder on his passion for the woman. Had he felt such passion for his first wife, dead these long months? Did he miss her the way Father missed Mama? Did he cry for her when he felt no one was watching?

Fanny looked at the floor, rather horrified by her thoughts and the emotions they brought up in her chest, including jealously for the former and possible future Mrs. Longfellow. "It was of great interest to me, I assure you."

They reached the top of the stairs, and she faced him, realized she didn't know what to say, and moved forward again, staying one step ahead of him while her mind raced.

She felt as though a covering had been pulled away from something that few people were allowed to see. It was exciting, but unnerving, too. What would she do with all he had told her? How would it change her, and did she want to be changed?

Seven

Schaffhausen

Fanny crept into the room of the rented house in Schaffhausen where Tom sat with William, who was sleeping. She sat on the settee next to her brother, who was reading an expired copy of *The Boston Statesman.* That morning their father had retrieved the mail that had been waiting for the family at a posting station. They had spent the morning getting caught up with family and friends, as well as the current events of their city, though the events were not so current. The correspondences were from almost three months ago, but still they were pieces of home that all of them were glad to indulge in.

Fanny watched William's withered chest rise with a rattle and fall with a gasp for several seconds before she spoke, giving Tom time to fold the paper. "Did he eat anything at all?"

"A few bites of bread," Tom said. "Now that we have reached Schaffhausen, I don't think he will indulge us so much."

Fanny suspected that what William had eaten the last week or so had only been to appease them, not because he had any desire to prolong his life. They had arrived in Schaffhausen yesterday afternoon with heavy hearts. There was no longer anything to keep William from giving into the failing of his body.

Tom put an arm around her shoulder and gave her a squeeze. "We shall be alright," he said with the brotherly wisdom that was not his nature. "He shall join the others he loved so much in this life. He shall be at peace, and his earthly struggles will be over."

Fanny nodded but could not speak. Believing in a life after this one—a life free of pain and sorrow—was certainly a balm for her aching soul, but it did not take away the regret at losing her dear cousin. One more piece of her history taken from her and buried in the ground. She did not want another empty place in her heart that would ache for someone loved and lost.

The sound of someone in the doorway caught her attention, and she and Tom looked to the servant standing there. Adelè had been with them since Havre and would remain with them until the completion of their journey, along with a cook, a footman, and a valet for the men.

Adelè kept her head bent and her eyes on a spot on the floor a few feet in front of her. "Mr. Longfellow is awaiting you in the front parlor, Mr. Tom, Miss Frances."

Fanny had not heard the bell, but perhaps in light of William's condition, Mr. Longfellow had knocked lightly enough to get the attention of the servants rather than disturb the household.

Their father had wasted no expense in their lodging for this stay and had rented a three-level house with servants' quarters and two parlors filled with exotic collectibles. It was finer than the other rentals they'd had on their trip and not far from a Protestant church their father had communicated with while they were still in Zurich.

As Fanny and Tom made their way to the front parlor—the company parlor, as Fanny thought of it—she wondered why Mr.

Longfellow had included her in the request. Their private conversation in Zurich had led to Fanny feeling a connection to him, and she had wished for more private conversations that had not come. As he had been lodged some distance from their hotel, and her days had been filled with packing, traveling, and unpacking it was not surprising. She hoped that Germany would provide more opportunity, but William would be gone by then, and she could never think on that for long.

"Longfellow," Tom said when he reached the parlor a step ahead of Fanny. Her brother's voice did not betray the family pain as he crossed to his friend, who rose from where he'd been sitting near the window. The men shook hands. "It is good to see you, my friend. How are your accommodations? Better than Zurich, I hope."

"They are very well, Tom, thank you." His tone was somber, and Fanny noted his furrowed brow and regretful expression.

"Is something wrong, Mr. Longfellow?" she asked. "Has something happened?"

Mr. Longfellow let out a breath and held Fanny's eyes a moment before turning his attention to Tom. "I'm afraid I've been summoned back to Heidelberg by Miss Crowninshield, my . . . my wife's companion who undertook this journey with me. She has been with friends in Germany while I traveled through Switzerland."

"Is Miss Crowninshield unwell?" Fanny asked. She had asked Tom about her at one point, wondering at the propriety of Mr. Longfellow having traveled for months with an unmarried woman. Tom had chuckled and shook his head. "I assure you that you need not worry about competition for Henry's affections," which Fanny assured Tom were no concern at all. Fanny had been embarrassed at Tom's inference that there was any affection between her and Mr.

Longfellow, but secretly glad to know that there was none between him and Miss Crowninshield either.

"She is in good health, thank you." Mr. Longfellow attempted a smile, but it did not stay long. "She is ready to return to America and has found us passage on a ship set to leave London in early October. We have just enough time to travel to the port without having to rush through the last few cities she would like to see en route."

"We had hoped you would continue our tour with us," Tom said. "Could she not return with some other traveler? I'm sure Father could help with such an arrangement."

Mr. Longfellow shook his head. "It would be unkind for me to expect her to make the trip without me. She was a good friend to me when Mary died." He looked out the window. Fanny had never heard him speak of his wife, and the light from the window made him look very much like the troubled widower he was. He turned back to them. "I am disappointed not to continue on with your family, but I feel I must return to Boston with Miss Crowninshield and see to her comfort. I came to you as soon as I realized my situation. Your father is out?"

"Yes," Tom said. "He had a meeting with the local clergy here concerning . . ."

Fanny looked at her brother when he didn't continue and felt a lump in her throat. She reached for her brother's hand and gave it a quick squeeze of understanding and support. "We shall give Father your regrets," Fanny said, smiling at Mr. Longfellow. "Of course, you should return with Miss Crowninshield. Father will understand."

Mr. Longfellow nodded slowly. "I also received word regarding my position. They need me in Cambridge by the end of the year and, then, Mary's father sent me word of his eagerness to give Mary a proper burial." His words sounded as though he were trying to convince them, and himself, of why it was necessary to return. "I should have returned before now. I feel I have not done well by her." When he met Fanny's eyes, his pain was laid bare before her. Did he truly blame himself for his wife's death? Did it haunt him? He looked away and changed the subject. "If we make passage on the ship Miss Crowninshield has indicated, I could return to Cambridge in time to bury Mary very close to the anniversary of her death. It feels right and best."

"Of course it is," Tom said. "You are a good man."

Mr. Longfellow said nothing, only stared at the carpet in silence.

"When will you leave Schaffhausen?" Tom asked.

"First thing tomorrow morning," Mr. Longfellow said. His agitation seemed to unstick his feet, and he began pacing between them and the window. "My trunks are still packed from Zurich, and I have settled my account with the landlord for my rooms, but I had hoped to sit with William this afternoon as I will be unable to stay until . . . the end. I would like to read to him—the Dewey sermons, I think." He stopped his pacing and faced Tom with an expectant expression.

"Certainly," Tom said. "But he took a dose of opium not more than an hour ago. I'm afraid he will not be alert for some time."

"That is all right," Mr. Longfellow said. "It is not his ears and mind I will recite to. I only hope his spirit might hold my words and take them with him." He looked up with tears in his eyes that he did not try to hide or blink away. "There is such unfairness in this life at times. What would we do if not for a belief in Deity?"

Neither Tom nor Fanny answered the rhetorical question, but Fanny nodded, blinking back tears of her own.

"You may attend him for as long as you like," Tom said. "And stay for tea and supper as well. We shall all miss your company. You have been a great comfort for us these weeks."

"As you have been for me," Mr. Longfellow said. "I am without words to adequately express my gratitude for your friendship." His eyes flickered to Fanny, but she looked away, unable to carry the burden of sentiment his glance might hold. "May I go to William now?" Mr. Longfellow asked a moment later.

"Of course," Tom said. "I shall have Fanny see that you receive some refreshment."

"That is not necessary," Mr. Longfellow said, shaking his head. "I simply thank you for allowing me to stay a bit."

Tom showed Mr. Longfellow to the back of the house while Fanny ordered some tea and bread to be brought to him. When the tray was ready, she took it to the parlor herself, setting it quietly on the small table.

Mr. Longfellow did not acknowledge her entry. He sat beside the lounge where William slept, breathing his rattling breaths. Mr. Longfellow leaned toward William and began to read the sermons he had brought with him, his voice soft.

A feeling of reverence washed over Fanny as she prepared Mr. Longfellow a cup of tea—cream only, no sugar—but she accounted her feelings to the sermons, not the man reading them with such feeling.

She placed the cup of tea on the table beside Mr. Longfellow, but still he did not look up, so intent he was on his task. Unsure what to do with herself and unable to ask Mr. Longfellow his wishes, she chose to stay in the room, as she had during numerous discussions when William was awake.

She settled into a chair and gave into her tears, allowing them to drip from her chin and stain her dress as she drew comfort from the sound of Mr. Longfellow's voice. She sent out her own prayer that William's suffering would not continue much longer. She allowed herself to feel the fullness of her love for her dear cousin and imagined the welcome such a kind soul would receive when he arrived in Heaven. It had brought her comfort when Charles passed to imagine her mother embracing his return, and she was glad to think of both Mama and Charles waiting for William now.

She closed her eyes and let Mr. Longfellow's voice lull her to a place of comfort, a place where believing in God's love was enough. A place where her own heart could find peace somehow.

Eight

Strasburg, France

Fanny looked out the carriage window at the imposing tower of the Strasburg Cathedral and marveled that after all that had happened this last week they found themselves here. Strasburg was often called "Little Paris" and served as a natural stopping point for a traveler journeying between Germany or Switzerland and the *actual* Paris and all the distractions it offered. The gothic architecture of the cathedral, with spires stretching toward heaven, made Fanny think of William and the blessed rest he had finally earned. She let out a sigh that betrayed, despite her faith, how much she missed her cousin.

The family had stayed with William through his final moments and attended his burial two days later. Rather than travel to Germany without a proper guide, Father decided they would go to Paris for the winter in hopes that the distraction of the city would revive them. The shadow cast by William's death could not be ignored, and Fanny wished she had asked Mr. Longfellow for advice on how to bear it. Tom had written to Mr. Longfellow's hotel in Paris, where he would go after collecting Miss Crowninshield in Heidelberg, to tell him the sad news.

"Perhaps we shall see Mr. Longfellow again before he leaves for London. He was going to Paris, too," Fanny said with an absent air. It was not *impossible* that their paths could cross since their destinations were the same. The Appletons would stay in Strasburg for only a few nights before continuing their journey, however, so there was a limited window of opportunity.

"Perhaps we shall," Molly said. "If not here in Strasburg, then perhaps we might meet up with him Paris. Did he say how long he would be there?"

"He didn't," Fanny replied. Mr. Longfellow had been such a comfort, especially the last day he'd spent at William's side, and she imagined the balm his words could give to her now as she struggled to make peace with her family's loss. Beyond her desire for solace, though, Fanny missed the way he talked to her and the way he listened to what she said. As the carriage made its way to the center of the city, she looked at every man they passed, wondering if it might be him, even though she knew it was improbable.

The hotel was full, but there were some guests preparing to leave, and so the Appleton family was directed to the salon where they could wait for their rooms to be readied. Fanny was tired and hungry as she fell into a seat near the window and took off her bonnet. It had been a long day of travel. Father buried his face behind a Paris newspaper while Molly and Fanny watched the street outside the hotel window. It was a fine day, and there were a lot of people about.

"It seems that *Norma* will be performed at the Paris opera house again beginning next week," Father said after a few minutes of silence.

"Shall Fanny and I get a new opera dress?" Molly asked, turning hopeful eyes toward her father. "You did say we could have some new dresses for winter."

"Yes, of course," their father said with a nod. "You must have some winter dresses, and another for the opera, too. We shall find a reputable dressmaker as soon as we are settled in the city."

"I would like a new coat in the French style," Tom said, betraying his love of fashion. "I did love Henry's fine red coat. He gave me the name of the tailor who made it for him. Perhaps the tailor would have a reference for a dressmaker too."

"Very good, Tom," Father said. "I shouldn't mind updating my wardrobe either. I am not too old to dress like a Frenchman."

Molly laughed and the sound lightened the mood considerably. How long it had been since any of them had laughed, even Tom who was the most lighthearted of them all? "What else shall we do once we arrive in Paris?" Molly asked.

"I am looking forward to another tour of the Louvre," Tom said. "I plan to spend a week at least this time after Henry helped me realize how much I had missed."

"I should like the additional art classes we discussed," Fanny said, joining the conversation. She stripped off her gloves and flexed her stiff fingers. "I should like to do my own rendition of a classic painting before we leave. It is all the rage to bring home your own interpretation, you know."

"Yes, yes," Father said. "I shall see to those lessons. I would also like both of you girls to improve your French with a tutor. As we will be in Europe for some time longer, it would be a credit to take full advantage of the educational possibilities." He paused for a breath. "Hearing Mr. Longfellow speak of how learning other languages expands your ability to learn all manner of things intrigues me. He attributes his own intellect to having learned so many languages in his youth. As you both learned French in school, I do not think it would take much to restore your skill and increase it to that of conversation level. I've already sent ahead to our boardinghouse to see about a teacher."

Fanny considered this revelation a moment and wondered how it had come about. Her father hadn't shown interest in his daughters learning the language when they were in Paris the first time. "Did Mr. Longfellow *tell* you to have us take French lessons?"

"Well, he recommended it," Father said as though nothing was strange about Fanny's question. "We had an interesting discussion one afternoon where he spoke of the importance of education, even for women." Father did not say it the way Fanny *knew* Mr. Longfellow would have. "The more I thought on what he had to say, the more I realized that women with greater education are well-suited wives for educated husbands. As I only want the very best of men to seek out my daughters, it is perfectly reasonable that I should educate both of you in such a way as to improve your appeal."

"Won't men find it intimidating for us to be educated?" Molly asked, her eyebrows pulled together as though sorting out in her mind what kind of man would be intrigued and what kind would be intimidated.

"Which is why learning French is the perfect solution," Father said with a note of triumph. "Most men of our class learn French, as Tom and Charles did when they were in school, and so to speak a language men already know would not put you above them in any matter of intelligence. It would, however, keep unsuitable men at a distance, I think. And what better place to learn French than in Paris?" He said *Paris* like the French did—*Pairee*—and Molly laughed again.

Fanny smiled politely, turning her gaze back to the window and her memory back to her conversation with Mr. Longfellow regarding education for women. Not once had Mr. Longfellow asserted that the reason for a woman to be learned was to attract a husband. Nor did he express concern regarding a woman having a greater intellect than her husband. Rather, he had focused on how a woman could be edified by her own education, and how two educated parents—as a partnership—could then influence their children.

Remembering that discussion renewed Fanny's appreciation of the confidence Mr. Longfellow had inspired within her. He had spoken as though any woman was capable of learning and that all women would be bettered for it. He had called Fanny articulate and well-spoken, and she had felt complimented for her own individual merit, rather than hopeful that an education would serve as an element of attraction for a suitable man.

Molly, Tom, and Father began to talk of their expectations for Paris while Fanny watched the people promenading down the *Route du Polygone.* She hoped their rooms would be ready soon. She longed for a nap—after a good meal, of course.

When a familiar form on the street outside the window caught her eye, Fanny startled and blinked. She shook her head and wondered if she'd nodded off, but then she focused her gaze more intently and gasped too quietly for anyone else to hear. The man who had caught her notice was Mr. Longfellow! He was walking with three women—one older and two younger, one of whom was quite pretty and holding on to Mr. Longfellow's arm.

Fanny told herself it couldn't be him. The odds of seeing Mr. Longfellow here were slim, but as he and his party drew closer, Fanny's heart rate increased. She smiled in anticipation, already imagining the way his blue eyes would look when he would see her. She had longed for this chance to talk with him and began to rise from her chair, drawn by her desire to reconnect with his compassionate heart. Then the pretty girl on his arm said something and he laughed with such levity that Fanny returned to her seat in an instant, the warmth and excitement she'd felt upon seeing him vanishing.

Fanny had not had many occasions to see Mr. Longfellow laugh, and the contrast of his gladness when she was so steeped in mourning made her chest heat up. She looked away, trying to make sense of the instant envy and irritation she felt. She reminded herself that he did not even know William had died; Tom's letter was waiting for Mr. Longfellow in Paris. She could not judge his lighthearted mood based on information he was unaware of, and yet a sense of betrayal took root in her stomach and sent her joy at seeing him into the shadows of her aching heart.

Fanny looked back at Mr. Longfellow in time to see him nodding while leaning closer to his companion at his side as though to better hear what she was saying. Seeing him with the girl made Fanny realize that he had rarely talked with Fanny so easily; only that one day in Zurich had he been so casual. To see him so different, so comfortable and easy, sparked both envy and embarrassment. She had thought perhaps Mr. Longfellow fancied her, and she had allowed herself to feel flattered by that perceived affection.

Anyone looking at him now would assume he fancied the girl on his arm, and perhaps he did. Perhaps he took a liking to whatever young woman was in his company at any given time. Perhaps he complimented her mind, too, made her feel special and particular. The thought left Fanny's chest cold and her neck hot.

"Your rooms are ready, Mr. Appleton."

Fanny turned away from the window in time to see a servant bowing out of the doorway. She took a moment to control her thoughts and straightened her spine. Thank goodness no one knew of the foolish fancy that had been growing in her since Mr. Longfellow left their company in Schaffhausen. At least she would not have to endure Tom's teasing or Molly's pity at having seen more in her interactions with Mr. Longfellow than she should have.

As Fanny picked up her gloves from the table beside her chair, she glanced out the window one last time. Mr. Longfellow's back was to her now—showing the fine cut of his coat—and she lifted her chin.

It could never be like it's been, she told herself, following her family from the room. *And you are not a silly girl who does not understand the world. Enjoy the memory, take his encouragement to expand yourself, but do not let these weeks become anything more than that in your mind.*

Nine

Reunion

Henry read the note, his heart heavy in his chest. William Appleton had passed and had been buried in Schaffhausen a week ago. Henry knew when he had last parted company with the Appletons that William did not have many more days, but knowing of his death increased Henry's sorrow. He would have liked to have been there. He had known William for only a few weeks, but he had come to love him. Henry's greatest regret was on behalf of the Appleton family. He understood the pain of their loss too well and mourned alongside them in his heart.

Following the revelation of the sad news, Tom Appleton had included an invitation for Henry, and whomever might be traveling with him, to join the Appletons for breakfast at their hotel. The Appletons' hotel was not far from the more modest accommodations Henry and his company had chosen, and he felt sure that Clara, Mrs. Bryant, and her daughter would be glad to join them. Had Miss Bryant not said just yesterday that Henry seemed to have fallen in love with the Appletons? And hadn't Clara teased him about how

Switzerland and the Appleton family had been the cure for his melancholy?

Henry himself would not go so far as to say he was cured—every thought of Mary still brought with it a stab of regret—and yet his time with the Appletons had taught him a great deal. First, that he was not the only person to lose someone he loved, and second, that there was hope he could be a happy man again someday. He'd come to realize more fully that Mary would want his happiness. That was not to say he knew how he might find that fullness and joy, but he could hope for it. The restoration of his spirit would be something for which he would always credit the Appletons. He had needed time apart, with people who would not share thoughts of Mary, in order to see the possibility of a life without her. He would be forever grateful for the role they had played in that discovery; Fanny most of all. The opportunity to see her again—the whole family, of course—helped relieve the sting of William's loss.

He quickly scrawled an acceptance of the invitation to Tom, then went around to the room the Bryants and Clara were sharing on the women's floor of the hotel to make sure they were agreeable, which they were. Once it was confirmed, he gave the message to the clerk with instructions to have it delivered to the Appletons' hotel as soon as possible. They would need to leave within the hour to be there on time.

When they arrived at the hotel, they were shown into one of the private dining rooms, surely the finest the hotel had to offer. Mr. Appleton, Tom, and Molly were already seated at the table, and Henry introduced one group to the other.

"Your husband is William Cullen Bryant," Mr. Appleton said to Mrs. Bryant after the introductions concluded.

"Yes," she said with a nod. "Do you know Mr. Bryant?"

"Of him only, I'm afraid. But I have great respect for his work at the *Post.*"

"The Bryants have become dear friends," Mr. Longfellow added, drawing Mr. Appleton's attention. "Clara and I are indebted to them for all the help they have extended toward us since meeting them in Heidelberg."

Mrs. Bryant waved away the admiration. "It is a joy for us to spend time with our fellow countrymen, and we all got on so well, we were glad to lend the necessary company and allow Mr. Longfellow and Miss Crowninshield the opportunity to continue their tour."

As happened frequently, Mary had become an invisible topic of conversation. Henry could not travel alone with an unmarried woman, but Mrs. Bryant had been both willing and gratified to assist, as her husband was kept quite busy and her teenage daughter was growing rather bored of just her mother's company.

"Are you the family Miss Crowninshield stayed with in Germany?" Tom asked.

Mrs. Bryant shook her head. "She stayed with a German family so she could better learn the language, but we had rented a house nearby for the winter."

The group continued to make small talk while Henry watched the door. Mr. Appleton had mentioned that Fanny would be joining them, and Henry's anticipation grew with each passing minute. Part of him was frightened by his interest in the youngest daughter of Mr. Nathan Appleton—there were so many reasons why he should not feel as he did—but another part of him, the part that had come alive since becoming acquainted with such a remarkable young woman, was relieved to be so affected. Parting company with the family had only confirmed his interest in Miss Fanny. Where his particular interest in her would lead, he did not know; this feeling was too new and unexpected. He only knew he enjoyed her company and wished for more of it. As the party served themselves from the buffet and the minutes ticked forward on the clock, Henry found himself worrying that Fanny was not coming.

He was halfway through his plate of ham, eggs, and mushrooms before the parlor door opened and Fanny entered. The men stood for her arrival, but she'd no sooner stepped over the threshold that she came to a stop and looked over the crowd with wide eyes. "Oh," she said, looking first at her father and then moving her gaze to Henry, who smiled in response. "I—I did not realize . . ."

"I only learned Henry was in Strasburg last night, after meeting some other Americans at a pub down the street," Tom explained.

Fanny seemed to realize they were all waiting for her, so she stepped forward and let the door close behind her.

The men returned to their seats, and Tom continued his explanation. "I sent 'round an invitation and here they are."

"It was a wonderful surprise," Molly said.

"Yes," Fanny said in an even tone. "Indeed it is."

"Let me introduce my traveling companions," Mr. Longfellow said.

Fanny greeted each woman cordially and then excused herself to the sideboard where she filled her plate.

Henry's awareness of her movements, though she was behind him, was strange but not unwelcome. Just being in the same room with her made him feel more alive, more keen, more assured. She took a seat at the far side of the table, between Molly and Miss Bryant, and immediately engaged the young woman in conversation. He envied Miss Bryant the attention and realized, somewhat surprisingly, that she and Fanny were near the same age. Fanny seemed so much older, more worldly and self-possessed. Henry watched them without being obvious. He was too far away to speak with her, but a smile from Fanny would be the crowning pleasure of his day.

"Did you arrange passage back to America, then?" Tom asked.

Henry turned his attention from Fanny to her brother, who sat directly across the table. "We did. A ship sails out of Liverpool on October 12."

"That will not give you much time to spend in Paris."

"A week or so is all," Henry said. "Long enough to finalize the arrangements."

"Would you have time to join us for the opera?" Mr. Appleton asked. "We quite liked *Norma* the first time we saw it."

"Thank you for the invitation," Henry said, trying to keep the regret from his tone, "only we hadn't planned to take in much entertainment."

"We're quite turned out," Clara cut in, causing Henry to wince. She was a good woman and he was grateful for her insistence that they continue their tour, but her manners were not as they ought to be. In Portland it didn't matter so much as everyone knew of her illegitimate heritage and forgave her for it. She was wealthy and personable after all, but now and again she showed a lack of refinement that embarrassed Henry and made him too aware of what kept her apart from company the caliber of the Appletons.

"What Clara means," Henry said, casting her a look he hoped she understood but was not offended by, "is that every minute of our time there will be filled with the details of transatlantic travel. We'll be sending most of our things—including all my books and papers—on a different ship so we have to determine what we will need with us on the journey."

"It was less expensive to ship our belongings on a cargo vessel,"

Clara said, proving that she had missed Henry's pointed look. "It also allowed us better accommodations on the passenger ship."

"A wise decision," Mrs. Bryant said, though Henry was unsure whether she was trying to rescue them or simply joining the conversation. "I always say that proper rooms aboard a ship are worth every ha'penny it costs."

"I agree wholeheartedly," Tom said. "Though I do not mind sea travel very much." He looked down the table to Fanny, who was no longer talking with Miss Bryant but seemed rather intent on her plate. "Fanny and I handled the voyage out of Boston like sailors, did we not?"

Fanny glanced ever so quickly at Henry before focusing on her brother. "Indeed," she said with a nod and a polite smile. "You would think we'd been on deck our whole lives."

"Not me," Mrs. Bryant said. "I am already dreading it."

"Mama spent every day of the trip in her cabin," Miss Bryant added with a sympathetic frown. "The rest of us felt better after a few days." She turned to Fanny. "Were you truly not ill at all?"

Fanny smiled at the girl. "Not a bit."

"Oh, I do envy that," Mrs. Bryant said. "How about you, Mr. Longfellow? Do you do well with seafaring?"

"It takes me a day or two to get my bearings, but everything else is an adventure. There was a storm on our way here, however, that certainly tested my mettle. Do you remember it, Clara?"

"How could I forget it?" she said with a shake of her head. "Mary and I had to tie ourselves into our berths to keep from falling out at night. I've never seen anything like it."

Mary again—that prick of awareness, the momentary flag in conversation as everyone thought of her simultaneously. Henry looked at Fanny, and she gave him a slight smile of sympathy before asking Clara about Germany.

That smile was exactly what he'd hoped for, and he took it as a sign that the hope for his future would have something to do with Miss Fanny Appleton. Not for a while yet—she had a year or more left for her Grand Tour—but Henry knew that when she returned to Boston, she would be a part of his future somehow. He did not fully understand his awareness of this fact, but that it was fact was absolutely certain. By the time she returned to Boston, he planned to be ready to step into that future more fully than he could now.

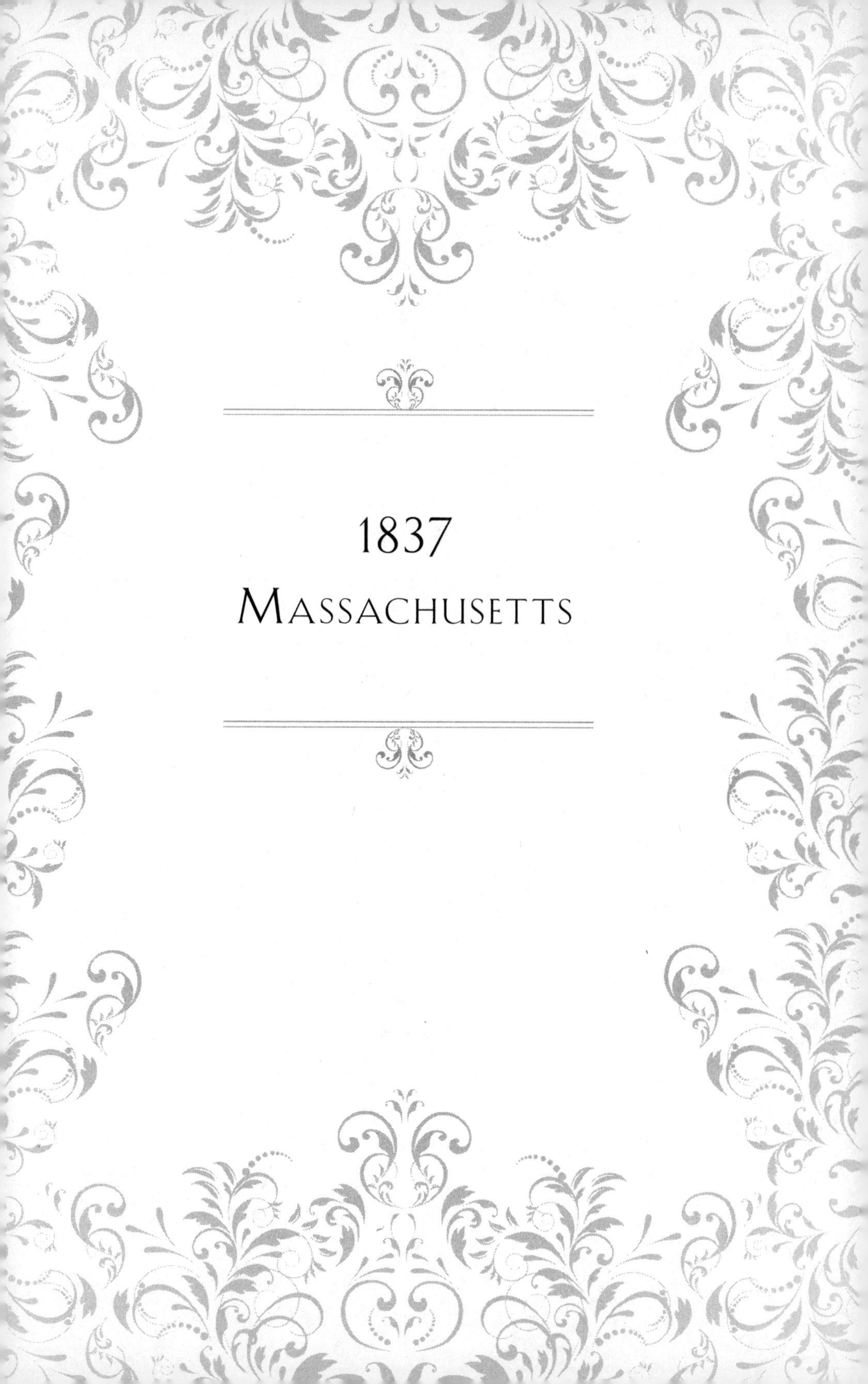

1837
Massachusetts

Ten

Home

Fanny and Molly filed out of Federal Street Church with the other parishioners while chatting with Aunt Sam. Their Uncle Sam's wife was actually named Mary, but they had somehow fallen into calling her Aunt Sam. A similar thing had happened with Aunt and Uncle William.

Aunt and Uncle Sam had no children and so she doted on her nieces and nephews, something that had only added to the sweetness of being home again for Fanny and Molly.

It was their first Sunday back in Boston, and Fanny found the congregation as comfortable as ever. The tour of Europe had been wonderful, beyond what she could have imagined. She would always cherish the memories, but it was good to be home. She and Molly stopped to converse with several acquaintances intent on taking turns to share an embrace and welcome the family. The August heat was stifling, but the sisters did not want to be rude to their friends by begging off after their two-year absence.

After several minutes, Aunt Sam excused herself with the reminder that they would be joining her for tea that afternoon. It would be the third visit they'd had with their aunt and uncle since their return, but if the audience was willing to listen—which Aunt and Uncle Sam seemed to be—Fanny and Molly were eager to continue chattering on about all they had seen and done on their tour.

Fanny and Molly began walking toward home but were delayed by yet another neighbor.

"You shall have to come to dinner," Mrs. Wilton said after welcoming both Appleton women back to "the fold of the Lord." "We look forward to hearing about your trip, and my nephew, Phillip, is staying with me. I would so like to introduce you now that your adventure is past." She dropped her head and said in a conspiring tone, "I imagine your futures are looming rather heavy before you these days, are they not?"

Fanny kept her smile polite, but her shoulders tightened along with her grip on the handle of her parasol. "I believe our futures are as bright and welcoming as ever, do you not agree, Molly?"

"Certainly," Molly said, also smiling politely at Mrs. Wilton. They had known her all their lives and did not dislike her, even if she was a bit of a busybody. "We would love to come to dinner. Please send us 'round an invitation. Does Phillip speak French, by chance? Both Fanny and I are quite desperate to *parler en français* again."

Fanny pressed her lips together to hold back her smile while Mrs. Wilton tried to keep her own smile in place. "I shall send an invitation," she said, though she was not nearly as excited as she had been. "All the best as you get settled in." Mrs. Wilton hurried after her husband, who waited on the corner and seemed eager to get home and out of the humid heat of the New England summer.

"How do you know Phillip doesn't speak French?" Fanny asked Molly as they continued toward home. Father was talking with some friends under the shade of a yew tree, and Tom had left as soon as services were over—the political and financial tensions of the United States had quickly drawn the men's attention upon the family's return. The women were used to finding their own way home, however, and glad to avoid political talk if they could.

"According to Mr. Longfellow, no one *speaks* French even if they know the language." Molly gave a single shrug and a satisfied half-smile. "And Phillip did not even go to Harvard."

"You certainly can wield a sword when you choose to, can't you, Molly?"

"C'est la vie," Molly said, looping her hand through the air. "Father had wanted French to be a useful skill, and if it keeps unworthy gentlemen off our doorstep then I say it has fulfilled its purpose. Besides, Phillip is twenty-one years old. Too young to be hunting for a wife unless he is looking to line his pockets."

Molly had no sooner finished her explanation than an old family friend, John Peterton, was bowing before them. "Is it not the Appleton ladies returned from their travels abroad," he said with a wide grin that both women responded to in kind. John was Tom's age and had been a playmate of his when Tom and Molly were young. Their families still dined together, though John had lately been in New York learning the banking business from an uncle. "Might I walk you ladies home?"

"It would be a pleasure," Molly said, stepping to the side so he could move between them. He put an arm out for both sisters, and they all fell in step together. He asked after their voyage and then listened as they shared the highlights of their tour. He had been to Europe some years earlier, but had visited only London and Paris.

When they reached 39 Beacon Street, John—Fanny could not think of him as Mr. Peterton though she knew she should—brought them to the door and bowed over their hands. First Fanny's, then

Molly's, which he lingered over. Fanny caught the subtle cue and excused herself, leaving John and Molly alone on the doorstep, though she waited just inside until Molly came in. When she did, her cheeks were flushed in a way that spoke of more than the summer heat.

Fanny raised her eyebrows, and Molly took hold of her arm, hurrying her into the parlor as though someone might overhear them. The butler should have greeted them upon their entry, but they had returned home from Europe to find that he had run off weeks earlier. Fanny and Molly had not yet had time to interview a replacement. There were all manner of things regarding the household that needed to be set to rights, but they would have to wait. It was the Sabbath after all.

"He's invited me for a stroll on the Commons tomorrow evening," Molly said, her eyes wide with excitement. "Only the two of us."

"Indeed," Fanny said with a grin. "And did you accept?"

"Of course," Molly said. "He has grown into a *very* handsome man, and his family is well respected."

"My, my," Fanny said. "You *are* excited."

Molly shrugged and looked a bit embarrassed as she walked to the window, perhaps to catch a glimpse of John's retreating form. "I am almost twenty-four years old," she said, her voice suddenly serious. "I would be a fool to not be flattered by the attention of a man like Johnny. I would not want Mrs. Wilton to know it, but now that we are returned, I *am* eager to secure my future."

"A man like *Johnny*?" Fanny repeated, raising her eyebrows at the familiarity of her sister's address. Even though Fanny called him John in her mind, she would never address him as such, much less an even more familiar version of his name.

Molly blushed again. "I suppose I can't call him that any longer, can I? It was what I called him when we were young."

"Perhaps he will give you leave to be so familiar soon enough."

Molly flashed her sister another grin and then headed for the stairs. "I should like to change my dress before we go to Aunt Sam's. Are you coming up?"

"I shall be there shortly," Fanny said.

Only after Molly disappeared through the doorway did Fanny let her smile fall. Any man would be lucky to have Molly for a wife. She had an easy nature and a genuine goodness that would only benefit the man who asked for her hand. But for all of Fanny's appreciation for Molly's virtues, she was not ignorant of the areas of charm in which her sister was lacking.

Unfortunately for both sisters, they were not great beauties. Fanny had come to accept it for herself, especially as her appreciation of more intellectual matters had increased. Molly, on the other hand, often regretted her plain features. She did all she could with her hair and even a bit of rouge now and again to soften her features, which Fanny felt only seemed to draw more attention to the beauty she did not possess.

John Peterton, on the other hand, cut a very fine figure. He was tall with broad shoulders, bright eyes, and a fine face. He was also charming and never lacking for female attention. Why would his interest suddenly spring up toward Molly after all these years? He had never given her such notice before their trip; rather, it was Tom's company he sought out back then.

Fanny had come to realize during their travels how very wealthy her father was and through him, his children. Now that she was an adult, Father had explained to her the investments he had made in her name—money that belonged only to her. Her father would control her money until she married or reached the age of thirty, of course, but she was officially an heiress in addition to the significant dowry set aside for when she married. With the knowledge of her financial security also came the understanding that her money would be an attractive feature for young men.

Molly was similarly situated, and with the growing economic concerns of the time, Fanny wondered if she too felt rather conspicuous. Did she not know she might catch a man with a silver hook she did not mean to put in the water? Just this afternoon she had expressed suspicion of that very thing regarding Mrs. Wilton's nephew.

Fanny hated feeling suspicion toward John, however, and doubting Molly's potential to make a good match based on her excellent character made Fanny feel like a very bad sister. While Fanny questioned her own desire to marry—she had been increasingly vocal about such things since learning of her inheritance—Molly wanted nothing more from life than a husband and children. While Fanny felt the need to protect her heart, which still ached with the loss of those she'd loved, Molly's heart remained hopeful and optimistic.

"Do not look for ghosts," Fanny told herself, repeating a phrase her mother would often say when they were exaggerating an insult or looking for someone to blame for a foul mood.

Molly and John had known each other their entire lives, and it was certainly possible he had missed her during her absence and come to better appreciate her virtues. Fanny would not look for ghosts in John's motivations. He was as good a man as the family had ever known, and if he were to make an offer to Molly, Fanny would be the first to congratulate her sister on a very good match.

Having given herself a good talking-to, Fanny made her way to her bedchamber, thinking of the people she had seen for the first time in two years and allowing the comfort of being home again to truly seep into her bones. She loved Boston—the richness of its history, the breadth of its opportunity, and the quality of its people.

In remembering friends she was eager to see again, she included Mr. Longfellow. There had been plenty of time to ponder on their time together once they were apart—it had been almost exactly a year since they had seen one another in Strasburg—and she was *convinced* of her full recovery from any foolish fancy she may have imagined between them. Her only expectation was that of friendship and intellectual discussions.

Fanny had seen Europe differently after having met Mr. Longfellow, searching for the influence and the beauty within the cultures they saw. She had looked at herself differently, too, and realized the fulfillment of study and learning she had taken for granted before. It was also because of him that she had applied herself so intently to her French lessons. She was eager to show him what she had learned, eager to see the pride in his eyes, confirmation that she had met his expectation—an expectation no one else seemed to hold for her.

At some point, Mr. Longfellow would be invited to Beacon Street. She looked forward to such a meeting but did not allow herself to look forward to it *too* much. Too much attention toward a reunion might tempt her to wonder if there was a deeper connection between them, and she had already made her decision about that.

Fanny forced herself to think of other friends she had not yet seen—Emmeline Austin, for instance, who had grown up just one street away but who was visiting family in Pennsylvania until next week. And Susan Benjamin, who would love to hear of all the fine art Fanny had seen. And of course there was Fanny's dear friend Robert Apthorp, who had written Fanny faithfully throughout the entire two-year trip. So many people to see, so much history to share. And there would be dances and dinner parties and afternoon teas. Fanny had not lost her appetite for fashion and entertainment, and she yearned for the energetic company of her young friends. Learning had not deadened all her other interests.

Her maid was waiting for her in her bedchamber. Molly must have sent her; she was such a good sister. Fanny turned so the servant could undo the buttons of her dress, glad for the comforts of home all over again. Yes, it was very good to be home. Very good indeed.

Eleven

Renewed Acquaintance

Henry stood in the parlor of Craigie House—a stately Georgian mansion on Brattle Street where he'd lodged for nearly four months—and watched the front walk, waiting for Tom Appleton to appear.

Has it truly been a year? he asked himself. Henry wished he weren't nervous about renewing the acquaintance, then again he would be an idiot not to be.

Now that he was a resident of Cambridge, Henry better understood the Appleton family's place in society and how it contrasted with his own. Not only was Nathan Appleton one of the wealthiest men in New England, he was also politically active, a faithful member of the Federal Street Church, and respected to the point of devotion among many. He and his partners had actually founded the town of Lowell when they brought the modern-age of textile production to the area and an entire settlement grew around it.

Beyond that, Nathan Appleton stood as proof that the entire premise of the United States worked. That the son of a church deacon could change his circumstances justified the fight for their independence from Britain, who still marginalized their citizens based on the society of their birth.

Being part of a new nation, however, did not remove the distinction of class between its citizens. Born or earned, one's situation prescribed their society. That Henry had ever been included in the Appletons' circle—even abroad where the choice of company was so limited—was a thing to be appreciated. The Appletons were kind and accepting, and Henry doubted they would purposely reject him now that the tour was over, but he would not be a part of their social circle unless they wanted him to be.

While awaiting the Appletons' return from Europe, he had become acquainted with additional members of their family, specifically William Appleton and his wife, with whom he shared a mutual friend. Mr. and Mrs. Appleton were polite and accepting, giving him hope of further acquaintance when Nathan Appleton and his family returned.

Which is why Henry had been excited to receive Tom Appleton's note two days earlier, requesting they take a meal together and become reacquainted. Henry was glad for the opportunity, but anxious too. It was not Tom's friendship alone that Henry hoped for. Miss Frances Appleton was returned to Boston as well, and though Fanny would not be joining them for dinner, she would surely know of it.

Henry had spent the last year coming to terms with his interest in Fanny and knew that the opportunity to renew his acquaintance with Fanny would be determined in part by how well he and Tom got on tonight. The awareness made him feel disingenuous regarding his excitement to see Tom again, which served only to increase his anxiety.

Movement outside the window caught his attention, and Henry focused on the handsome carriage that stopped in front of the house. The coachman jumped down from his seat and opened the door so Tom could step out. Tom said something to the driver and then moved up the walkway that led to the front doors of Craigie House. Henry felt a dash of pride as he watched Tom's eyes take in the splendor of the house. Tom saw Henry through the window and lifted a hand. Henry raised his as well and hurried to meet his friend at the door.

Henry expected a handshake of greeting and so was surprised when Tom pulled him into a quick embrace, slapping Henry on the back. "Oh, it is good to see you again, Longfellow," Tom said, smiling as wide as the moon.

"Good to see you as well, Tom. I cannot tell you how happy I felt when I received your note. Do come in, dinner will be served shortly. We have the dining room to ourselves tonight, which is a happy accident to be sure."

Henry led Tom into the dining room to the right where the two men sat on the plush chairs at the far end of the hand-carved table. The table could accommodate twelve but rarely did since Mrs. Craigie, the woman who owned the house, often kept to herself for meals, and the other tenants often had their evening meal elsewhere. Miss Sarah Lowell, the only female tenant, was out tonight as well.

"So how fares the Maine-land boy exiled to Cambridge-town?" Tom asked, reclining against the back of the chair.

"Well enough," Henry said, not wanting to expound on his complaints too early in the renewal of friendship. "The society is excellent, and I have made good friends here."

"Oh, I agree, society does not get better than Boston." He lifted his eyes to look around the room, complete with heavy velvet drapes and well-crafted furniture. "What a fine house. Built by that Redcoat-lover Vassall, wasn't it?"

"Indeed," Henry said. The history of the house was part of what had drawn him here. Another attractive factor was that Henry felt Craigie House looked like an Italian villa. "After Vassal fled in '74, the house was occupied by the Marblehead regiment. It even housed General Washington and his family for nearly a year."

Tom grinned throughout Henry's explanation, prompting Henry to remember that Tom had grown up only a few miles away. "I'm sure you know better than I the history of the place."

"Likely not," Tom said, shaking his head. "It is one house of legacy in a place fairly dripping with it. I did know Washington stayed here before it was sold, of course, but where else would he stay but the finest house on Tory Row?" Tom gestured toward the front of the house. "And with such a view of the Charles River to boot?"

"Yes, it was surely fit for a president," Henry confirmed, turning the familiar phrase of "fit for a king" to one more appropriate in a free nation. "In fact my rooms are the very rooms Washington himself stayed in. I sleep where he slept and work in what was his sitting room."

"Well then, I fully expect you to raise up an army and overthrow some nation's repressive control within the year."

"If only that were not so near my situation," Henry said, a rueful laugh in his voice. "I am attempting to overthrow the antiquated regime of Harvard College and usher in a new age of linguistic merit. Alas, I am not the general Washington was and fear I may have to surrender."

Tom's smile remained, confirming Henry's trust that he was a safe confidante. It seemed Tom took few things seriously enough to be offended.

"What sort of attitude is that?" Tom asked as Miriam—the serving girl of Craigie House—brought in their dinner plates. Tom pulled back so the plate of lamb and roasted squash could be set before him, but did not stop speaking. "Where would our nation be if the forward thinkers of our grandfathers' generation had felt the fight was not worthy of engagement? I say, stay the course, Longfellow. Dig in, and fight to the death to liberate the imprisoned minds of our New England youth!"

Henry laughed out loud, then sobered enough to thank Miriam and request a red wine to go with the evening's lamb. "You are a breath of fresh air, my friend. Now, tell me of the rest of your time in Europe. What portions did you like best?"

Throughout their meal—and the bottle of wine—they spoke of the second half of the Appleton tour. Tom's interest had focused on the people, entertainment, and food as much as the literature and culture, but he was a natural storyteller and Henry felt transported back to the places he dearly loved. Tom mentioned Fanny with the same level of inclusion he mentioned Molly or his father, and Henry had to keep himself from asking about her specifically. What did she think of Germany? Did she ever think of the man who had wanted to serve as the family's guide there?

It was nearly ten o'clock, the hours disappearing easily into the late summer night, when Miriam came to tell them that Tom's carriage had returned for him.

"You *must* come to dinner on Beacon Street," Tom said to Henry. "I shall need to see when we might have you, but I know we all look forward to seeing you again."

"I would very much enjoy seeing the rest of your family as well," Henry said, hoping he didn't sound too enthusiastic. "How is everyone adjusting back to Boston life? How is Fanny faring?"

Tom's smile held, but he cocked his head to the side. *"Fanny?"* he repeated. "When did you begin addressing her as *Fanny*?"

Henry felt his neck turn hot at the slip. The wine had loosened his tongue and mind to the point that his usual reserve was in repose. "My apologies," he stuttered, trying to find a way to explain himself. "I fear that my memories of your family are so well that I have fallen into too much familiarity."

"*Fanny* is faring well," Tom said after another moment, still scrutinizing his friend with uncomfortable attention and his ever-present smile. "She and Molly are setting the household to rights. The servants became sloppy and idle in our absence, I'm afraid. And then my father ordered some reconstruction that had my sisters quite at odds with him. They did not like the changes as much as Father thought they would." He rolled his eyes.

Henry turned his wineglass on the table. "I imagine the line of suitors ready to greet them must extend the length of Beacon Street." Even as he spoke he reprimanded himself for his transparency.

"The length of Beacon Street is a fair comparison," Tom said. "I believe Fanny alone has received one or two cards every day since our return. Molly has already secured a beau."

Henry swallowed. He'd expected Fanny would have her pick of gentlemen, but the confirmation was difficult to hear.

"Unfortunately for the hopeful lads hanging about Fanny, she is rather opposed to marriage at present. I can't say I blame her," Tom said with a shrug. "Why anyone should want to saddle themselves with matrimony I cannot imagine. For my part, I would never want to narrow my focus to such a degree as one woman day in and day out." He let out a breath, seemingly ignorant to Henry's growing discomfort of the topic. "What of travel? What of keeping one's own schedule and pursuing one's own interests?" He shook his head. "Perhaps she and I are Appletons who are not the type to marry—too independent and set upon our own course."

Henry could not tell if Tom was trying to discourage his interest in Fanny specifically or simply share information. Regardless, the words fell heavy.

"I am sorry, Longfellow," Tom said suddenly. "I did not mean to be insulting."

Insulting? It took a moment before Henry realized Tom was likely thinking about Henry's marriage to Mary. It felt like it had been ages, rather than not quite two years since her passing.

"I am not insulted," Henry said, shaking his head. "But I fear you and I differ quite a lot on that matter. There is a comfort to matrimony that is very inviting to me."

"One can find such *comfort* without clamping an iron around one's leg." Tom winked.

Henry shook his head at Tom's implication. "I am speaking of the companionship, of the shared pain and pleasures, to say nothing of children and legacy. I have lived both sides, and while I can acknowledge the appeal of independence, I shall always come down on the side of a life shared with someone you love and admire."

Tom's smile grew thoughtful, then it turned into a grin and he shook his head. "I must stand my ground. There is nothing marriage can offer that would be worth the sacrifice. I shall leave it for better men such as you, Henry, to populate future generations and extol the virtuous promise." He drank the last of his wine in one swallow, then set the glass on the table and smacked his lips. "I shall send 'round that dinner invitation, Longfellow, and eagerly anticipate the event. I would caution you to refer to Fanny as *Miss* Fanny, however, especially in my father's company." He winked again, and Henry felt his face flush. If not for Tom's continued smile, Henry would fear he had overstepped his bounds.

Henry walked with Tom to the street. "It was wonderful to see you again," he said, clasping Tom's hand in good-bye. "Thank you for coming this evening."

"The pleasure was mine, I assure you," Tom said with a quick nod. "All the best to you, Longfellow. We shall meet again soon."

Twelve

39 Beacon Street

It was nearly a week before the invitation to dinner on Beacon Street arrived and another week before the event at the Appletons' mansion in Beacon Hill. Henry sent his acceptance right away, eager to renew his acquaintance with all the Appletons, but Fanny especially. Knowing she was back in Boston had spurred his affections forward, and he could not wait to see her again.

On the night of the dinner, Henry arranged for his émigré assistant to oversee his students' language recitations for the evening, and then set off on foot from Brattle Street, across the Boston Bridge, to Beacon Hill. He didn't mind a long walk, and the mid-September night was pleasant. He reached the house and took a deep breath before knocking on the imposing front door. His eyes traveled up the three levels of the house, taking in the bow windows and the front door framed by an ornate Doric portico. Even being accustomed to the grand style of Craigie Castle, Henry found this house intimidating.

A butler wearing a black uniform opened the door. He showed Henry into the parlor where Tom waited. The men exchanged greetings and had been visiting for a few minutes when Henry heard movement from the direction of the doorway. He turned, and his breath caught to see Fanny walking toward him. The smile on her face warmed him to his toes.

"Mr. Longfellow," she said as she approached, her hands clasped in front of her. She stopped a few feet away and curtsied, prompting him to bow in greeting. When their eyes met, his chest grew hot. It had been a year since they had last seen one another and yet he felt sure that her features were more developed and that her carriage reflected greater self-assurance and poise. Even her hair was styled in such a way that bespoke a maturity he did not remember from their time in Europe. He realized she was speaking only after she'd said something he did not hear. " . . . in Cambridge?"

"I beg your pardon," Henry said, shaking himself back to the present. "What did you ask?"

She smiled, somewhat indulgently. "I asked how you have liked your time in Cambridge."

"Oh, I like it just fine," he stammered. "Just fine indeed. I have a fine boardinghouse and fine rooms." He paused for breath and to cut the word "fine" from his current vocabulary. "You look very well, Faaaa—Miss Fanny. I am very glad to see you again."

"As I am to see you," she said, giving him a strange look before turning toward the doorway. "Molly is on her way down, and Father sent a note that he would be along as soon as he finished a matter of business. Shall we retire to the dining room? Dinner is ready, and I should hate for it to grow cold."

The men agreed, and the three of them moved to the dining hall, a splendid room with thick curtains, silk wall coverings, and a marble hearth. Henry could feel his nerves increasing. He was out of his element and feared everyone knew it. Molly joined them just as they were seated and the conversation soon began regarding the second half of the family's European tour. Henry had heard some of the accounting from Tom but was glad to hear the women's impressions about this piece of art and that specific site. Dinner was served—fish in a lemon sauce with asparagus and parsnips—excellent, of course.

Henry had just taken a bite when Fanny turned her attention to him.

"Voulez-vous plus de vin, Monsieur Longfellow?"

"I would, thank—" He stopped when he realized Fanny had asked if he wanted more wine in *French.* He stared at her with wide eyes, questioning whether he had heard her correctly.

Molly was the first to laugh, followed by Tom. Even Fanny put a hand to her mouth to hide her laughter at his reaction.

"You learned French?" he said, thrilled to the point where he could feel the smile on his face stretching to his ears.

"Oui, oui," Molly said, pulling his attention to her for a moment. *"Papa a insisté."*

"But we are very glad Father did insist," Fanny said. "It was immensely helpful for the second half of our tour, and it allowed greater exploration for both of us even outside of France, I daresay."

"Wonderful," Henry said, nodding eagerly. "Of any language you can speak in Europe, French is the most useful."

"We knew you would be impressed, Mr. Longfellow," Molly said, glancing toward her sister. "Fanny and I have been so excited to show you."

"Well, now I must test you," he said, leaning back in his chair. He looked around the room for a subject. His gaze settled on his dinner. "What is on this plate?"

Fanny and Molly exchanged a confident look, and then Molly told him exactly what was on the plate. Henry laughed—the sound was strange to his ears—and then asked them to describe what Tom was wearing. Fanny took on the challenge, and though one of her conjunctions was not exactly right, he was quite impressed.

"Here is the final test," Henry said, raising one finger. "Can you read it and know what you have read?"

The sisters shared another glance, and then Molly got up from the table to retrieve a book from the buffet. They had anticipated him. She held it up to him so he could see it was a book of Racine's work, then she opened to a marked page, cleared her throat, and read the first few lines of what Henry recognized as part of the play *Bérénice*.

When Molly came to a stopping point, she explained the passage—a lament of time lost—and handed the book to Fanny who read a few more lines and then provided a *translation*, not just a summary. She did very well finding the English words to convey the heart of the French.

He asked her to read more and she did, transfixing Henry as the words washed over and around and through him. Henry could have listened to her read all night long, and though the play she was reading from was a great tragedy, he did not know when his heart had felt so light. When Fanny finished, all was silent for a few moments.

"I am speechless," he said, his eyes still on Fanny until she began to look uncomfortable. She glanced at her sister as though in supplication. Henry reluctantly moved his attention to Molly before he continued. "You have both put such effort into this learning."

"We did," Molly said, returning to her meal with a pleased air. "After our first few lessons, Fanny and I agreed to only speak French to one another."

"Which was beyond irritating," Tom said. "They sounded terrible when they first began—like pigeons fighting over a crust of bread."

"You said we did very well," Fanny said to her brother as she put down her knife and fork in protest.

"I simply did not want to hurt your feelings," Tom said with a wink.

"But you shall hurt them now?" Molly said, raising her eyebrows.

"Nothing I can say would take away from Henry's praise of your efforts. I do believe he is genuinely impressed."

"I am," Henry said, forcing himself not to stare at Fanny any more than he already had this evening. "Beyond measure." He turned to Molly. "Didn't you once question how I could enjoy speaking another language, Miss Molly?"

"I did," she said with a humble ducking of her chin. "And I now better understand the freedom of speaking the same language which surrounds you. To understand a language well enough to participate in conversation and speak with curators and performers was beyond exquisite."

"And to read it," Fanny said, allowing him to meet her eye without feeling conspicuous about the attention. "You told me once how reading literature in the language of the author allows a greater understanding of their motivation and specific meaning. I found that to be true, and I loved exploring the French literature we discovered."

"Have you read Victor Hugo?" Molly asked.

Henry could not hold back a smile at the possibility that he had *not* read Hugo. "Indeed."

"Fanny also liked Chateaubriand, but I found him too political."

Henry felt as though his heart had sprouted wings as he turned back to Fanny. "You liked Chateaubriand?"

Fanny shrugged modestly. "He was more difficult to read, but his perspectives on the French Revolution were rather profound."

"French bluestockings, Henry," Tom said, shaking his head and swirling the wine in his glass. "That is what you have created. I for one cannot wait until the language fades and they are once again silly Bostonian girls who prefer frocks to soggy French books."

Henry bit back his abhorrence of Tom's suggestion and instead kept his attention on the women. "No, you must continue to practice," Henry said passionately, looking between the sisters. "If you do not use your ability, you will lose the level of skill you have developed. I would encourage you to keep reading it and keep speaking it to one another. It is a gift, a precious gift."

Both sisters smiled with just enough unease that he feared he had come across too strong. Muting his passion, he asked about their tutor in Paris, a severe man who would slap the table when they misconjugated a verb. He laughed with them over the inevitable *faux pas* they encountered when they used the wrong word, such as when Fanny asked a shopkeeper if they had any gloves, but used the word for teeth instead.

Henry tried not to give too much attention to Fanny, but found it difficult to keep his gaze from straying to her face. Had he never seen her so fully until tonight or had she changed so much in the year they had been apart?

Nathan Appleton did not join them until they were enjoying dessert, a delicious fruit tart perfect for the late summer evening. The patriarch was served his dinner, and the family lingered at the table, repeating many parts of the prior conversations for his benefit. Before Henry knew it, it was past the polite hour for him to have already left, and he could not delay his departure any longer, never mind that they had never exited the dining room.

"I cannot tell you how much I have enjoyed this visit," Henry said, hoping they sensed his sincerity as he pushed back from the table. He turned to Fanny and Molly. "Thank you for the wonderful meal and the even more delectable French. It has touched my heart to hear that you both found joy in something so very dear to me."

"We would not have done so without your encouragement," Fanny said, smiling so softly that he wished he could capture it in a portrait. He had once thought she was not particularly beautiful, but looking at her tonight, her hair soft and her expression so joyful, she was surely the most beautiful woman he had ever seen.

"After hearing you proclaim the virtues of language, how could we not feel such enthusiasm?" she said.

The sentiment caused Henry's heart to race in his chest. "As you have learned one language, your minds are conditioned for another." He was unable to look away from Fanny even though good manners dictated he should. "Do you recall the translations of Uhland you enjoyed when we were in Switzerland? I wrote to you about continuing your German—did you get that letter?"

"I did," Fanny said. She opened her mouth to say more, but Henry's passion caused him to interrupt.

"I would be happy to teach you German so you might read those great poets exactly as they were intended to be read." Belatedly he realized he'd left Molly out of his offer and turned to her. "And you as well, Miss Molly. I would very much enjoy tutoring you both."

"Not me, though I thank you for the offer, Mr. Longfellow," Molly said, shaking her head. "French is enough for me, and Fanny enjoyed the German translations far more than I did."

Henry turned his eager attention to Fanny, who looked at him with surprise; she must be feeling overwhelmed at such an undertaking. "With such a strong foundation in French, you will have a much easier time with German. I think you would find it a fascinating venture."

"Oh, well," Fanny said, shyly. "I'm not sure that—"

"Oh, just do it," Tom said, waving toward his sister. "You can then be the only girl in New England who speaks not one but two foreign languages. Think of how your friends will admire you."

"I don't think our friends are all that impressed that we speak French," Molly said. "These things do not amount for much among women, and Fanny is already well on her way to being deemed a bluestocking as it is."

"But you *could l*earn it," Henry said, his eyes focused squarely on Fanny. "What do you say, Miss Fanny? Friday afternoon, around two o'clock here at Beacon Street?"

"Yes, what do you say, Fanny?" Tom teased, raising his eyebrows at his sister.

"Give the man an answer," Mr. Appleton finally said, scooping a spoonful of parsnips. "It's late, and he likely has an early class in the morning."

"Well, I suppose I could try," Fanny finally said, looking down and smoothing the tablecloth in front of her.

"You will adore it," Henry said, unable to suppress his grin. "We shall have a wonderful adventure."

Thirteen

Uncomfortable Attention

Fanny waited until the door had shut behind an exuberant Mr. Longfellow before she glared at Tom and Molly who stood in the parlor with her. Tom smiled while Molly seemed surprised by her sister's ire.

"I do not want German lessons," she said, focusing on Tom, who was the greater villain. "You backed me into a corner so that I could not deny him."

"Oh, don't be so disagreeable, Fanny. Could you not see how excited he was to teach you? It was your idea to do your little French performance; you should have been prepared for the consequences of such a display."

"I should have been prepared for the consequence of learning to *speak German,*" Fanny said, throwing up her hands before putting them on her hips. "I swear, Tom, one day your pranks are going to put *you* in the soup."

"For now, I shall appease myself with the pot you find yourself in," Tom said, not the least bit irritated by her anger.

"What am I to do now? Take lessons I have no interest in?"

"Why have you no interest?" Molly asked, sounding genuinely curious. "You *did* pick up the French very well, and you and William loved the German translations of that dark stuff. With Mr. Longfellow's help you could learn German and read those for yourself just as you have with the French. Why are you so set against it?"

Fanny did not have an easy answer. She had never considered learning *another* language, and though French had come easier for her than it had Molly, it had been difficult to resurrect what she knew from her youth and then expand it to the level of fluency she now possessed. She could not imagine how Mr. Longfellow could read so many different languages; it seemed to her that all the words and interpretations would get tangled up in her head like a knotted ball of string. Failing at such a challenge would be embarrassing.

Even so, she would likely welcome the lessons if it were anyone but Mr. Longfellow teaching them. He watched her. Closely. And it both flattered and discomfited her. He'd become acquainted with Aunt and Uncle William while she'd been in Europe, and Aunt William said he was particularly fond of Fanny's portrait when he had the occasion to visit Aunt William's house. Fanny feared his interest in her went beyond his hope for her to speak German. To even think such a thing made her feel arrogant, as though she were such a woman as to draw the attention of every man. And yet, since returning to Boston, it seemed as though every eligible bachelor of her family's acquaintance had been paying her a visit. She was always eager for entertainment and had gone out with a few of the young men, for a walk or a drive, but was hesitant to encourage individual time with any one of them.

Now she had Mr. Longfellow coming for a *private* lesson on Friday. He would want to come the next Friday, too, and the next and the next. She would have to either turn him away, which would feel wretched—she did like the man and did not want to hurt him—or endure the lessons with the fear that he was interested in more than her linguistic merit. There was also the lingering fear that too much time in his company might remind her of all the things she had liked about him in Europe. Even tonight she had been so aware of him, the graceful way he moved, the depth behind his eyes when he looked at her. She had already made her decision that they would only be friends, and yet she worried about his interest, and her own, if she were truly honest.

"I have no interest in the German language," she said again simply. "And I should not have been pressed into a position where I could not refuse the lesson. He is a professor, his days are likely filled to the brim, and now he shall make the trek to Beacon Street to teach a student who does not want to be taught."

"I think he is *more* than happy to make the trek," Tom said with a wink, causing Fanny's neck to flame hot. Tom had noticed Mr. Longfellow's attention and he had still put her in this position!

"I am not interested in being pursued," Fanny clarified, her voice low and her anger only barely in check. "I believe I have been quite clear on that count."

"Pursued?" Tom repeated, his eyebrows lifting in mock surprise. "I think you may overestimate your charms, dear sister. Henry wants to teach you German. Why on earth would you interpret it to be anything more than that?"

"Oh, Tom, I could throttle you!" Fanny said, stamping her foot and wishing she could slap him. Maybe she should. Perhaps a physical attack would show him the level of her frustration.

He put a hand to his chest and gasped. "My, my, what big claws you have." He grinned and moved toward the front door, unaffected by her glare. "Tell Father I shall return in a few hours. I want to take a pint at the corner."

He let himself out, and only then did Fanny take her hands from her hips. Father was still finishing his dinner, but Molly stood to the side of the foyer, watching Fanny with concern. "Are you really so against the lessons?" she asked.

"Yes," Fanny said, her voice tired. "I have no interest in anything of such a personal nature with a gentleman right now. I am feeling rather suffocated by the attention I've received thus far, if you want to know the truth."

"Everyone is simply excited to have us home," Molly said, waving away Fanny's concerns. "And Mr. Longfellow is just passionate."

"Which is exactly why I do not want individual time with him." Fanny took a breath and decided to admit to her discomfort. Of anyone she could confide in, Molly would be the best at seeing Fanny's perspective. "Did he not seem particularly attentive to me this evening?"

"He has *always* been particularly attentive to you, Fanny," Molly said with a smile. "That you pretend not to have noticed before is rather silly."

Fanny let out a sigh. "I do not want such attention."

"Why not? He is an amiable man, and poets are so very romantic."

"Poets are poor, Molly." Fanny hated how it sounded when she said it out loud, but she had taken the time to compile all the reasons Mr. Longfellow was ill-suited for her, and since no one else seemed to have done the same, she had no choice but to be direct.

Molly laughed. "I remember you told Tom that, back when he fancied himself making a living as a poet. Mr. Longfellow is not some bedraggled poet singing for his dinner, however. He is a professor, a distinguished one and well-regarded. Why, I think Father would welcome a match for you with a man like him."

"Well, *I* do not welcome such a match," Fanny said, raising her chin as her determination strengthened. "Mr. Longfellow is ten years my senior and . . . and not the type of man I imagined I would marry. It is not fair for me to lead his affections when we could never make a suitable match. I have been too spoiled to live a lifestyle less than this." She waved her hand through the marble foyer, complete with an original painting by Goya that they had brought back from Spain. It was not evil for her to want nice things, was it?

"So he is not a man of fortune. He *is* a man of virtue, and Father's investments for you will make up for whatever Mr. Longfellow might lack by way of comfort."

Fanny was already shaking her head. "I would resent it," she said stubbornly. "I know it makes me seem horrible, Molly, but I would. As my husband, he would have access to my money, he could spend through it, use it on all manner of endeavors—we both know situations where exactly that has happened. The only way to have security in marriage is to enter on equal ground with your husband. I know my mind well enough to know what I can bear, and what I cannot."

"I think your judgment is severe," Molly said. "What of love? What of affinity for one another?"

"Can such exist if you question the man's motivation?" Fanny was irritated that she could not seem to convince her sister of her perspective. "You can't understand. John is of our station; he does not need your name or place in society. He has no other motivation but his feelings, and therefore you have every reason to feel secure."

Despite Fanny's concerns regarding John's attention in the beginning, Molly had blossomed under his attention, and he had been nothing but kind to her. A kindness she deserved. The couple walked the Common three nights a week, had attended the theater two weeks ago, and had had dinner with his family twice. In just three weeks, it had become all but certain to Fanny that Molly was falling in love, and there was no reason to doubt that John was feeling the same.

"I do not think Mr. Longfellow would use you so poorly, Fanny," Molly said as she turned to the stairs, bringing an end to the conversation. "Don't make up your mind too rashly. Perhaps he is exactly the man who would make you happy."

"I don't need a man to make me happy," Fanny said, causing Molly to look back at her. "I am happy as I am, with my family, in my family home, and surrounded by friends and culture. I see no reason for me to risk that security for a match that could not promise me the same happiness. That is all. I mean no offense to Mr. Longfellow—I have great admiration and respect for him—but he is still a man, influenced by the world as we all are. I do not want to encourage him when I know it will only lead to causing him pain."

"Then tell him you have no wish to study German," Molly said, as though it were that simple. "If you are so determined to be independent, then hold your ground and nip this in the bud before his heart becomes more engaged than it already is."

Molly moved up the stairs, leaving Fanny alone in the foyer with her arguments and justifications.

"I do not need a man to be happy," she said again before heading toward the kitchen. She wanted to compliment the kitchen staff on the evening's tart, which had been particularly good. She also needed to discuss the broken lamp in the upstairs hall. It would need to be replaced, but she was curious as to why it was not working in the first place and whether or not the staff knew when it had gone dark. How would the household function without her, really? Especially when

Molly married John and Fanny alone would be attending to these matters.

Someone must care for Father, and someone must manage the household.

"I do not need Mr. Longfellow or anyone else," she said under her breath to fortify her position. "I shall not give up my independence for any man. Not yet. Perhaps not ever."

And yet did she have enough confidence in that decision to tell Mr. Longfellow she did not want his kindly meant lessons? He would be disappointed, and the anticipation of such a reaction made her stomach tight. He had been *so* excited to teach her, and he had never been anything but kind and considerate toward her. She did love his insight on literature and language. Was that reason enough to *accept* the lessons?

Fanny took a breath and decided she would take the lessons one week at a time. If she did not reciprocate his attention, he would surely tire of the pursuit and a natural boundary would develop between them. She knew how to flirt when she wanted to, but she also knew how to close herself off and *not* draw a man's interest. She felt sure that, if necessary, she could be very determined in showing Mr. Longfellow all her worst parts so he would not want her for anything—not a wife, not a student.

It should not be so hard to be an independent woman, she thought as she reached the lower level and turned toward the kitchen. She should not have to justify her feelings to everyone, including herself.

Fourteen

Language Lessons

"Came-air-eh-den," Fanny repeated, trying to make her mouth form the strange sounds of the German word. How could they flow so easily from Mr. Longfellow's tongue and be so rocky and jumbled upon her own?

"Yes," Mr. Longfellow said from his place beside her on the settee they shared. "*Kameraden.*"

"It's sounds lovely when you say it," Fanny said, trying not to sound petulant. "Fluid."

"I have been speaking and reading German for nearly a decade, Miss Fanny."

She had to look away from the half smile that accompanied his comment. There were certain expressions on his face that made her heart still or race without warning. To avoid the feeling of emotional vulnerability that followed the physical reaction, she reminded herself of their differences. A decade ago, when she still wore skirts above her ankles, he had been a grown man, traveling the world and only a few years away from marrying Mary Potter.

"I've had more practice," Longfellow continued. "Let's say it again."

Fanny returned to the page they each held with one hand between them and focused on the lesson. *That is why he is here,* she told herself, *to teach.* She tried to mimic Mr. Longfellow's pronunciation. It still came out garbled.

"Much better," he said.

Fanny could not help but give him a rueful laugh. "It is deplorable," she said. "You are being dishonest."

"Certainly not," he said. "But you need to trust that I have heard hundreds of students learn the language. If I say you are doing well, then you are. Now, let me explain the full sentence in context and how it would translate into English while still keeping its meaning and texture."

He began to explain the sentence—the opening line to one of Uhland's most famous poems—while pointing to the words on the page, but Fanny was watching him, not the paper. This was their fourth lesson, and it was not going well in more ways than one. To start with, German was much harder than French and required more memorization and study. Mr. Longfellow was patient with her, but she knew she was not making the progress he had hoped for.

The other failure, however, was more profound. Spending time together as they did, with Mr. Longfellow so confident and impressive in his knowledge, had weakened Fanny's resolve to remain unaffected. He was so patient, so kind, and so determined. How could she not be attracted to such things? And yet her attraction frightened her and pushed her toward continual reminders on why they were not a good match. He was too old, and widowed, and poor, and smart. She was too young, and frivolous, and rich, and while he continually complimented her intellect, the German lessons seemed to show how far below him she truly was. She was not his equal of mind, and she never would be.

By the time Fanny realized Mr. Longfellow was no longer speaking, she worried the silence had stretched on too long. She had been staring at him, watching him without his knowing—at least at the beginning—but now he was meeting her gaze, and the intimacy caused her cheeks to burn with instant fire. She blinked and faced forward again, focusing her gaze on the poem.

"The Good Comrade," she said, grabbing at the last thing she remembered him saying. "Not a direct translation."

"Not direct, but clearer," Mr. Longfellow said. He was still watching her; she swore she could feel his gaze burning through her skin. Reading her mind? Could he sense her conflicting thoughts?

She forced herself to take a deep breath to calm her racing heart and tried to renew her objections. There was no room in her heart to love this man. No room in her life to make space for him either. Yet she had not cancelled the lessons and in the process knew she had led him to believe she felt things she did not feel. Or, rather, felt things she would not admit to feeling. The feelings he inspired were not enough to override her objections.

Yet she could feel the heat of his closeness, a contrast to the rain outside the window, and the warmth of his eyes every time they lingered upon her. The briefest thought wove into her mind—what if he put his hand over hers just now? What if he touched her face, traced her lips with his long and elegant fingers . . .

"And this second line," Fanny asked quickly, pointing to the words and trying to regain her focus. "What is the direct translation compared to the clearer one?"

"Repeat after me," Mr. Longfellow said. He shifted closer to her, and his shoulder brushed against her, causing her to shiver. He surely noticed it—he had to—but he didn't pause to savor it as she was tempted to do and instead began saying the German words.

This time she purposely mangled the lines when she repeated them.

"It's hopeless," she said, leaning back in her chair and crossing her arms over her chest like a child. "German is too difficult." She did not meet his eyes. She didn't dare.

"Instead of repeating it, say it with me."

He began to say the words, slow and lyrical in his mouth, and though she hesitated, she fell under the spell and began to say them, a moment behind him. When they finished that line, he moved to the next, and she followed along, the words blending and dancing like children around a maypole.

A few words stood out—words she already knew—and as she read with Mr. Longfellow, she could better understand how the words worked together, where the cadence was set within the lines. She began to see the *shape* of the poem. Even if she did not understand all the words, she felt a tremor of discovery in her chest.

She leaned forward, feeling the depth of the poem written about a fallen comrade during battle, feeling the words they both spoke as though they were singing. His voice was low and rumbling; hers was light and sweet. No more was the recitation choppy words that made no sense, rather it was playing out in her mind with a beat and a rhythm and a flow like waves on the sand.

Mr. Longfellow finished, and a syllable later Fanny did too. But she continued to stare at the page. She had never experienced anything like this and did not know how she would explain the sensation. The words still surrounded her somehow, like hummingbirds or a silken drape.

"Do you feel it?" he asked with a caressing tone as though he was unwilling to break the magic they had spun together.

Fanny looked at him. His eyes were eager for her answer, his eyebrows lifted with expectation. She wanted to resist him, and yet she didn't. Her defenses were down, and she was suddenly a willing victim of the spell he had cast.

"How can I feel it when I don't even know what it says?"

"Because you *do* know," Mr. Longfellow answered. "You know enough of the words for your mind to bind them together, like mortar between bricks, until it is not bricks anymore but a wall, a structure with its own identity and substance. It does not matter that those bricks could have been used for a prison or a hospital or a house, they were used for *this* place. *This* experience. They are forever changed by their use. That is the beauty of poetry, Fanny, ordinary words bound together with heart and soul and measure."

Fanny swallowed, feeling overwhelmed by the whole of it—this poem, yes, but also this man who represented both freedom and captivity. Their eyes held one another's, and Fanny felt a growing panic as the air between them warmed. What was happening to her?

She was *not* falling in love—that was a blissful, light, and flowing feeling. Not a heavy, fearful, burden. Wasn't it? But did she *only* feel fear, or was there bliss, too? Frightening bliss? Burdening lightness?

The chime of the grandfather clock in the hall broke her free—finally—and she jumped to her feet as the clock chimed twice more. "It is three o'clock," she said too loud, clasping her hands behind her back and clenching her fingers tightly together. "The lesson is over." She smiled, but her legs felt shaky, and she was not herself.

"I can stay longer," Mr. Longfellow said, looking up at her from the settee. Looking through her. Seeing too much.

Fanny walked toward the window and pulled back the sheer drapes. "I am meeting my Aunt Sam at a shop," she said somewhat sharper than she meant to. Her defenses snapped back into place, one slat at a time, building a fence, then a wall. Too much risk. Too much potential pain. She continued to explain and justify. "We are both in need of new gloves, and I'm afraid I am unable to prolong our lesson today, though I thank you for the offer to extend."

He was still watching her, and she feared he would open his mouth and say words that could not be retracted.

"I shall have Mathews call you a carriage," Fanny said, looking up at a sky filled with gray clouds. "It looks like we may get rain this afternoon. Perhaps even snow. I would hate for you to be caught in a storm."

"I prefer to walk."

She searched his tone without turning back to him. Was he disappointed? Bemused? Finally she heard him stand and gather up his books. She stayed at the window until she heard him approaching. She steeled her nerves and lifted her chin before she turned toward him, determined to be polite, cold if necessary. He could not know her thoughts. He could not know her fears.

"You did very well today, Miss Fanny," he said, bowing slightly, holding her in his gaze.

"I was appalling, but I admire your determination to be a gentleman about it."

She could tell he was frustrated by her response. He wanted her to feel good about her progress, but she didn't. Not in German. Not in her self-preservation.

"Might I walk you to the shop where you are meeting your aunt?" he asked. "Perhaps through the Commons?"

"Thank you, but I must refuse," Fanny said, keeping her demeanor tight. "I do not think it would be appropriate for us to walk together alone. It would give the wrong impression."

His eyebrows came together and he opened his mouth to speak, but she cut him off, though it pained her far more than she would ever admit not to hear what he might have said.

"I shall see you for our lesson next week?" she said quickly.

Mr. Longfellow held her eyes a moment longer and then smiled. "Next week," he said with a nod. "I shall count the hours."

Fanny swallowed as he left the room. She returned her attention out the window. The front door opened and shut and then Mr. Longfellow appeared on the street. He looked back, and she stepped away quickly so he would not see her.

What are you doing? she asked herself when she dared step forward again. She caught the last of him before he moved too far from view; she could swear he was smiling.

He had seen this lesson and the shared intimacy as a great success, whereas Fanny's eyes filled with tears as she embraced her failure to keep her heart at a distance. She tried to think of how she could possibly fix it. Why could her head not rule her heart? How did her heart dare to love anyone when it had been broken so thoroughly by those she'd loved before and lost too soon?

Fifteen

An Open Heart

Henry skipped up the steps of Craigie House, checked his watch, and then went directly to the dining room. It was five o'clock, and he'd told Mrs. Craigie he would be attending dinner before his evening's recitation—Italian on Thursdays. He entered the room and nodded a greeting to the other lodgers at the table.

Jared Sparks was a former pastor and the McLean Professor of Ancient and Modern History at Harvard, so they interacted a great deal. Sarah Lowell reminded Henry of his maiden aunt, Lucia, who had helped his mother raise ten children. The two were good company on every front, and Henry was in the mood to fully enjoy his time with them.

"Good evening," Henry said as he took his seat beside Sparks and across from Miss Lowell. "How are we this fine day?"

"Apparently not as well as you," Sparks said. "You are in a very bright mood."

"It is Thursday," Henry said with a broad grin.

"Yes," Sparks said with a nod. "Of course, why did I not realize the happy nature of a *Thursday*?"

"He gives lessons to Miss Frances Appleton every Friday," Miss Lowell said knowingly. They had spoken of his tutoring over their shared breakfasts of toast and tea. "This shall be your fifth lesson?"

"Indeed," Henry said, reaching for a roll from the basket in the middle of the table.

"What kind of lessons?" Sparks asked.

"German," Henry said. "You know I met the Appletons in Europe. Well, after I parted their company, Miss Fanny and her sister took French lessons in Paris, and she would now like to learn German. It has been a most invigorating experience."

"What a strange girl to want to learn German." Sparks grinned as he looked over his spectacles. "Is she a lunatic?"

Miss Lowell laughed, and Henry shook his head. "Do try to contain your envy that a lovely young women is interested in my work, Sparks. I know it shall be difficult."

Sparks hooted at that, and Henry went on to explain the nature of his tutoring while dinner was served around the table. Beef stew, a simple meal but one of Henry's favorites.

"If you ask me," Miss Lowell said a few bites into their meal. "I suspect the lessons are nothing more than a screen to hide the true intent of these meetings."

"I have only just learned of these lessons, and I agree with you completely, Miss Lowell," Sparks said as he broke open a roll. "No one gets this excited about tutoring."

Henry smiled into his bowl and then wondered what reason he had to deny his feelings. He looked up at his companions. "Miss Fanny is a most remarkable woman. She is smart and witty and so very self-possessed that every minute spent in her company is a moment of pure pleasure."

"Oh, goodness," Miss Lowell said. "I think you are quite smitten, Mr. Longfellow."

"Completely," he said with a nod.

"And when shall you confess the depth of your feelings?" Sparks asked with a single arched brow. "So that Miss Lowell and I might wish you happy."

"I have yet to determine my timeline for that," Henry said. "We have had four lessons thus far, and two dinners with her family, but I asked her to walk the Commons with me last week and she refused, claiming she was unsure it would be appropriate."

He caught a shared glance between Sparks and Miss Lowell and hurried to alleviate their concern. "I think it is because she has been rather beset with suitors since her return to Europe and worries that being seen in individual company with me should set up an expectation with other men who would like to pursue her."

"She has *many* suitors?" Miss Lowell asked, a crease between her eyebrows that he did not feel was warranted.

"*Would-be* suitors," Henry clarified, using another roll to sop up the stew in his bowl. He had such energy and knew it was because of Fanny and the light she brought into his life. The hour-long lessons in her company felt as though time stopped completely. And last week! Oh, the glorious moment of discovery when she felt the fullness of what poetry could do. It had been as invigorating a moment as Henry had ever experienced. That ability to feel a poem would now be a part of her, and it would paint the world with colors she had never seen before.

Each time Henry made his way home from Beacon Hill following their Friday lessons, he was already eagerly anticipating the next week. Saturday was his longest day, knowing he was six days away from seeing her again, but his anticipation would build each day, stronger and stronger, until Thursday when he was ready to burst. He would count the hours—twenty-four hours from now, eighteen, sixteen—then he would wake up Friday and know that in seven hours he would be knocking at the door of her home and ushered into sunshine all over again.

"And she is not troubled by the attention of a poor college professor?" Sparks asked. "As I understand it, the Appletons could buy the whole of Boston if they were of a mind to."

Miss Lowell laughed at the exaggeration but did not correct him.

"I do not think Fanny cares for such things," Henry said. "She understands my work and does not put on airs. She has been encouraging of my attention." He paused and reflected on a deeper level of his feelings before looking up at the faces of his friends. "I have not felt such invigoration since the early days of my marriage to Mary, and I never expected to feel such again." It still hurt to talk of Mary, but not as it once had. "I thank God for extending to me a second chance to feel such happiness I once believed was lost to me."

The teasing left the faces of both of his companions, and Miss Lowell reached over to pat the back of his hand. "Such love as that is a gift, Mr. Longfellow," she said reverently. "I wish you the best in your pursuit."

"As do I," Sparks said with a nod. "Would that we could all be so lucky."

Sixteen

A Broken Heart

It was autumn in New England, and Fanny and Molly spent the day with Aunt Sam purchasing items they would need for winter and ordering those things not immediately available. The sisters would celebrate their birthdays next week, only a day apart. On October 17, Fanny would turn twenty and enter a new decade of her life. The next day, Molly would turn twenty-four, an age that was not quite as exciting to celebrate.

Aunt William had also attended them for part of the day, and they had luncheoned at the Union Oyster House. After sending the packages to the house and saying good-bye to their aunts, the sisters enjoyed a walk along the wharf, despite the cold, and watched the ships come in and leave port, each of the vessels moving so smoothly it was like they were speaking to one another.

The sisters had been back in Boston almost three months and had enjoyed every moment of the summer and fall, knowing a hard winter would be on them soon. Once the snow and ice came, they would warm themselves with memories of more pleasant days like this one.

They walked arm in arm and spoke of an upcoming ball, a past dinner party, and when Molly would next see John. He had gone to New York the previous week to assist in a business transaction for his uncle. There seemed to be no end to the virtues which Molly so easily extoled for John, and they speculated when he might propose. They both agreed that was where his attention was pointed. Perhaps there would be a wedding to usher in the New Year.

Fanny kept to herself how much she would miss her sister—it wouldn't be the same without Molly on Beacon Street—but she was happy for Molly. Marriage was exactly what Molly wanted and deserved. As for Fanny's own thoughts on love and a marriage of her own, she found great frustration regarding the topic.

She had not yet determined what to do about Mr. Longfellow, but after last week, she knew she must do something. She could not lead him on, nor could she risk her own heart becoming exposed. Thinking about him, and tomorrow's lesson, filled Fanny's stomach with butterflies, so she instead looked forward to the ball tomorrow night. She would wear one of her Italian ball gowns and dance every dance!

When the sisters arrived home, both dusk and the temperature had fallen, and they were ready for a good thaw in front of the fire. They let themselves in through the front door and were chattering about numb fingers and toes when their father came down the stairs, his footsteps heavy. It was unusual for him to be home so early, but a welcome surprise.

"Good evening, Father," Fanny said with a warm smile. She gave her coat to Mathew and then crossed the foyer to kiss her father's cheek. "It is such a lovely evening, have you—What is wrong?"

Father's expression was harsh, his mouth tight.

"Molly, I must speak to you," he said, moving immediately toward the parlor.

Molly looked at Fanny, handed her own coat to the butler, then followed their father. Fanny's heart pounded. It was rare for Father to request a conference with either of them separately, but Fanny had certainly *not* been invited. After Molly entered the parlor, Father held Fanny's eyes with a serious look. Whatever he needed to discuss with Molly was grave indeed. He closed the door.

At a loss of what to do with herself, Fanny went to her room and changed into her house shoes—it was cold enough that they wore boots when they were out—and checked to see that dinner would be on time. She was lingering in the warmth of the kitchen while thinking of which upstairs fire might be the best laid when the sound of running feet on the family level above startled her.

Fanny lifted her skirts and hurried up the stairs to the main floor and then to the parlor. Father stood before the fireplace, his forearms resting on the mantel and his shoulders slumped in defeat.

"Papa?" Fanny asked cautiously, staying in the doorway.

"I never expected my success would become such a bitter draught for my children."

Fanny stepped into the room, feeling dread building in her chest. "Your success has been nothing but a blessing." Had Molly said otherwise? What on earth had they discussed?

"Not in this," he said wearily, shaking his head slowly. "Not in regard to seeing my daughters properly cared for by good men of virtuous character."

Fanny's mind was hesitant to interpret the meaning though the possibilities struck her cold. "What's happened?" she finally asked.

"He is a wastrel."

"Who?" But she knew who. Her stomach sank.

He turned, his face showing the heartache he felt. "John Peterton has accrued substantial debt these last years. Gambling, along with the costs of a woman he has been keeping in New York."

Fanny put a hand to her mouth and felt her stomach finish the descent to her toes. *Oh, Molly.*

Father continued. "He has managed to use his family's reputation to hold back his creditors, but the word is out. I received a visit from his father this morning, hat in hand and heart in his throat. It seems courting our Molly was but a solution to the enormous trouble John has made for himself. He has moved quickly in hopes of securing her before his character caught up to him." He shook his head and looked at the floor. "She is devastated, Fanny. I think she truly loved him."

Silence fell as Fanny blinked back tears, imagining how the words had landed upon her dear sister's heart.

After a few moments, her father met her eyes again. "Will you go to her? I said all I can, but what she needs is her mother . . ." His eyes filled with tears, and he turned back to the mantel. "I cannot give that to her either."

Fanny awoke Friday morning with an exhaustion she had not felt since the days of keeping vigil beside her mother's deathbed. She had slept in Molly's bed last night, and Molly's still swollen eyes stood as proof of her sorrow.

Fanny got out of bed carefully, still wearing the dress she'd worn the day before when Molly had spoken so brightly of her dear John. John, who had a kept woman. John, who owed thousands of dollars to the most seedy men in the country. John, who had broken the heart of a woman who could not even comprehend such deceit.

Fanny tiptoed out of Molly's room and asked the upstairs maid to alert her as soon as her sister awakened. Then she hurried through her own toilet. The inside of her eyes felt lined with sand. She splashed lavender water on her face and patted it dry, hoping it would refresh her skin. If only she could refresh the rest of herself so easily.

Once revived, Fanny sat at her writing desk, where she usually loved to write letters, and extracted a sheet of the fine linen paper. She was not eager to write this letter, and yet, perhaps, a bit relieved to have reason to do so.

The morning had brought to Fanny a greater resolve to do what had to be done regarding Mr. Longfellow. Molly's situation convinced her that the sooner she cut ties, the better for everyone. Her sister needed her, and Fanny dared not divide her attention.

Dear Mr. Longfellow,

Though I regret to send you such news in a letter, I am unable to meet for our appointment today. A circumstance has occurred which demands my immediate attention. Furthermore, as much as I appreciate your attention and all I have learned, I feel it the best course to discontinue our future lessons. I have a great many commitments vying for my time, and though I have enjoyed learning German, I do not foresee the mastery of the tongue in my future and feel I must focus on other responsibilities.

I am grateful for your friendship and wish you every good thing.

Sincerely,
F. Appleton

Fanny looked over the words with a heavy heart and then wrote another copy of the letter. She hesitated only long enough to reassure herself this was the only reasonable course before she folded and sealed both letters. She took the letters to the new butler.

"I need these letters delivered to Cambridge immediately, Mathews. One goes to Craigie House on Brattle Street and the other to Mr. Longfellow's department office at Harvard College. It is imperative that one of them finds the recipient within the hour so he does not come to Beacon Street at the usual time. Send them however best insures their quick arrival."

"Very good, ma'am," Mathews said, bowing slightly before heading below stairs to arrange for the delivery.

Fanny ignored the increasing prick in her heart and instead looked up the staircase. She wished she knew what to say to Molly that could bring her comfort. Were there even words for such a thing?

Seventeen

Rejection

It had been four days since they had learned the truth about John Peterton, but by now it seemed that everyone in Boston knew. To protect Molly from well-meant—but intrusive—condolences, Fanny had kept her sister to her rooms and asked everyone who inquired to simply pray for Molly and Mr. Peterton. The request that they pray for the lecherous man was not born of Christian devotion, rather Fanny knew he would need the prayers of good-hearted people if he were *ever* to receive forgiveness for what he'd done.

Fanny professed to everyone that, of course, Molly was shocked, but that they were all relieved to have learned of John's true nature before any arrangements had been entered into. Fanny assured their friends that Molly was recovering and would be as good as new in no time.

In truth, Fanny was quite concerned. Molly stayed in bed all day and night, some days unwilling to even change from one nightgown to another. Fanny had tried every manner possible to comfort her, but nothing had worked.

Tuesday morning, after taking a breakfast tray to Molly's room herself, only to have Molly roll away and face the wall, Fanny returned to her desk and began a letter to her Aunt Frances who lived in Pittsfield. Perhaps they could come for a visit; she needed time away from the probing eyes of a society far too interested in the goings-on at the house on Beacon Street. Fanny had just signed her name to the letter when there was a knock on the door of her room. She turned to see Mathews in the doorway.

"Mr. Longfellow to see you, ma'am," Mathews said.

Fanny put a hand to her forehead and let out a heavy breath. What was he doing here? He had responded to her note on Friday with a request to better understand her reasons for canceling the lessons, assuring her that he would fit his schedule to hers in order for the lessons to continue.

She was forced to send him another letter with even more explanation, which had resulted in another response where he requested to meet with her. That letter had come yesterday, and she had chosen to ignore it. She did not appreciate his insistence, and she had far more important things to deal with at the moment. That he had ignored etiquette and come to the house for a meeting she had not agreed to was grating.

There was no room for Mr. Longfellow in her life right now. She was as sure of that as she had ever been. Amid Molly's sorrow, and the increasing realization of how much vulnerability their fortunes provided, Fanny felt she had finally managed to close her heart against Mr. Longfellow completely. Only she hadn't expected to have to face him so soon.

"Shall I tell him you are indisposed?" Mathews asked when Fanny did not answer straightaway.

Yes, she thought. "No," she said out loud. He was here, and Fanny would have to confront the situation between them sometime. Her stomach felt like hot metal as she stood from her writing desk.

If Molly were not so miserable, Fanny would ask her to attend the conference, but Molly was not up to it and no one else was home. Perhaps that was for the best. Tom was amused by Mr. Longfellow's attention to her, and Father would think her rude for the things she would have to explain. Perhaps, like their timely discovery of John's character, this conversation was happening just as it should.

Fanny took the stairs slowly in the hope she would feel more prepared if she took her time in getting there. She paused outside the parlor door and took a breath.

"Mr. Longfellow," she said, entering the room and smiling politely.

He immediately stood and turned toward her, an almost frantic look in his eyes. She stopped some distance from him so as not to give the wrong impression; she worried she had done that too often. How many times had she leaned in too close while he helped her read the German texts he brought? And on more than one occasion, she had praised his interpretation of a phrase or verse quite strongly. She had not reined in her own feelings soon enough, and in the process, she had given rise to his interests. She would never forgive herself for being so unfair to them both.

"I hope you will forgive my unannounced visit, Miss Fanny," he said with a slight bow. "How are you this fine day?"

"Well enough, Mr. Longfellow. Thank you." She waved toward the seat. "Please do sit down."

He did so, and Fanny sat in one of the satin-covered chairs across from him, trying to hide her building tension. She thought of the comfort they had found with one another these past weeks and hated knowing they would never find it again. She should not have allowed such companionship in the first place.

"What can I help you with, Mr. Longfellow? I believe I made myself quite clear in my letters."

He took a deep breath, bracing as if preparing himself for something, and Fanny felt herself tense even more. He cleared his throat and straightened his shoulders. "I was disappointed to read your letters. I had enjoyed the time we spent together very much."

Fanny looked away from his probing gaze, collecting her thoughts and preparing her response. "You were kind to make the time for them." She was careful not to sound overly gracious. "However, as I said, I am unable to continue. In fact, I expect to be traveling to Pittsville soon to visit my aunt for a time."

"I did not come to discuss the lessons," he said, pausing to lick his lips. "I have come to speak with you on another matter—a matter of dire importance."

"Dire?" she repeated, lifting her eyebrows but keeping her polite smile in place.

"I only use such a word to help communicate the importance."

"As I assumed," Fanny said. "I do not expect that you often say what you don't mean, Mr. Longfellow."

"I do not," he said, shaking his head without taking his eyes off her face. "Nor do I take words lightly. To me they are objects, placed as needed but solid and physical. Therefore, I hope you will understand my deep intent for coming here today."

"Why, Mr. Longfellow, you have me quite eager indeed to hear these words you have so elevated," Fanny said, trying to keep her tone light even as his became heavier. She could not imagine what he had to say to her unless it was regarding Molly, but that did not explain his intensity.

He looked at his knees clad in his signature black trousers, seemed to line them up, and then looked at her again. "Miss Fanny," he said with such seriousness that she found herself holding her breath. His expression was raw, almost pleading, and she struggled to hold his gaze that seemed to cut through her. "I hope you will forgive me for being so forward, but . . ." He took a breath. "I was not exaggerating when I once told you that my time in Interlaken was akin to a rebirth for me. I had been in such a place of darkness, and you lifted me from it."

"I think you mean my family helped to lift you from—"

"No, it was you."

Oh, dear. Fanny's smile fell.

"When you returned to Boston, I experienced the same rejuvenation—the same sense of new life and sunlight I had felt the first time we met. Once again I find my mind clear, my senses keen, and my future open. I feel certain that your company is the best medicine for my troubled soul, and I am here before you now asking that you will fulfill the hope of my heart and agree to become my wife and rescue me from my heavy solitude."

Fanny blinked at him, feeling as though her vision had narrowed so that the only thing she could see was his anxious expression staring back at her. This could not be happening! She had to repeat what he'd said in her mind twice more before she believed it.

"Mr. Longfellow," she said carefully, "I—I—You have taken me off guard and—"

"As the strength of my feelings for you have taken me off guard every hour I spend in your presence." He rose from his chair and moved toward her like a bird of prey. She pressed back against the chair cushion, and he stopped a few feet away.

Her mind spun. What could she say to him? She grabbed at any explanation for why she could not—*would* not—entertain his request. "Mr. Longfellow, I do not feel you have thought this through."

"I have thought of nothing else for days."

"Days of consideration are unmatched toward the decision of a lifetime."

"My life is empty without you. I tire of bachelorhood and long to move forward with you beside me."

His hurried words only served to impress upon her the frantic nature of his proposal. It could not be considered. Not seriously. Fanny lifted her chin an inch higher. "I believe what you feel is loneliness."

"Yes."

He did not seem to understand her inference that loneliness was an insufficient reason to marry. If nothing else, she would have imagined a more romantic offer from such a man, which prompted Fanny to be more direct. "I think you miss your wife, Mr. Longfellow, and are looking to return to a happier time in your memory."

Mr. Longfellow furrowed his brow in confusion, which frustrated Fanny even more. He did not seem to be listening to her, not comprehending what she said.

"Certainly I am lonely," he said as though eager to move through her concerns. "It is not for that purpose alone that I have come. I mean to convince you of—"

Convince me? Fanny thought. She sat up a bit straighter. "You are also ten years my senior, Mr. Longfellow."

He stared at her a moment. "It is not such a distance. Many marriages span a greater difference than ten years. I am ready to marry again." He spoke with a tone of conclusion as though wanting to put an end to any argument and expecting her to simply agree with him.

The shock Fanny felt passed, and in its place a restored confidence took root in the fertile field of growing irritation. What a bad action it was to put her on the spot like this!

Mr. Longfellow continued, "And you and I are so well-suited."

"I do not agree," Fanny said strongly. He had not spoken to her father and had never given any indication his interests were so serious. His proposal was completely inappropriate. "The very fact that you would come to me with such a presumptive request is proof of how little you know of my true nature, Mr. Longfellow. We have never spoken of such things."

"But our love of literature and poetry," Mr. Longfellow said, his own shock reflected in his tone. "The enjoyment we have in one another's company."

"Yes, we have been well-suited *friends*, but I must be quite honest with you—I am not of a mind to marry." *Especially not now.* The idea of entertaining any man's feelings when Molly had so recently been wronged by such a heartless cad was impossible. Thank goodness Fanny had not let her affections toward Mr. Longfellow grow beyond what they were. Thank goodness she had not considered a match or spoken of her deep feelings with him. How would Molly feel to have her younger sister with a beau after all John Peterton had done?

Mr. Longfellow looked down and fingered the lapel of his coat.

Fanny wished she dared run away. Even with her irritation so sharp in her chest, Fanny had no wish to cause him pain.

"You do not mean to marry—or you do not mean to marry *me*?" he asked, quietly, forlornly.

"I have no wish to be cruel," Fanny said, softening her tone and wishing it could also soften the blows she was landing. "But I feel sure any interest you have in me comes from the fact that we met when the wounds of Mary's death were quite fresh. I believe you have misinterpreted your feelings toward me and given me the credit for having had your spirits restored through your friendship with my family. I believe you see me as a ticket away from your grief, but such a thing cannot replace the mourning of your wife."

His gaze came back to hers. "With all due respect, I do not agree with that opinion." His tone was unexpectedly bold. "I very much admire you, Miss Fanny, for your own merits. And I *have* mourned my wife. I cannot, however, be expected to live within that mourning all my days. Mary would not want that, and I would not want it for her if our places were reversed. I am prepared to step eagerly into my future again, and I feel to the depth of my soul that you are the woman with whom I can find happiness."

What of my happiness? Fanny wondered. *Has he any regard for what would make me happy, or is he incapable of thinking past his own desires?* Like John Peterton. Like any number of other young men who saw money or position or, in Mr. Longfellow's case, his own relief.

"I am grateful for your friendship, Mr. Longfellow, to me and to my family, especially to William when he was fading. I think you are a very good man with great compassion and intellectual merit, but I am not interested in marriage, not to any man." She paused, took a breath of confidence, and then said the horrible truth she knew would put an end to his hope. "And should my feelings regarding marriage change in the future, it would be unfair for me not to make it clear that I expect to marry a man very much like my father in situation and achievement."

Mr. Longfellow's neck turned red, and he looked at the rug beneath his feet for several seconds, long enough for Fanny to feel the razor of her words. None of her thoughts had been said as smoothly as she would have liked, but he had put her on the spot. She'd had no time to prepare, and yet she *had* told the truth.

Finally, when the agony was becoming thick, Mr. Longfellow

raised his head. "I understand." Had he said it with a tinge of anger or pride, Fanny would have become even more defensive. But his tone was sorrowful and full of humility. "I hope, however, that you will not dismiss my affections as that of a lonely man who does not understand his mind or heart. Instead, please accept them as a compliment to the woman you are. I shan't take back any of what I said, even as I wish you happiness on your course. Good day to you, Miss Fanny."

He didn't wait for her to speak and instead gave a quick nod before crossing the room and disappearing into the foyer. A moment later, she heard the front door open and close. Fanny sat looking at the doorway where he'd disappeared and reviewed their conversation over and over in her mind until she could not hide the fact that in the face of her rudeness he had been nothing but kind.

Tears rose in her eyes—tears whose source she would not define. She had done the only thing she could do. It would have been unkind to have said anything different. She wiped at her eyes, berating herself for such a reaction, then took a deep breath and assured herself that, though not as well-stated as she would have liked, she had said what was necessary. Mr. Longfellow should not have gone about it as he had. She'd had no choice but to reject him.

If only her rejection of his suit didn't sit like a rock in her stomach.

Eighteen

Pathways

Henry did not go home. He had told Mrs. Craigie of his planned proposal and received not only her blessing but also her agreement to rent rooms to both Henry and his new wife upon their marriage. She would even consider selling the house to them if an agreeable arrangement could be reached. Henry was only one year into his position as Smith Professor and did not have the means to give Fanny a home in the manner she was used to, but Craigie House was as near equal to her father's house as any could be, and Henry had felt certain she would be comfortable there.

How would he explain to Mrs. Craigie that he was the most idiotic fool? How would he preserve his pride in light of the old woman's pity?

He went to his office and attempted to occupy his thoughts with mindless tasks until the hour was late and the sky was dark. He'd had his émigré take the evening recitations because he'd expected he and Fanny would be celebrating. How many of his friends knew he was planning to propose? Four? Six? He had not been shy once he'd made his decision.

Putting the collar of his coat up against the cold wind blowing off the Charles River, Henry hunched forward and walked home, his humiliation raw. He encountered no one when he entered the back door of the house, for which he was grateful. He headed to the back stairs and was at the landing before he heard movement. He looked to the top of the steps where Sarah Lowell stood as though about to come down. At least she was unaware of his planned proposal, unless she'd heard it from someone else.

Henry did not want to engage in conversation but he was a gentleman. "Good evening, Miss Lowell."

"Good evening, Longfellow," she said, smiling easily. "Are you coming to the parlor for a visit?" Henry and his friends often ended the day conversing and debating in the parlor, and although the topics were a bit more staid when Miss Lowell joined them, it wasn't unheard of her for her to hold her own.

"Not tonight, Miss Lowell. I'm afraid I am not feeling well."

She pulled her gray brows together beneath the lacy mobcap that rimmed her head. "Shall I have Miriam make you a tonic? She made one of rum and anise for me last month that was exactly the thing for my sour stomach."

"Thank you, but I'm sure I just need to lie down." In the dark. For the next eight weeks.

"You do looked a bit peaked," she said, cocking her head to the side. "I should think a tonic would be just the thing—"

"No, thank you," he said firmer then he meant to, prompting him to offer a hasty apology. "Forgive me, Miss Lowell, I am not myself this evening. I should prefer not to see anyone, not even Miriam."

She regarded him another minute, and then turned toward her rooms, waving him to follow. "I have what you need, Longfellow. Come with me."

Henry let out a breath of surrender and followed her. He could not refuse her any more than he could refuse Aunt Lucia, but he was in no mood for this. He needed solitude, and darkness, and perhaps a wall to bash his head against. Instead, he followed Miss Lowell to her apartment on the opposite side of the house from his own.

He stopped in the doorway of the sitting room, which was filled with delicate furniture and knickknacks. Miss Lowell moved to her desk, shuffled through a drawer, and then lifted a bottle of brown liquid he hoped was—

"Whiskey," she said as soon as he'd thought it. She moved to another table where there were two glasses on a brass tray. When she finished filling the glasses, she turned toward him, still standing in the doorway, and raised her eyebrows. "It is only my sitting room, Mr. Longfellow, and the door shall remain open to ensure propriety. We are friends, are we not?"

He was not entirely comfortable being in a woman's sitting room, but he did not want her to come to him so he crossed the room and took the glass she offered. When it came to drinking, he preferred wine, the best he could afford, but he was in no mood to savor the rich flavors and subtleties of wine tonight. He threw back the whiskey in a single shot, then grimaced at the burn that raced through his throat, chest, and shoulders. He coughed once into his hand, his eyes watering.

Miss Lowell regarded him. "I suspected it was not illness that had you out of sorts." She took a quick drink of her own glass without making a face. "A man who drinks like that is suffering from a very different ailment. Would you like to talk about it?"

Henry stared into his glass for a few moments before meeting her eyes. If he were to talk to anyone about his circumstance, it would be his Aunt Lucia, who had a practical wisdom beneath her stern demeanor. Miss Lowell was not as stern as Aunt Lucia, but he knew he could trust her. "I would like another drink first."

She did not hesitate to fill the glass a second time. And, though it did not burn as hot as the first drink had, he still cringed against the spreading fire.

"She does not want me," he finally said, feeling each word as though it was being peeled from his heart in long, bloody strips. The tears that rose in his eyes were no longer from the drink, and he placed the empty glass on the tray.

"Miss Appleton?" Miss Lowell said. "She no longer wishes the German lessons?"

Henry looked about for a chair and, upon spying a worn leather settee, moved to it on unsteady legs. He sat and then dropped his now-swirling head into his hands, bracing his elbows on his knees. He had not told Miss Lowell and the others that Fanny had cancelled their lessons.

He had obsessed all weekend until coming to the realization that Fanny simply did not understand the level of his affection. Fanny thought he was a man who did not know his own heart or mind; she may even have been testing his level of interest to see if he were truly devoted. Such justifications seemed like nonsense to him now, but up until the horrid meeting in her parlor that afternoon, he had believed that once he declared himself, Fanny would reveal her feelings to be the same as his own.

"I fear she never wanted my attention," he said, mournfully. "And now she is lost to me forever."

"Now, now." Miss Lowell sat beside him and softly patted his shoulder. "You have been attending to her for weeks now, surely she has welcomed your visits. Why would she be *lost* to you?"

"I asked her to marry me, and she refused my suit."

Miss Lowell's hand froze on his shoulder. "You proposed to Miss Appleton?"

He nodded.

"You proposed without courting her?"

"I *was* courting her," Henry said, looking up at his unlikely confidante. "I was teaching her German every week. We get on so well and have so many shared interests. I felt sure that rejecting the lessons was her way of being coy with me—wanting to see if I would be bold in my affections." He shook his head, dumbfounded at how wrong he had been. "But today . . . today . . . I don't understand it. Why would she have encouraged me?"

"*Did* she encourage you? Were you given false promises?"

Henry considered that but had no answer. He had *felt* encouraged. He had *believed* their affections were mutual. "We share such a love of literature, and I feel such a depth of admiration for her. I don't understand what's happened." How could he have felt so hopeful and been so horribly wrong?

"Did she give you a reason for her rejection?"

He thought back to Fanny's words and huffed in irritation. "She said I am too old for her."

"How many years are between you?"

"Ten," Henry said. "It is not so many." *Was it?*

"For a young woman, it can seem like twice that. You are nearly as close to her father's age as you are to her own."

Henry hadn't thought of it like that but resisted giving the idea merit since age was of no consequence to him. "She also feels that I am simply pining for Mary." Henry felt the heaviness in his chest when he thought of his first wife. He was at peace with Mary's death, wasn't he? "It has been two years."

"But you loved her," Miss Lowell said as though it were an accusation.

"Of course I loved her," Henry said, meeting Miss Lowell's eyes. "Should I say that I did not?"

"Miss Appleton is young and possibly believes the romantic notion that people only have one portion of love to give. If she feels you have given it to another, what is left for her?"

"That is ridiculous," he said sharply, then cleared his throat and took a calming breath. "Would she rather I *hadn't* loved the woman I married? Would that make her feel *better*?" The idea made no sense to him at all.

"I don't think she has thought of it in that way," Miss Lowell said with a sympathetic smile. "It is a credit for you to have loved Mary, but it may make Miss Appleton question your ability to love her as well. In fact, are you certain she understands that you *do* love her? Without courting her properly, perhaps she does not know your true feelings."

"I asked her to marry me—does that not prove my love for her?" He didn't apologize for his tone this time; his shock had turned to anger. "Am I to be sentenced to a life of solitude because I *dared* love Mary?"

Miss Lowell smiled kindly, softening Henry's heart and tempering his anger. He blinked back tears again. "The heart is not always reasonable," she said. "I am so sorry."

"She also said that she would marry a man like her father." He had to pause to keep his voice from betraying how the words had cut him. "I am not good enough for her. Not rich enough, not successful enough." He dropped his head into his hands again, this time clenching his fists around his hair and pulling until it hurt.

"Oh, I am very sorry she said such a thing. That was unkind."

Henry wanted to agree with her, expand upon Fanny's insult, and then think only of her unfairness to him. But *was* it right for him to expect her to accept a lifestyle so below what she was used to? She had servants and luxury; he could offer her only a modest life on the wrong side of the Charles River.

Mary had been the daughter of a judge, wealthier than the Longfellows of Portland, and adjusting to a simpler life had been difficult for her. More than once, she had asked her father for money so she might have new furniture or clothing that Henry could not afford. The comforts that Fanny was used to were well beyond that of Mary's family. Could he be so surprised that she was hesitant to give up such comfort? Did he expect she would abandon everything she had known for love alone?

Love.

Henry raised his head and stared at some point in front of him with unfocused eyes. "She does not love me," he said, verbalizing the discovery as though it was an artifact he had dug from the earth and was inspecting for the first time.

If Fanny loved him, their age difference would not matter, she would not feel threatened by Mary, and she would not be so reticent to accept a lowered lifestyle because she would *know* that love could make up for any want. Henry had seen love resolve all manner of discrepancies; it was truly the great healer. That Fanny was unwilling to negotiate even one of her objections made it clear to him that the love he felt for her was not returned. In some odd way the realization was a relief . . . and a challenge.

He looked at Miss Lowell sitting beside him. "How do you make someone love you?"

"*Make* someone?" Miss Lowell said, lifting her eyebrows and causing her cap to shift back on her head. "I'm not sure that's possible, Mr. Longfellow. Or advisable."

"I am *so* certain of my love for her," he said, putting a hand to his chest. "That can't be a mistake. God would not give me such feelings if not to have them remedied. She is my salvation, Miss Lowell, she embodies everything I need to be whole. I know this to my very bones."

"I fear your poetic heart may be creating a stumbling block for you in this, Longfellow," she said sadly. "Not all love is returned. Not every desire is answered. You are not the first to be crossed in love nor feel the sting of being pushed aside. I do not discount your feelings, but neither do I think it wise to interpret them as prophecy."

Henry wondered if Miss Lowell had once been in love. Had she had her heart broken, too? For a moment, he pictured himself fifteen years from now, as alone in the world as Miss Lowell, living in rented rooms and seeking purpose in his life. He felt bad for judging Miss Lowell's situation, but he did not want to live the rest of his life as he had this last year—without companionship, without a family of his own. He could *only* picture his future with Fanny. To remove her from the vision caused the entirety of it to fade away.

"What can I do?" he whispered, wondering at the wisdom of asking a spinster for advice in love. "I cannot give up."

Miss Lowell regarded him for some time. "Well, if giving up is not an option, then perhaps the best you can do is learn patience. She is young. Give her time to better understand the world and to see your virtues."

Henry nodded. Yes, he needed patience. She was barely twenty years of age. She enjoyed dancing and parties—frivolous things that Henry had no interest in. As she matured, she would turn more fully toward her intellectual interests, and then Henry would be an asset.

"But you must respect her wishes," Miss Lowell added. "You cannot force her heart to change."

He frowned in frustration. "Her wishes are to marry a rich man who has never been married before and is closer to her own age. I can change none of those things, but I feel certain—to my very core—that she is the woman who can make me happy." He stilled, allowing the passion he felt to be rejected by any part of him that did not agree. Nothing disagreed. He and Fanny were meant to be together.

"To truly love someone means that you place their happiness above your own. Thus far I have only heard you speak of your happiness."

Henry thought on that a moment. "You think I am being selfish?"

"I think that if you said to Miss Appleton what you've explained to me, she may have felt that *your* happiness was your only objective."

Henry reviewed what he'd said to Fanny and felt the painful truth of Miss Lowell's assessment. He had told Fanny she had healed him, lifted him, and remedied his solitude. Of course his intent had been to compliment her, but had it come across as selfish? *Was* it selfish? The rising self-recrimination brought panic into his chest. Had he acted rashly and destroyed whatever chance he might have had if he'd gone about things differently?

He turned to Miss Lowell with new anxiety. "Have I ruined everything? What can I do?"

She smiled at him in a motherly way. "Well, you cannot change her heart, but you may be able to influence it."

"How?" He felt the desperate need for a solution rising in his chest with every passing minute.

"As you said, you can't change the fact that you're ten years her senior and widowed, but perhaps you *could* increase your income. Remedy that one objection as much as possible. It is the only aspect over which you have control."

"There are specific salaries afforded each department, and they are not generous," Henry said with a shake of his head. "Increases are mandated and nonnegotiable."

"But you are not *only* a professor," Miss Lowell reminded him. "What of your writing? Why have you not published another book?"

Henry stared at her.

"Do you remember the night when we discussed the possibility of America having its own Milton, or Austen, or Scott? You were the one who felt there was finally enough literary interest from Americans to support such an artist—we needed only to raise one up. I believe it was Felton who suggested *you* could be that man—America's first great poet. The man to change the course of American literature and usher in a new cultural age that is not dependent on European voices." She paused and then smiled shyly. "My nephew, James Russell, spoke to me of your work not long ago, something you shared during one of your lectures. He also felt that you had real potential to change the landscape of literature here in America. I tell you this only to show that it is not only your friends who encourage you."

"I have so little time to write," Henry argued, though without much heat. He remembered the discussion he'd had with Felton and Sparks that Miss Lowell was referencing, remembered how exhilarating their encouragement had been, and yet how intimidating it was as well.

He had several poems in his desk, bits he had worked on here and again, but he had not given his full attention to any of them. He also had the outline of another novel. But what if he were rejected? Could he withstand the rejection of his mind after the shredding his heart had experienced this very day? Yet how could the rejection of his writing possibly hurt like Fanny's rejection had?

And what if Miss Lowell were right? What if he could remedy his situation to the point where Fanny would not have to lower her standards, to where he could offer her the lifestyle she deserved? Success would give him confidence and security, two things he did not have now and therefore could not offer. It was a heady consideration and played easily into his insecurity, already so well fed today.

"My time is stretched so thin," he protested again.

"Not to pour salt on the wound, my dear, but you shall now have one extra hour a week on your hands. Three, if you count the time you spent going back and forth between Beacon Hill and Cambridge. Why not use that to begin with and see if immersing yourself in your writing doesn't help you find even more time for it."

Henry said nothing. On a day where he had gone from hopeful to hopeless he had very little left to draw from. He pondered Miss Lowell's suggestions and thought deeply of the risk of such a venture. He had works he could polish. He had relationships within the publishing industry he could strengthen. He had an audience in his students. Miss Lowell's nephew was one of those audience members, a student who would come out for lectures and who would be eager to see an American rival the acclaim of the British writers.

"What if it is not enough?" he asked in almost a whisper. "What if I fulfill every hope of my writing, and her heart remains closed to me?"

"Then she is a fool," Miss Lowell said, nodding her head for emphasis. "But you finding success might lessen the sting of her foolishness."

"She is not a fool," Henry said. He pictured Fanny in his mind. Not as she'd been today—anxious and guarded—but as she'd been in her dining room two months ago when she'd surprised him with her French. That was an evening of pure joy. As had been their last lesson—when she'd felt Uhland in the fullness of his emotion and depth.

For Henry, watching her discover such a thing had affirmed how desperately he needed her in his life. How could she *not* feel the same? But he knew the answer. She did not love him, nor did she fully understand his love for her. He had bungled his proposal, put the cart before the horse and expected all would move forward simply because he wanted it to.

"If she is not a fool, and you are so certain that you are meant to be hers—not only that *she* is meant to be *yours*—then you have no reason not to move forward with your career and see where it might take you. Pour all the feelings of your heart and soul into your words, Longfellow. Let this setback make you stronger and better. Let her see you moving forward. You will be better for the journey with or without her, if you use this difficulty to push you toward a better future."

Stronger.

Better.

With her.

Henry took a deep breath and nodded slowly, taking hold of the one spark of hope he had left. If he and Fanny were truly meant to be together—and he believed with his whole heart that they were—finding success in his writing could only help that happen. He could learn from this failure and better prepare for another chance to proclaim his love in a way that did not discount her wishes or poorly communicate the depth of feeling he had for her.

And perhaps he *could* find greater fulfillment in pursuing his own writing than what he found in the classroom. Perhaps he could.

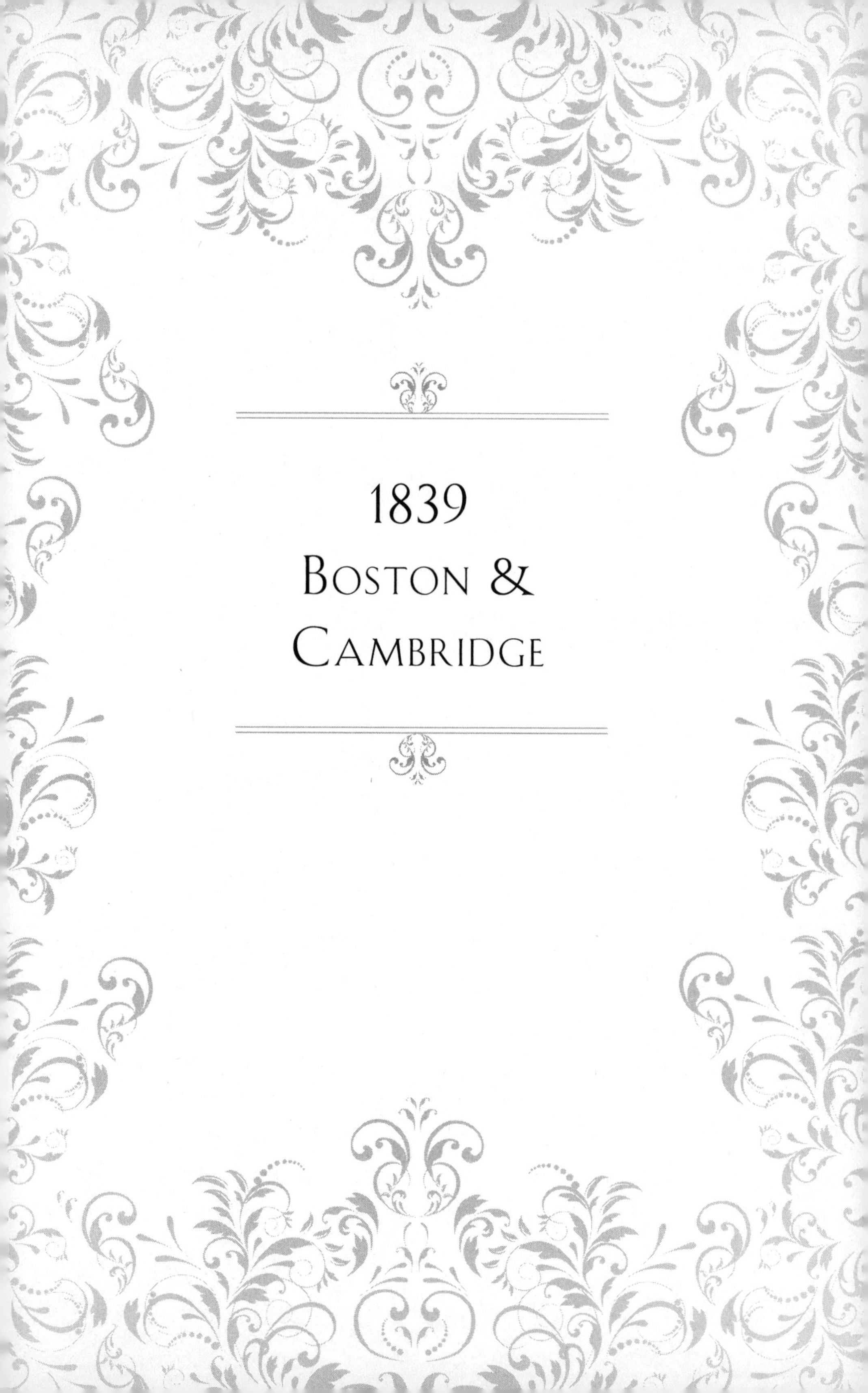

1839
Boston & Cambridge

Nineteen

Mrs. Appleton

Fanny sat amid the other wedding guests and took a deep breath through her nose before letting it out slow and steady through her mouth. *Is this truly happening?* she asked herself. Tom, sitting beside her, put a hand on her knee that she hadn't realized she'd been bouncing up and down. She stopped the nervous habit and covered his hand with her own. She was glad he was here. She knew his feelings for this marriage were not much different than her own. That her discomfort was understood if not shared assuaged some of her guilt.

The organ began and everyone stood and turned toward the back of the chapel to see Fanny's soon-to-be-stepmother come down the aisle. Harriet Coffin Sumner . . . Appleton. Fanny was embarrassed that Harriett had insisted on a full church wedding, despite the fact that her groom had three grown children and was twenty-two years her senior.

Father stood at the front of the chapel dressed in a top hat and tailcoat, waiting for his bride as though he were a young buck.

This is *happening,* Fanny said to herself as though until that very moment she had not believed it would. *My father is getting married.*

Harriet walked down the aisle like the blushing bride she was—though she was thirty-five years old—and Fanny worked hard to keep a polite smile on her face. Nothing would be helped if the other guests knew her discomfort, and she had decided months ago to act as though she were accepting of her father's choices. The alternative was to vocalize her objections and draw even more gossip to an awkward situation.

When Father had begun paying particular attention to Jesse Sumner's spinster daughter, Fanny had warned him that his interest was drawing notice, and whispers, which were increasingly uncomfortable. Fanny did not feel it appropriate for him to court a woman nearly the age of his children.

Father had held her eyes a long time, then crossed the room and put a hand against her cheek. "I have been alone for six years, Fanny," he said tenderly. "If this old heart of mine can fall in love again, I hope my children would wish me happy. Harriett is a fine woman. It would be an honor if she returned my affections."

Fanny had been shocked, and a little embarrassed, by his response. Without raising his voice or justifying his feelings, he had made clear that he expected her support. Fanny had not shared her concerns again even as the relationship deepened between Father and Harriet, but he knew her displeasure. She acted too formally when Harriet was around, never dropping her hostess persona. Through months of courting, Fanny had felt sure one or the other would see the error of their decision and put an end to the relationship. But they had not, and so here she was, with Tom on one side and Molly on the other, watching their father make vows to a woman who was not Fanny's mother. She felt tears well up in her eyes, grateful to know the other guests would think they were tears of joy.

Dr. Channing conducted the ceremony, but Fanny looked at

the floor when the time came that they were pronounced man and wife. She could not understand her father's reasons for this marriage. Everything was going well with their family, business was strong, everyone was in good health and good spirits. Why disrupt the accord?

A mutual sigh came from the crowd now that the deed was done, and Fanny looked up to see the new Mr. and Mrs. Nathan Appleton face the crowd—legally and lawfully married before the state of Massachusetts and God Himself.

Molly leaned toward Fanny. "Doesn't Father look happy?" she whispered.

Fanny hated to admit that he *did* look happy. Happy and carefree and . . . in love. It hurt her heart to admit it. What of Fanny's mother, six years in the ground? Where did she fit now?

The wedding couple walked down the aisle together, and the wedding party filed after them—immediate family first—into the frigid January morning. It wasn't snowing and for that Fanny was grateful as she looked over the line of hired carriages waiting to take the guests to a wedding breakfast at 39 Beacon Street.

She kept her smile in place and accepted the congratulations of people she passed as she moved toward the second carriage. Her father and Harriet were in the first. She was glad when Molly took her hand, gave it a squeeze, and held tight until Tom lifted his sisters into the carriage. The three siblings settled into their seats in silence, shivering in the frosty cold. The warm bricks placed in the carriages were not much remedy for a New England winter.

"Could they not have waited until June or some such month that is at least pleasant?" Tom said after he shut the door of the carriage. He shivered dramatically. "Do you know they never get snow in Barcelona? Rain every day, but never snow."

"Is that where you will go? Spain?" Molly asked, settling the skirts of her new dress about her legs.

Tom had become an attorney last year but mostly worked hard at not working very hard. He had recently announced he was going to close his office and sojourn in Europe to recover from his failure. He had never wanted a legal career, and his mind was more and more focused on writing and the study of the arts—an occupation Father did not find acceptable. Now that Tom could say he'd tried his father's way and failed, he would plot his own course. Fanny felt sure, however, that part of him removing to Europe was because, with a new woman in the house, things were changing. Like Tom, Fanny also questioned where she fit into her father's new life and if she would be welcome there.

"I hope to go to Europe as soon as I can," Tom said. "But I will miss the company of my sisters." He slid his gaze to Fanny, who looked out the window to avoid his eye. "Or at least one of them. The other sister has been a bit of a bear these last weeks." He kicked playfully at Fanny's leg, and she drew her feet back against the seat, out of range.

"Do not tease me, Tom," she said in a quiet voice that shook a bit, prompting her to take a steadying breath. "I shall not get through this day if you break me apart."

Molly and Tom were silent for nearly a minute, during which time Fanny dabbed at her eyes with her handkerchief while she tried to control her emotions. She needed to recover before they arrived at Beacon Street where she and Molly would share the role of hostess, perhaps for the last time. Molly scooted closer to Fanny on the bench and put an arm around her shoulder, prompting Fanny to lean against her older sister for comfort.

"It's going to be all right," Molly said. "Can you not find some peace in Father's happiness?"

"I *should* find peace in his joy," Fanny said, staring into her lap. "But I cannot seem to."

"You must try," Molly said. "It is done and all will be well, but you must try to find that peace that Tom and I have found, Fanny. Promise me you'll try."

I have tried, she said to herself. But that would not do. She had no right to make Molly feel worse. "I will try," she said finally, lifting her head and taking a deep breath. She managed a shaky smile for Molly's sake, and avoided Tom's eyes.

The carriage began to slow.

"We are nearly there," Tom said, as though they couldn't have guessed that on their own. "Fanny, would you rather go to your room when we arrive? We can give your excuses."

Fanny looked at her brother in surprise but shook her head. "It wouldn't look right."

"But if you cannot lend your heart toward this union, then perhaps it is unfair to expect you to pretend."

Fanny didn't like the idea that she should be left out, but she understood what Tom was saying and appreciated that he was giving her an option. "Thank you, but I will be fine," she said. "I will do right by Father and honor his choice."

"Sometimes," Tom said in a careful tone, "I feel you think too deeply, Fanny. You ponder too much on things we cannot make sense of in this mortal life and create obstacles that are not really there."

Fanny was tempted to take offense, however there was truth in his words. "I wonder at his love for Mama," Fanny said. "Do we not believe in being reunited in heaven with the ones we love? Will Father have to choose between them?"

"Oh, Fanny," Molly said. "We don't know the answer to that, but we know that God is all that is good and beautiful. Do you not believe that Mama—more than anyone—wants Father to be happy? She would not want him to live the rest of his life alone."

"He is not alone," Fanny said, looking between her siblings. She truly wanted to feel as they did. She ached for such acceptance of this change. "He has us, have we not cared for him?"

"Not to be indelicate," Tom said. "But a wife is different than a child."

"Oh, Tom," Molly said, her cheeks turning pink. "We need not speak of that."

"It is the truth." Tom waved his hand toward Fanny. "Father would never ask *you* to give up your happiness for his, Fanny. Molly is right—Mama would want him to be happy, of course she would, and the Bible says that it is not good for man to be alone. We have no more claim than Mama or God on Father's choices."

Fanny said nothing, only turned to the window as the carriage came to a full stop. She tried not to hear her own words spoken to Mr. Longfellow more than a year ago come back to her regarding *his* first wife. She had accused him of being lonely and trying to replace Mary. The professor had told her that he *had* mourned, that he was prepared to move forward. But what about the woman he would move forward with? What of Mr. Longfellow's potential second wife? What of Harriett? How could a man love two women equally? How could Harriett not feel part of a contest? It was not only Fanny's mother she felt sorry for, it was Harriet, too, and their father whose heart must now be divided.

Yet Fanny could not deny that her father *did* love Harriet. Fanny could not understand it, but she knew it was true. Could Mr.

Longfellow also love another as he did his first wife? Was that right? Fair?

It was all so confusing, and she tried to push the thought from her mind. Perhaps Tom was right—she did think too deeply and create unnecessary conflict. There was plenty of natural conflict to keep her mind quite occupied without inventing more worries.

When the newlyweds returned from their honeymoon—a three-month tour of the Southern states—Harriett would assume the position of mistress of the house. Fanny took great pride in her management of the household alongside Molly and, specifically, in taking care of her father. What would she do now? What would her purpose be? She was twenty-one years old, too young to live independently, but too old to act the role of a daughter for a woman only twelve years older than herself.

As her thoughts grew heavier, Fanny *was* tempted to retire to her room. But she didn't want to make a happy day a sorrowful one for her father, who would notice her absence and suspect the cause. She would hate to cause him pain and so, until she could feel true acceptance in her heart of this necessary turn, she would continue to act as though she already had. She was Nathan Appleton's daughter, and she would not give him reason to be disappointed in her.

She took a deep breath, sat up as straight as she could, and nodded to the door. "I hope the pastries are fresh," she said. "I told the caterer to make them this morning rather than prepare everything the day before."

Tom smiled. "There's the Fanny we know and love."

The door opened, and Tom exited first so he could help his sisters down the steps. When she took his hand, he gave it a squeeze. "We should all want happiness for each other," Tom said quietly. "We know better than anyone how fleeting it can be. I, for one, do not want to waste a drop, nor deny anyone else their share."

Fanny still felt argumentative, but she nodded her understanding of what Tom was saying. Two hours from now she could collapse on her bed and cry out the anguish she felt. Until then, she would act her part. She was becoming quite good at pretending.

Twenty

Hopeful Romantic

Cornelius Felton cleared his throat and lifted his wineglass above the table, scanning the other occupants until his gaze settled on Henry, who smiled back at his dear friend.

"A toast," Felton said with a smile. The other men raised their glasses. "To Henry. May your heart and your pen put the stepping stones of success at your feet for the journey yet ahead."

Cheers and agreement rang out from the other men as they tapped their glasses together and then drank in both celebration and reverence for the accomplishment Henry had finally—gratefully—achieved. Almost six years after the release of *Outré Mer,* Henry had published another book. This one was a romance, though perhaps a tragic one. He had loosely based his new book—*Hyperion*—around his second European tour, and he was eager to see how it would be received. He'd picked up his own copies that very afternoon from the publisher, and, since it was not yet in bookstores, it was unspoiled by critical review which would likely follow.

But tonight was not a night to dwell on pessimistic possibilities.

Tonight was a night to enjoy good friends, fine wine, and the glow of accomplishment.

"I should be saluting each of you," Henry said to the company at the table. "I could not have done this without your support."

"Ah, not true," George Hilliard said with a shake of his head and a shrug of his shoulder. "Then again, who am I to dispute the possibility that you owe every bit of success to the rest of us?"

The men laughed, and Henry marveled at how close he could feel to these men who a handful of years ago were strangers. Now they were like brothers: united, ready to spar or tease or give whatever they could for another brother's mercy.

"Do you think you'll hang up your cape?" Felton asked once the meals were set before them. They were staying in the St. Charles Hotel, taking a few days to live above their privilege, though Henry Cleveland could afford such style on a more regular basis if he had a mind to. Charles Sumner and Hilliard were both lawyers, the former more successful than the later, while Felton was a bachelor professor at Harvard just as Henry was. "Now that you're publishing again, will you give up teaching?" Felton clarified.

When Henry had started his serious pursuit of a writing career nearly two years earlier on the heels of Fanny Appleton's rejection, he had expected to give up teaching as soon as he could afford to. Now that the opportunity was upon him, however, he was not so eager. "I would be a fool to turn my back on a solid career, at least this early on."

"But you *will* quit eventually," Sumner said in that direct style that was his own. "You won't let sentiment hold you back from your destined course."

"Your faith in me is well-appreciated," Henry said with a dramatic hand to his chest that made Sumner's mouth twitch in a rare smile. "But I'm hesitant to expect my pen to buy bread for the rest of my life."

"But you still hope to make a living of it, do you not?" Cleveland pressed. "What was it you said last week? That if you had one more ninny-hammered freshman ask how it could be poetry when the lines did not rhyme, you would let the college see the back of you for the last time."

More laughter. More jokes, which were never in short supply when it was talk of students on the table. Finally Felton brought the conversation back around to the topic at hand. "Or has teaching gotten into your blood now so you cannot see the possibility of leaving it behind?"

"I can't say, exactly," Henry said, seriously pondering the comment. "I expected I would be glad to be done with the classroom—you all know my frustrations."

The men nodded and chortled, confirming that they were well-aware of Henry's ongoing displeasure regarding the educational institutions of America. Whatever reticence he felt at sharing his negativity had long been set aside with these men. They all agreed with him on some level and were all hopeful of improvement, which would occur only through faculty and society supporting a higher standard until that standard became the new expectation.

"When faced with the prospect of *not* teaching, I have discovered three things." Henry sat forward in his chair and held up one finger. "First, there is no saying that *Hyperion* will be a success. Tonight may be the only night of acclaim." His friends made argumentative noises, but he pushed forward and raised another finger. "Second, I enjoy my writing more when it is an outlet for my frustrations. I fear that once it is my focal point, I shall have to take up another hobby and writing will become as tiresome as teaching."

"Oh, don't take us round a serious turn," Felton said, leaning back in his chair and pulling his eyebrows together above his spectacles. "You are a poet, not a philosopher."

"A poet is also a philosopher," Cleveland said mildly. Felton rolled his eyes to the ceiling. Jared Sparks faced Henry. "And the third reason, Longfellow?"

Henry kept his expression sincere, though his words were nothing of the sort. "The students *need* me so *very* much. What on earth would they do without me?" He leaned back in his chair while letting out a dramatic breath. "I feel it both my patriotic and Christian duty to bless these tender lives, gentlemen, and I cannot deny it."

The men guffawed, and Henry waved the waiter over for another round of drinks. It was as fine a night as any he had ever had, and he was glad for every moment of it.

After dinner, they decided to walk through Central Park, lit up with gaslights that reminded him of the Boston Commons, though Central Park was easily ten times the size. When they came across a man selling roses, Henry bought five and tucked one rose into the breast pocket of each man's coat as a token of his appreciation. Sumner scowled at his flower but did not refuse the gesture since the other men took it as a compliment, though a silly one.

The group eventually exited the far side of the park and came upon a cheese vendor pulling his cart in for the night. Henry stopped the man and asked after his collection. "Anything European?" he asked, an idea coming to mind that seemed brilliant—though so had that third glass of wine. "I would like to take a gift to some friends in Boston."

"Your friends are all here," Felton said. "I'm sure you don't have more than the four of us."

The men laughed.

"If you must know, I plan to call on the Appletons when I return," Henry said, avoiding the shared glances of his friends. They knew who he meant to call on, and he was used to their continued confusion regarding his feelings toward Fanny. "I want to make a gift to the Appletons of *Hyperion,* and a nice cheese will serve as a reminder of our time in Europe."

Someone muttered under his breath, though Henry did not press for clarification as he turned his attention to the vendor. Sumner stepped away to light his pipe while the vendor described his selection of European cheeses.

Writing about his second European tour had been impossible without revisiting memories of the time he'd shared with the Appletons, and Fanny specifically. He saw her from time to time about Boston, of course, and she was polite, but he could feel her defenses raised against him. His acceptance of her feelings—but his hope for a change—had become so much a part of him that he didn't often feel the passionate rushes of emotion he'd felt when she'd first returned from her tour. Rather, thoughts of Fanny had become quite ordinary, like the way his hair fell to one side or the swing of his arm when he walked.

He loved Fanny Appleton, he would love her all the days of his life, and he believed wholeheartedly that one day she would return his feelings. And so he continued to call, continued to greet her pleasantly, continued to enjoy her company when it blessed him, but he did not pursue her with the energy he once did. At times his mind fell into hopelessness and he wished he could exorcise her from his memory, but other times—such as now—when his mind was clear and his heart light, he was glad to have such a fine woman to think of and hope for. The longing itself was sweet.

"Now this here, sir," the cheese man said, pulling up a rather large wedge sealed in wax, "is a Swiss cheese straight from Zurich."

"Zurich?" Henry repeated, flooded with happy memories of that place. He and Fanny had rowed the lake with William in Zurich; he and Fanny had spoken of his feelings regarding education in America. They had been so free and easy with one another there.

"I'm afraid it's rather expensive, seeing how it's imported and all," the vendor continued. "But it is the real thing—Swiss cheese from Switzerland. Ya can't get much more European than that."

"I'll take it." Henry reached into his pocket for his purse. "It's just the thing." Surely the Appletons would love this symbol of their time together, and perhaps Fanny would recall their specific exchanges in Zurich, just as he had.

"You bought her a cheese?" Felton said from over Henry's shoulder while the cheese man wrapped the wedge in paper and tied it with string.

"A cheese from Zurich," Henry said, not the least bit chastened by Felton's teasing. "Perhaps she will remember fondly the time we shared there, as I do."

"Oh, Henry," Felton said, shaking his head and putting a hand on Henry's shoulder. "You are a hopeless romantic."

The clerk handed Henry his cheese and his change, and as the men resumed their walk down the sidewalk, Henry took the opportunity to clarify Felton's accusation. "*Hopeful* romantic, Felton. Ever hopeful."

Twenty-One

The Dark Ladye

Fanny looked at the wax-sealed wedge of cheese and then lifted her confused gaze to meet the laughing eyes of her cousin, Isaac Appleton Jewett, who everyone called Jewett. "Mr. Longfellow gave you a cheese?"

Jewett shook his head and waved toward the parcel. "He gave *you* a cheese. I am only the messenger, but I must say the look on your face is worth every moment this task has required of me. Is it not as rank a gift as the man who sent it?"

Molly cleared her throat, drawing Jewett's attention for a moment, which allowed Fanny to look back at the cheese on the table and try to make sense of the very odd gift. Had Mr. Longfellow gone mad? Who gives a gift of cheese? The other half of his gift was a copy of his new book, which Molly held in her hand, appraising the canvas cover.

"You said he gave these items to you in New York?" Molly asked. "This morning?"

Jewett nodded. "I was on my way to the train when I encountered Longfellow and his companions quite by chance. When he learned the two of you were removing to Pittsville soon, but that I was coming here upon my return, his companions suggested he let me take his offering to you and save him from cutting his time in New York short in order to reach you before you left." Jewett looked at Fanny. "Perhaps he relented because he knows how tiresome his visits are after all."

"They are not tiresome," Molly said, sparing Fanny from having to reply. "Mr. Longfellow is a dear man."

"That is not what Fanny says." Jewett waved toward Fanny, whose cheeks were suddenly on fire. "Why, I believe she has called him a pest."

"I was in a snit," Fanny defended, though she was terribly embarrassed.

Fanny attempted to shield her older and far kinder sister from her more caustic impressions of the world. Jewett, on the other hand, was as big a tease as Tom was and often managed to goad Fanny into saying some of the most horrible things. Mr. Longfellow was unfortunately the common topic of these discussions as his public proclamation of his feelings for Fanny had caused her a great deal of embarrassment and frustration these last two years. Jewett was an easy person to vent her irritation to, since he found the professor rather pathetic, but more than once Fanny would reflect on their conversations and feel shame over something she'd said. Jewett was usually more circumspect in sharing her impressions than this, however.

Fanny turned toward Molly. "You know I value Mr. Longfellow's friendship, Molly, only he has caused me some hardship with how blatant he's been regarding his affections."

"And he *obviously* values your friendship too," Jewett said, making a dramatic gesture toward the cheese. "Equal, no doubt, to the value of this fine cheese."

Fanny couldn't keep from smiling as the humor of the situation refused to be ignored. "Surely he explained himself," she said, looking into her cousin's face. "Surely he did not hand you a book and a cheese and say, 'Please give this to the Appletons with my regard.'" She might not like the way Mr. Longfellow continued to hover about her as though hoping she would change her mind, but she did not think him a loon.

Jewett shrugged. "There was something about Swiss cheese reminding him of his time with you—"

"Me? Or our family?" Fanny broke in—it was an important distinction. "Did he not say something specific, or send a note to explain himself?"

Jewett pulled his eyebrows together and patted his pockets. "I do think there was a note." He stopped searching and shrugged. "Or maybe not. No note. Just the cheese and his book." Jewett leaned in a bit and lowered his voice as though telling a secret. "I may have made your departure seem more imminent than it was in hopes of sparing you an awkward visit."

"If he were going to sit here as you are now and present me with a cheese, it would have been awkward indeed," Fanny said. Yet as she thought over what Jewett had said, and looked at the odd gift on the table, she had a burst of understanding. The gift was not just cheese, it was *Swiss* cheese. From Switzerland. The country where they had shared so much joy. So much comfort. Her heart ached with the memory even as she berated herself for feeling such nostalgia. That was a different time and place. Too much had changed, not the least of all how she'd hurt Mr. Longfellow by rejecting his proposal nearly two years ago.

In desperate need to prevent Molly or Jewett from suspecting her sentimentality, Fanny put out her hand for the book. Molly gave it to her, and Fanny turned it over. "The production of the book seems very fine. I am glad to see he's moving forward with his writing. He's told me as much, of course, when our paths cross, but one never knows if a writer will ever actually finish his works."

"Yes, he does seem to be making progress with his writing career. But you cannot judge a book by its cover, now can you?" Jewett winked.

"And since we have the book in hand, we do not have to," Molly said, sounding annoyed by the continued disparagement of the professor. "Thank you for bringing us the . . . gifts, Jewett," she said with a pointed smile. "We shall both very much enjoy them, I daresay, and accept them in the generous spirit in which they were most certainly given."

"Of course, of course," Jewett said. He stood and gave each of his cousins a kiss on the cheek, but before he pulled away from Fanny, he whispered in her ear, "Let me know what you think of the dark lady. I feel sure you might recognize her as someone we know. She appears in the second half."

Fanny looked at him curiously, but he did not explain, only winked before turning toward the door. "Have a safe journey to Pittsville," he said. "I shall let you know when I might be able to come for a visit."

With the good-byes finished, Molly said she would take the cheese to the kitchen before she left to luncheon at a friend's house. Fanny thanked her sister and then returned to her seat in the drawing room. She opened the book, the binding creaking in a most satisfying way, despite the fact that she was not the first to open it. Jewett had obviously read at least some of it already. Still, she was glad it still felt like a new book.

Fanny raised the book and inhaled deeply, the clean scent of ink and paper tickling her nose. After indulging in one more breath, she lowered the book to her lap and began skimming chapter to chapter. Her gaze scanned the pages until she found the reference Jewett had pointed out to her. She backed up to the first of that chapter and began to read. A lady—spelled "layde"—in black who the main character—Flemming—met. The "dark layde's" name was Mary Ashworth. Mr. Longfellow's first wife was named Mary. Is that who Jewett meant when he suggested the character might reflect someone they knew? Somehow Fanny doubted it, and her anxiety to answer Jewett's riddle coiled inside her.

"Do not look for ghosts," she told herself, but she feared it was not ghosts at all.

Fanny finished the chapter and had begun the next before the first dawning of awareness lit up her mind. Flemming was in love with Miss Ashworth. Miss *Ashworth?* Miss *Appleton?* Fanny read faster, skimming passages that did not contain specific reference to Mary Ashworth but taking note of everything else said about her. Not beautiful. Read German poetry with Flemming. Would not return his affections.

Fanny's mind spun until she had to stop, look forward, and take a breath. "Good heavens," she said to herself before centering her thoughts. "Please tell me you did not do this, Mr. Longfellow," she said to the walls and curtains and sashes in the room. "Please tell me you did not put me in a book with your wife's name as my own."

Twenty-Two

Lenox

Fanny relaxed in the Puritan rocking chair before the window of the cottage where she and Molly had been for the last few days and smiled at the rolling hills of Stockbridge county that stretched before her. "I fear I could become quite used to this," she said, looking over her shoulder at Molly, who was on the couch, turning the pages of a magazine.

"The country?" Molly asked, screwing up her face as she regarded an advertisement.

"The freedom," Fanny said with something akin to reverence in her voice.

One improved aspect of Father's marriage to Harriet was that he had eased up on the need to keep his daughters under his watchful eye. He'd had no qualms with them going to Pittsville for the summer to stay with family, for instance. And when they'd written to request rooms of their own, rather than staying under a relative's roof or in a hotel, he simply asked that they have their Aunt Frances help them find a suitable apartment. Which she had.

The cottage could not be more perfect and was just the respite

Fanny needed from the heat and the whispers of Boston. Thinking of why Boston was whispering about Fanny caused her carefree mood to fade, and so she focused on the brilliant greens of the rolling hills outside the window. A starling swooped and darted beneath the eaves. It did no good to run away from a thing only to bring it with you.

"Better that we enjoy the independence while it lasts," Molly said. "I am still shocked Father allowed it at all—and until October?" She shook her head. "It's a marvel of his trust in us."

"I'm sure the fact that he and Harriet have the house to themselves was a factor in his support," Fanny said, trying not to sound dour but failing. "Which is why we may be able to convince him to let us stay."

"Here?" Molly asked, raising her eyebrows. "With Mr. and Mrs. Yates?"

"Goodness, no," Fanny said with a laugh. "I wonder, however, if Father would purchase a cottage of our own, or even build one."

For the time being they were lucky to have found a house arranged so that half the rooms could be rented out. Mr. and Mrs. Yates lived in the other half and provided meals and care for the carriage horses—also rented for the next few months.

The sisters came and went as they pleased, kept their own company, and accepted their own invitations without having to manage the household entirely on their own. But Fanny was fantasizing about even greater independence. She was twenty-one, but Molly made up for Fanny's youth with her twenty-five years, twenty-six in a few more months.

Fanny did not point out that her sister was nearly a spinster, but only because Molly didn't like such an accusation. She still hoped for a good match with a good man, while Fanny had become only more determined against such a thing. She'd had a number of beaus—as she and Molly referred to the young men who buzzed about them—but none of them sparked her interest, and now the publication of Mr. Longfellow's blasted book a few months ago had made her feel like a sideshow. She blamed her growing displeasure with the opposite sex squarely on the one man who seemed determined to draw her ire.

There it was again—baggage she had not meant to bring unpacking itself and sliding into her cupboards and cracks. She pushed up from the chair and turned to her sister, forcing a wide smile on her face. "Let's get together a party for an afternoon picnic," she said. "We could go to town and extend personal invitations and then walk up to the glen. It's a lovely day, and we have time to make arrangements. I'm sure Mrs. Butler would come, and we could request a recitation—Shakespeare or something."

Molly looked up. "I thought you were too tired for such entertainment today. That's what you said last night when *I* suggested we put together a luncheon."

"I don't want a luncheon indoors—shut away from the glorious day." Fanny turned back to the window. She hadn't wanted a picnic either, until she realized what poor company her thoughts were. "I want to be outside, with the breeze and the birds and the—"

"Rain?" Molly said.

The clouds in the east were indeed moving in, but Fanny was not deterred. "It might not rain," she said. "And if it did, we could simply bring the party indoors."

"And have a luncheon?" Molly shut her magazine and gave her sister a rueful look. "I'm teasing you, of course. I think it sounds lovely."

Fanny hurried toward the door that connected their rooms with the Yates'. "I'll have Mr. Yates get the carriage ready," she said brightly.

Thank goodness Molly had agreed to the diversion. They had

been in Western Massachusetts for three weeks and still she could not keep her thoughts from straying to the frustrations of Mr. Longfellow and "Mary Ashworth."

When she'd first read the book, she tried to take comfort in the fact that only she and her closest family and friends would draw the conclusion that Mary Ashworth was to Paul Flemming what Fanny Appleton was to Henry Longfellow. That had shortly proven to be an optimistic hope.

It felt as if everyone in Boston had made the same conclusion until Fanny could hardly bear to leave the house for fear some acquaintance would stop her on the street to ask her thoughts on the matter, or make a joke.

To Fanny, the comparison was not a joke, it was an insult, and whatever feelings of kindness and friendship she had retained toward Mr. Longfellow had been carried away by the stream of her humiliation. Publicly, of course, she pooh-poohed the entire situation, laughed it off, and acted as though she were flattered by the attention. Internally, however, she twisted and writhed against the embarrassment and anger she felt toward Mr. Longfellow. She'd tried so hard to remain friends after his ill-fated proposal—which he had also made public fodder for the gossips to dissect and share among themselves.

"See if Mrs. Yates also has time to help us put together a meal," Molly said, causing Fanny to start, her hand still on the door handle. Molly cocked her head. "Fanny?"

"Yes, yes," she said, bringing herself back from the past. She hoped this picnic would spare her mind the continual repetition of her situation. "I'll ask her." She disappeared into the shared portion of the house, determined—again—to keep her mind focused on the distraction rather than on the reasons she needed the distraction in the first place.

Twenty-Three

Mary Ashworth

"Mary Ashworth is not Fanny," Henry said. "*Hyperion* is fiction."

He and Tom Appleton had met for dinner at a restaurant along the wharf and, after a bit of small talk, Tom had asked Henry about Mary Ashworth from *Hyperion,* which had been out for two months.

"Fiction about a man who loses a dear friend, goes to Europe to recover, and meets a woman with whom he recites poetry?" Tom smiled and raised his eyebrows. "A man who loses his heart to a *dark ladye* who will not have him, and so he decides to live a solitary life?"

Henry looked down at his chowder. He could feel heat in his neck and chest and took a deep breath to calm himself. It wasn't the first time someone had asked him if Mary was a veiled version of Fanny—or unveiled, according to some. It was not the first time he had denied it, but this was Fanny's brother. Though Henry's protests when the comments were first directed his way were insistent, Henry himself had begun to wonder. If not for his own study of literature and the way an author's heart and experience tended to seep into the pages—with or without his notice—he could better argue his point. But he knew it was impossible for an artist of any medium not to personally influence his work, and so many people had suspected a connection between Mary Ashworth and Fanny Appleton that he feared Tom was right.

"I did not *intend* the story to be a reflection of your sister," Henry offered. Or did he? Henry's frustration with his feelings for Fanny had found their way into some of his poetry. Had he poured those same frustrations into the novel and then hid the truth of it from himself? Sometimes his mind felt as fractured as his heart, and he could not make sense of anything. He had hoped *Hyperion* would give him greater purpose and focus, but the reviews had not been as good as he'd hoped, and his publisher was hinting at money trouble that might delay Henry's first royalty payment.

Tom waved a hand through the air. "Oh, don't go throwing around 'your sister' and whatnot, I am not here to shame you, nor am I asking for any great confession, but you cannot blame me for asking."

Henry met his friend's jovial gaze. "You're not angry?"

Tom laughed and scooped up a spoonful of his soup. "Very few things make me angry, Henry, you know that. And I think Fanny could use a little introspection, if you don't mind my saying so. If this story helps her see herself more clearly, then it is for her good."

Henry took another bite of his soup, picturing Fanny in his mind and wincing internally over the embarrassment she must feel. "Is *she* very angry, then?"

"Oh, yes," Tom said, a laugh in his voice. He took a sip of his beer. "But she pretends as though she finds the whole thing silly and unworthy of discussion. Of course, that only prods me to introduce the topic into conversation any chance I can, which vexes her to the extreme." He put a hand to his chest. "As her older brother, however,

I feel that part of my responsibility is to vex her whenever possible. I am determined to do it well."

Henry's heart sank even more, and he wished, as he rarely did, that Tom was capable of a serious conversation. Was Fanny *truly* angry? At him? Was she hurt? Had Henry destroyed what little friendship was left between them? She'd been on summer holiday since he'd sent the gift of the book to her through her cousin, Jewett, and Henry had not seen her in all the months since.

"Do not take it so hard," Tom said. He smiled with sympathy instead of amusement.

Henry hated feeling pathetic in his friend's company.

"I read the book, and I quite liked it. If similarities between Mary Ashworth and Fanny exist, she should take it as a compliment—and perhaps a warning."

"A warning?"

"Fanny should give greater acknowledgment to your feelings for her, Longfellow. I am disappointed she has treated you as she has, and I hope she will come to a place where she will be capable of returning feelings she attempts to talk herself out of."

Henry's heart leaped in his chest, and he sat up straight. "*Her* feelings?"

"I would not go so far as to say she loves you. I'm unsure she is capable of such a thing right now, but there is *something* there. Be it attraction or connection or whatever, you strike her in a way that no other man does."

"Do not give me false hope," Henry said, laying down his spoon with trembling fingers. "You are a good friend to me, Tom, but you do me no favors to encourage me toward barren fields."

"I do nothing of the sort," Tom said, leaning in and fixing Henry with a serious look. "She does not know her own heart and mind—she's been wounded. Between the loss of people she loves and her romantic interests that have soured, she protects herself with a critical tongue and busy action. I believe her feelings are not so different from your own, only they are as yet unrecognized, and she does not trust herself enough to truly consider them."

"You are teasing me," Henry said, shaking his head. "What good are feelings unrecognized? It is a kind way to say she holds no regard."

Tom raised his eyebrows. "There are plenty of men for whom she holds no regard, and there are some she is sweet about, but there are very few who can draw passion from her heart of stone, and I am certain you, as a man of poetry, know that passion is not always properly attributed."

Henry picked up his spoon. "Enough. You are simply giving me greater grief. What you mean to say is that she is passionately against me, and while I appreciate you stating that her passion could be for the future good should it turn to more optimistic intent, I do not feel such hope. I do not want conflict, with Fanny less than anyone." He paused, considered his words, and then looked across the table at his friend. "Will you tell her that I did not intend to reflect her? That I am sorry to have caused her embarrassment?"

The amusement returned to Tom's face. "Sure I will."

The way Tom gave his word worried Henry. He felt as if he may have inadvertently thrown Fanny to the wolves a second time.

"Is the book doing well?" Tom asked. "Are you pleased with its progress so far?"

Henry was grateful for the change in subject. "The reviews have not been all that complimentary, I'm afraid."

"I've read them," Tom said with a nod. "But Poe cannot be trusted to give you a *crumb* of encouragement, and I am much more interested in public opinion, which seems to like the book. I think a man could take the book as a travel guide through Europe, so rich is the description and setting."

"Thank you," Henry said, immensely lifted by Tom's compliments. "I'm sure it sounds arrogant for me to say, but I take great pride in the book—never mind the critics."

"There are always plenty willing to point out flaws," Tom said. "It's better to pay them no heed. And you have another book coming out soon, do you not? Poetry?"

"Yes," Henry said, unable to hide his smile. To have two books published in a single year was an accomplishment, and in two fields to boot. Even with the disappointments surrounding *Hyperion,* he was hopeful he was moving toward a writing career that he had wanted since he was a very young man. "And I have high hopes for it."

Tom asked detailed questions about distribution, reviews, and the foreign rights. It was easy to talk with Tom, who was not the least bit threatened by Henry's success. Tom had confessed he had once dreamed of being a poet, but he seemed to have determined since then that he had little need to make a career of any kind. He'd already opened and closed his legal practice, and he preferred to travel, appreciate art, and avoid marriage—a full time job if ever there was one.

The server cleared the empty dishes and both men requested a plate of cheese and fruit. After the server left, Tom leaned back in his chair and smiled widely. "So you've done it then. You are the newest American writer. You've broken the bonds of European culture and brought a voice to our own victories."

"You flatter me," Henry said, but he was unable to contain a smile. "I am certainly nowhere near ready to give up teaching, but I *am* encouraged. Should sales do well here and abroad, and if I am able to follow up with additional works, I may very well be able to make a career of my pen one day."

"That is remarkable," Tom said.

"I could not have done it without the support of my friends. You, Sumner, Felton, Cleveland, and Sparks have been unfailing in your encouragement. You have lifted me when I've fallen low and given me reason to continue forward."

Despite the recognition of his many blessings, however, the last few weeks had begun to turn gray and curled at the edges. The pattern was familiar to Henry, too familiar, and he longed for sleep and wine and mournful literature that somehow made him feel less alone. Thus far he had avoided the worst of the depression, but the cloaked figure lurked around the corners, beating him with its blunted fists on nights that were particularly long and weary.

"I'm glad indeed to have such credit," Tom said. "And very happy for your success. Jewett and I are heading up to Lenox in a few days to see how Fanny and Molly are faring. They've rented rooms for the summer there while Father and Harriet stay in Nahant." He paused and his eyes twinkled. "May I share your success with Fanny? I'm quite certain she does not know you have another book being published this year."

Henry had never told anyone that part of his reason for pursuing publication was to make a life for himself that might be more appealing to Fanny. His face heated up, and he was glad for the appearance of their server with the dessert plates. After the disastrous connection so many people had made between his book and Fanny, it seemed unwise to hope anything would show him in a better light.

And yet, despite the discouragement following his hasty proposal in the parlor on Beacon Street, and the awkwardness of the meetings that had taken place since, the hope Henry felt never went away. Not entirely. It certainly was low tonight, hearing that she was upset with him about *Hyperion,* but it was still there.

On the dark days, he would think of how lost Fanny was to him, of how worthless his days were without her. And yet somewhere in the corner of his mind was that flame of hope, pushing him on, drawing him out, keeping him active. He could not explain it, and so he simply accepted it as proof that someday, somehow, she would find a place for him in her heart.

Twenty-Four

A Letter from Home

Fanny's face burned hot as she stared across the breakfast table at her brother, wondering how she could miss Tom so much when he was absent and be so vexed with him when he was near. Why had he discussed her with Mr. Longfellow at all?

"I, for one, am glad to hear of Mr. Longfellow's success," Molly said while spreading jam on her toast. Mrs. Yates had provided a very nice meal for the sisters and their guests, Tom and Jewett, who had come for a visit. The men were staying at the hotel in Lenox, but it was not so far from the sisters' rented rooms that a morning visit was cumbersome.

"To claim *Hyperion* a *success* might be doing it too brown," Jewett said, raising one eyebrow. "Have you not read the reviews?" He winked at Fanny, causing her to blush again but for another reason. Once again, Fanny had not been circumspect in sharing her thoughts with Jewett and wished she had guarded her tongue. She wondered how many people he'd shared her lashings with and wished she were not so quick to temper.

There was a tapping at the door that separated their rooms from those of Mr. and Mrs. Yates. Molly stood to open it.

"Mr. Yates brought the post from town a bit ago," Mrs. Yates said, handing over a small stack of letters. "Thought you might like to see them over breakfast."

"Thank you," Molly said. She took the letters and returned to the table where she set the letters beside her plate and picked up where the conversation had left off. "I think Mr. Poe was exceptionally rude. You know, I heard he's been particular in his criticism of Mr. Longfellow. Some suspect his irritation is not only based on literary interests."

"Poe is a singularly miserable man," Tom said, returning to his eggs. "The point is that Henry wasn't writing about Fanny in his book. We can lay that suspicion to rest."

When he looked at Fanny, however, he did not seem as though he were intending to lay it to rest. Rather he was baiting her, and she could feel herself rising to it even as she told herself not to. Nothing would irritate her brother more than if she *refused* to spar with him. Only she could not help herself. Perhaps because of her embarrassment, perhaps because of her own guilty conscience regarding her venting to Jewett, perhaps because everyone else seemed to see this as such a small thing when, in fact, it was not small at all to her.

She took a breath to steady herself before she spoke. "Surely you cannot ignore that this book is the perfect revenge for Mr. Longfellow to make upon me. Why would he admit as much?"

"Revenge?" Molly and Tom said at the same time, both of them looking at Fanny in surprise. Jewett took a bite of his ham.

"Yes, revenge," she said, encouraged to defend her position. "Because I rejected his proposal, he has created a caricature of me and put it on display so as to embarrass me. Does he not woo Mary

Ashworth with German poetry and say she is not handsome? Does he not have Mary dismiss Mr. Flemming just as I dismissed Mr. Longfellow himself?"

"You are *very* handsome," Jewett said. He winked again when Fanny gave him a curdling look.

Fanny put down her fork. "I know what I am, and I have never been a great beauty. I am not protesting for the sake of my vanity."

"Then what are you protesting?" Tom asked.

She almost believed he was sincere. "I have been wronged."

Tom snorted, and Fanny narrowed her eyes at him. She turned to Jewett and Molly. "Mr. Longfellow was most improper in his proposal to me, and then he has gone about town telling everyone the whole of it. A week has not gone by in Boston where someone does not make some sly comment about having seen him or his having asked after me—and that was *before* this blasted book was released."

"Mind your language," Molly said, taking a sip of her tea.

Fanny clenched her jaw a moment before she could speak again. Cutting into Molly would only weaken her argument. "He should not have made my rejection public. He should have afforded me respect then, and he should not have mimicked me in his book now."

"He says any similarity was unintentional," Tom said. "And I truly feel he was genuine in his claim."

Fanny sighed. The argument was going nowhere, and she was sounding like a ninny. "Do *you* think I am reflected in Mary Ashworth, Tom?"

When he did not answer right away, she turned to Jewett, then Molly. "Tell me truly, do you think Mr. Longfellow—on purpose or not—reflected me in his book?"

Everyone was silent, awkward amid the serious turn to the meal. Molly flipped through the stack of letters beside her plate by way of distraction. Fanny turned her full attention to Tom. He was the most likely to be honest since sparing her feelings was never his priority.

"Well?" she asked, cocking her head and keeping her focus on her brother. "Do you?"

"There are . . . similarities," Tom admitted.

His cautious tone irritated her all the more, but she knew how to force the truth from him. "Don't be a nincompoop. Do you or don't you think that the professor put me in his book?"

"Alright, then. Yes," Tom said. "I think you have nearly trod that man's heart into the ground, and whether intended or not, he attempted to exorcise his heartache through writing a mean-spirited woman who turns down a good-hearted man for no other reason than she sees him as beneath her."

Fanny was unsure if the sound of someone sucking in a breath was her or Molly or Jewett. Regardless, she stared at her brother who refused to apologize. The silence was numbing.

Fanny stood, threw her napkin in her chair, and ran from the room to the bedchamber. She locked the door before throwing herself on the bed as though she were some adolescent girl. She wanted to cry and rage, but the numbness Tom's words had brought on kept her from displaying her emotions. She buried her face in the quilt while Tom's words marched through her head like tin soldiers. *Exorcise his heartache. Mean-spirited woman. Good-hearted man.*

She clenched her eyes shut and turned her head so she didn't suffocate. Mr. Longfellow *was* a good-hearted man. She had never said otherwise, but that did not justify the embarrassment he had caused her. Not just with the book, but his continued attention and the fact that everyone in Boston seemed to know it. *He* was the one who proposed to her unexpectedly, without a proper courtship. He had not been a gentleman in his regard for her. If he had, he would not have wanted to cause her discomfort.

"For no other reason than she sees him as beneath her."

Fanny's stomach burned. Was that true? Was the primary reason for her rejection of the professor based upon her unwillingness to lower herself to his class?

She felt both embarrassed and defensive of the possibility, but then she wondered if it mattered what she thought if everyone else believed she was a spoiled rich girl looking down on a college professor. Did people think she was so afraid of not having fine clothes or nice carriages that she kept her heart locked to him?

Were they right?

Was it so wrong to want comfort?

Was she willing to give up every other happiness for that comfort?

How could she love a man who treated her so poorly?

Had he treated her poorly?

Could she love any man at all?

It seemed the men who drew her interest did not return it, and the man who was so blatantly interested in her, quite frankly, frightened her. He was so intent. So seemingly unaffected by *her* feelings regarding *his*. The moment in the dining room in Interlaken, when he had looked at her and made her feel so . . . noticed had only been the first time he'd done so, and the more time and clarity that grew between those experiences and the present, the more uncomfortable she was with the level of his notice. Who was he to understand her? And did he, really? He'd created a character made up of her and his dead wife. How was that anything less than objectionable? When she had rejected his proposal, she had stated that very fear—that he was looking to replace Mary Potter Longfellow. And now this?

These were thoughts she could share with no one, but they boiled inside of her and begged her to determine which part of *Hyperion* was most hurtful. That he'd reflected Fanny in the character of Mary Ashworth, or that he'd reflected Mary Potter as well? Did he see any distinction between the two? Did she even matter for her own merit?

Never far from her objections and irritation was the notice *she* took of *him*. The gentleness that was now at odds with what she saw as an attack against her, the keen mind she admired, and the affection she had felt toward him at times. Those things were tainted now, or so she thought, but now and again they would rise up and she would wonder if *she* had bungled this entire situation, not him. If she had opened her heart, would things be different? But it was too late for that. She did not want a man who would treat her as Mr. Longfellow had. She was entitled to her feelings.

Fanny had locked the main door to her room but hadn't remembered to secure the door that joined Molly's bedchamber to her own until she heard the hinges squeak. She was still sprawled over the bed and silently cursed Molly's entrance. She did not want to discuss this with Molly, her sister who'd been left so wounded by John Peterton that she had stopped speaking of marriage all together, even though Fanny knew Molly wanted it more than ever. And here was her younger sister, in hysterics because a man was *too* attentive to her, *too* sincere, *too* determined.

Fanny pushed herself off the bed before Molly could sit beside her or stroke her hair. She didn't want comfort—wasn't sure she deserved it. If only she could be like Tom and catch a ship to Europe and hide until everything had faded away. If only she had such control of her destiny.

Fanny came to her feet and tried to smile at her sister, who was not smiling back. Her expression was so serious, Fanny instinctively asked, "Are you all right, Molly?"

Molly sat on the edge of Fanny's bed and waved toward the chair beside it. "I think you should sit down. There's something I need to tell you, and I fear you will not like it."

"Did Mr. Longfellow publish another book?" Fanny said, still immersed in her ire but attempting to lighten it.

"I'm serious, Fanny."

Her expression *was* serious. Fanny sat, put her hands in her lap, and prepared herself.

Molly took a breath. "After you left the breakfast room, I opened a letter from Father."

"What has happened?" Fanny asked. Was someone ill, or worse yet, had they lost someone else they dearly loved?

Molly looked confused a moment, then shook her head. "Nothing has happened. Well, not exactly. He had news."

"What news?" Fanny asked cautiously.

Molly smiled, albeit weakly. "He is going to be a father again. In January, they suspect. They held off telling anyone until they knew all was well with, well, with Harriet and the . . . the baby."

Fanny blinked and leaned back in the chair.

"He said he had hoped to tell us in person, but it doesn't look as though they will be leaving Boston any time soon, now that they have returned from Nahant. At Harriet's age, you know, they have to be careful. He hopes, however, that we will share in his joy and return in October as planned to help Harriet in her final months of confinement."

Fanny looked at the braided rug beside her bed. A new wife. Now a new family.

"You are happy for them, are you not, Fanny?"

"Of course I am," Fanny said, looking up at her sister. "Do you think I am so heartless as to not be joyful for such a thing?"

"You did not approve of the marriage."

"No, I did not," Fanny said with a sad smile. "But Father is happy, and Harriet is a good companion for him."

The news made her thoughts even more complex. Her father had come to life with Harriett at his side. Though she struggled to find the words to explain it, Fanny could see that he still loved her mother, still missed her even. But he was happier than he had been for many years, and Fanny was genuinely glad of that. She no longer felt the same resentment toward Harriet that she did in the beginning, or feel that her mother had been replaced. Rather, she saw her father being given another chance at joy. And Harriett had been given the chance to be loved and, now, to have a family of her own.

So why did it all make Fanny's heart ache? Why was their happiness painful for her at times?

Molly moved her gaze to the side. "A child between them will displace us even further."

Fanny was surprised to hear such a thing from Molly, who had tried so hard to be cheerful and accommodating of their stepmother. The sisters had spent the majority of their time since the wedding traveling. Between the awkwardness of a new woman running the household and Mr. Longfellow's book, Boston had become uncomfortable. As grown women, they were entitled to such freedoms, but the fact was that the house on Beacon Street felt less and less their home.

"Fate does seem to be pushing us toward more independence, doesn't it?" Fanny said.

"It does seem that way, only our options are limited."

"I wouldn't say that," Fanny said, scraping for the positive. "We have means of independence, and Father is progressive. If we wanted to set up our own residence, for instance, I feel sure Father would support it—after the baby is born, of course."

"Oh, I disagree," Molly said, her voice strong as she shook her head. "He might be progressive in some ways, but not enough to release his daughters into the world alone."

"Perhaps you are right." Fanny took a deep breath and let it out as she reached for her sister's hands. "We shall be fine, you and I, and a baby is always a wonderful thing. I believe that is where our attention should be focused, on the good news this brings."

"Never mind the bruising?" Molly asked.

Fanny smiled. "Never mind the bruising. We have each other, and for that I am grateful."

Molly's brow puckered for a moment, as though something about Fanny's comment concerned her, but she repaired it quickly, and Fanny chose not to ask for an explanation.

"Indeed," Molly said with a smile. "We shall always have each other."

Fanny rose from her chair. "My, this has been a trying morning. I do hope the day's diversions are fine enough to make up for all this heavy talk. What is the agenda?"

"I believe Mr. Mackintosh will be calling this morning," Molly said.

Fanny looked over her shoulder, struck by the nervous tone in her sister's voice. "The Irishman?" While they had had any number of gentleman callers these last months, Fanny had found Mr. Mackintosh's company rather dry.

"He's Scottish," Molly corrected her sister, picking at a loose stitch on the quilt.

Fanny watched her sister another moment and then turned to

the window so Molly wouldn't see her concern. Had Mr. Mackintosh drawn her sister's interest?

Don't look for ghosts, she chided herself and then thought of Mary Potter Longfellow. Was Fanny trying to see ghosts where there were none? Had Mr. Longfellow properly mourned Mary Potter to the point that, like Father, he could love again? As whole and complete as ever? Harriet was not threatened by the fact that Nathan had loved before. In fact, she had told Aunt Sam that it encouraged her, proved to her that he was faithful and capable of loving her just as well as he'd loved Fanny's mother.

It frustrated Fanny how easily her thoughts turned to Mr. Longfellow. More than ever, she did *not* want his attention, so why must he invade her thoughts? She suspected the reason was due to how often he seemed to bring out the worst in her. From the very first night they had met, it seemed she was always putting her foot in her mouth or reacting in ways that embarrassed her later. Yet her poor behavior never seemed to dissuade him. It was irritating . . . but was there not something appealing about it?

How many times had Fanny reflected on the people in her life and felt as though they didn't really know her? She knew how to behave, how to react, how to carry and present herself. Even with Molly—her dearest friend—she was cautious about sharing certain thoughts and feelings she had for fear of disappointing her sister. Mr. Longfellow, however, seemed as accepting of Fanny's flaws as of her virtues.

"Fanny? Did you hear me?"

Fanny turned back to Molly. "I'm sorry. What did you say?"

"I said that we should return to Tom and Jewett," Molly said from the doorway. "We should put this morning behind us. Tom is simply defending his friend."

Fanny wanted to ask why he could not defend his sister, but the fight had gone out of her. Maybe she did deserve Mr. Longfellow's censure. Or perhaps he truly did not mean to reflect her and was as embarrassed by the connection as she was. Either way, looking for ghosts was exhausting and she was tired of the effort.

"Give me another minute to collect myself," Fanny said. "Then I will join you."

Molly exited the room through the adjoining door.

Fanny looked out the window over the fields and hills. She thought of Mr. Longfellow writing by lamplight at the end of the day when his teaching responsibilities were done. She thought of her father penning a note to his daughters, hoping they would share his happiness. She closed her eyes and dropped her chin to her chest. "Help me find peace," she whispered in desperate prayer as emotion stung her eyelids.

Twenty-Five

Mrs. Mackintosh

Fanny adjusted the slight train of Molly's simple muslin wedding gown and glanced up to find her sister watching her in the mirror. Fanny looked back to the dress, nervous for reasons that shouldn't matter and hesitant for the type of heart-to-heart that was requisite for a day such as this.

"You *are* happy for me, aren't you, Fanny?"

"Of course I am happy for you," Fanny said as though the alternative were completely ridiculous. "I could not wish a better man for you than Robert Mackintosh."

"You did not like him so much in the beginning."

Fanny stared at the pristine fabric for a moment before placing her hands on her sister's shoulders from behind and meeting Molly's eyes in the mirror. Today was Molly's wedding day, a day that would forever serve as a marker for her life, and Fanny's efforts in behalf of the celebration that would follow would count for nothing if her sister did not feel as though they had connected as they had always connected during life-changing events before.

"I will admit I did not enjoy his company all that much in the beginning," Fanny said, though this was hardly a surprise to Molly. She had been distressed at the idea that Fanny had not liked the man who Molly liked very much. "I found him arrogant and stuffy, but once you gave your heart to him, and he gave his to you, I came to view him in another way. I am sincerely grateful such a man has earned your love. I could not have parted from you for anything less than that."

Molly's eyes filled with tears. "You mean it truly?"

Fanny wrapped her arms around Molly's shoulders and gave her a tight hug from behind. "With all my heart, dear sister." They embraced a few seconds longer before Fanny released Molly. She stood beside her so they could look at one another side by side in the looking glass. Molly looked angelic in her high-waisted white gown, simple and elegant, just like her, while Fanny had chosen a lavender dress with the lower waist and fuller skirt of the current fashion.

Fanny thought of their dual portrait painted by Isabey when they had been in Italy nearly four years ago, of how well he had captured them. Fanny wished they could have another portrait done of the two of them today—older, wiser, and one of them meeting her destiny.

"You deserve every good thing, Molly," Fanny said softly. "And I could not be happier for you than I am in this. It is everything you have ever wanted, and my heart is full to bursting for the joy of it."

Molly responded with a watery smile and a few dabs of her handkerchief. "I wish we weren't going so far away from one another."

The reminder made Fanny's heart thump in her chest, but she was careful not to show the reaction she felt every time she was reminded of the distance soon to come between the sisters; they had never been parted before.

"You are to be married to an international diplomat, Molly. Far away is part of the bargain." Worried her attempt at a joke sounded severe, Fanny faced her sister and took both of her hands. "Perhaps it is for the best that you will go abroad," she said, though she did not necessarily believe her own words. Molly's eyebrows pulled together, prompting Fanny to continue. "We have been as close as any two people for all of our lives, and I'm not sure I could let you go enough to find your way with Robert if you were still in Boston. I would be on your doorstep every day, beside you at every meal, and continually entreating you to attend me in this thing or that." She laughed at the image of it. "Poor Robert would be beside himself."

"But how will I get on alone?" Molly said in a near whisper. "I have never had to run a household on my own. What if I am not equal to it?"

For an instant Fanny wondered why Molly hadn't thought about that weeks ago, when Robert had first proposed marriage. "You have cold feet, Molly. There is absolutely no reason why you should question your abilities. You will learn the way of it as every woman does."

It would help that Robert would not have a grand house, not like 39 Beacon Street. He was an envoy and would spend his career traveling between a variety of posts and living in whatever accommodations could be found. There would not be a great many servants to manage or society to entertain, not like it had been for Molly in Boston. Fanny did not think of the changes in a disparaging way, rather she believed Molly would find great comfort in a simpler life. Yet one more reason why Robert seemed the perfect man for her.

"I hope I will be equal to it," Molly said. She turned back to the mirror and seemed to take a deep breath while squaring her shoulders. She took in her reflection, without Fanny beside her this time.

Fanny stepped to the dresser and picked up the simple wedding bouquet of myrtle and lilies from the tray where it rested. She handed the bouquet to Molly, who held it in both hands and regarded herself in the mirror.

"I'm getting married," she said as though speaking to herself. "I shall be Mrs. Mackintosh."

"And one day soon, a mother," Fanny said.

"Oh, I do hope so," Molly said, a wide smile lighting up her features. "I hope you don't feel poorly toward me for this bout of nervousness."

"Not in the least. I'm sure every bride feels exactly the same. It is a good day, a happy day, the start of a new and wonderful future."

"Yes," Molly said, her spirits restored. "Yes it is."

Fanny helped Molly finish the last of her preparations, then left her with a kiss on the cheek so that Fanny could manage the few guests who would be in attendance.

When Fanny entered the parlor, which had been set up for the ceremony, Robert looked as nervous as Molly had been. None of his family were in America, and she was glad that the extended Appletons had embraced him fully. Fanny whispered words of encouragement to him before taking her seat between her dear friend Emmeline Austin and her Aunt Sam.

Tom and a very pregnant Harriet sat on the chairs opposite the aisle, with an empty chair for Father between them, while a dozen or so guests filled the chairs behind. Emmeline reached for Fanny's hand, which Fanny appreciated.

For all of Fanny's speeches and encouragement, part of her was absolutely heartbroken over Molly's marriage. She would miss her sister so much.

Dr. Channing took his place at the front of the parlor, the windows behind him overlooking the Commons. As the musician began to play a hymn on the pianoforte, Fanny allowed the last few years to weave through her mind: Mama's death, Charles's passing, traveling through Europe, burying William in Schaffhausen, Father's marriage—not quite a year ago. So many changes. So many struggles.

Molly had been there through all of them, smoothing out Fanny's edges, encouraging her to see the best in people, helping her keep her confidence and not fall prey to her fears that nothing would ever be right again. After each difficulty, life had once again gained its color and joy.

But was that because of Molly's influence? Had Fanny weathered the storms because Molly had pulled her through them? There were surely more struggles ahead, and Fanny would face them without her dear sister, her closest friend, the person in the world who Fanny believed knew her best and loved her anyway.

Dr. Channing instructed the guests to rise, and Fanny, along with the other guests, stood and turned toward the doorway.

Fanny held her emotions in check until she saw Father blinking back tears as he led Molly to the front of the room. Then there was no hope for controlling her own. Tears streamed down her face as Father and Molly made the slow walk down the aisle.

Standing before Dr. Channing, Father handed Molly to Robert, who thanked him, then took Molly's hand. Whatever nervousness bride and groom had felt before this moment disappeared in the bright hopefulness of their expressions as they looked upon their futures together.

Emmeline squeezed Fanny's hand again, and Fanny sent her friend a happy smile. It *was* a happy day, and Fanny's heart was full.

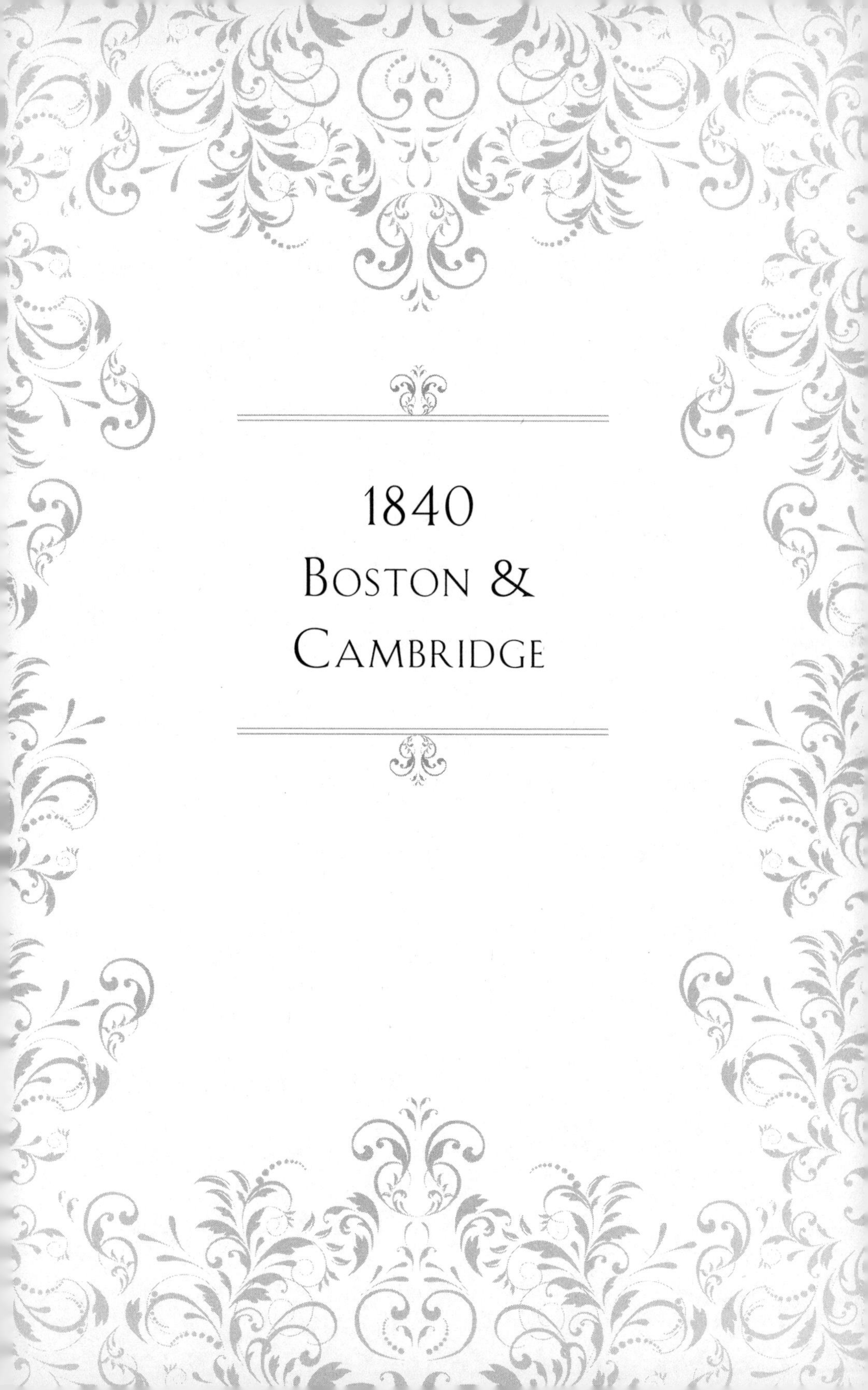

1840
Boston & Cambridge

Twenty-Six

A Scholar

Fanny gave her Aunt Sam a quick hug and a kiss on her cheek. "Thank you for such a lovely afternoon," she said as the carriage stopped in front of 39 Beacon Street. It was early November—Fanny had celebrated her twenty-third birthday a few weeks before—and cold enough to freeze fingers and toes, but not so cold to prevent the women from sprucing up their wardrobes for winter. Since Molly's marriage and removal to England last March, Fanny had become even closer to her aunts as they filled in some of the loneliness she felt.

"I am the one who should be thanking you," Aunt Sam said. "Such young company keeps me from feeling my age. Besides, what good is having a niece if I cannot spoil her from time to time?"

Fanny smiled, thinking of what a wonderful mother Aunt Sam would have been. It had not been her destiny, and so she bathed her nieces and nephews with love. "This niece will not complain one bit," she said, lifting up the hatbox hanging at her wrist. Inside was the most beautiful green velvet hat that matched the striped pelisse Fanny had ordered from the same shop two weeks earlier. "Thank you."

"Oh, never you mind," Aunt Sam said, waving Fanny from the

carriage. "Besides, I want you to look smart for your smart company tonight. Come for tea tomorrow and tell me all about the lecture."

"I shall," Fanny said, though she knew Aunt Sam was not all that interested in Mr. Dana's poetry. As Aunt Sam had said, however, she adored her niece and rarely needed a reason for a visit.

"I shall expect you at four," Aunt Sam said as Mathews opened the carriage door. He lifted Fanny down from the carriage, and she stood long enough to wave a final good-bye as the carriage drove off.

Mathews opened the front door for Fanny and then received her hat and coat. She instructed him to put the hatbox in her room.

She turned toward the sound of footsteps coming from the drawing room. "Good afternoon, Fanny," Harriet said.

"Good afternoon, Harriett," Fanny said with a smile. "How is little William faring today?" Her half brother, whom Fanny adored, was ten months old and an absolute delight. He was crawling now, and at times the house on Beacon Street did not seem nearly big enough to contain him. Harriet had a nurse come in every afternoon, but did all the rearing herself in the morning—a very unusual choice for a woman of her status.

At first Fanny had been annoyed with the disposing of tradition, but as time passed, she gained a new respect for her stepmother, and perhaps a bit of envy for William, who had his mother's full attention for hours every day. He had become a thread of connection between the women, giving them a safe topic of conversation.

"Oh, William," Harriett said, shaking her head. "He only napped half an hour this morning, and then he toppled down the first flight of stairs when I turned my back a moment too long."

"Oh, dear," Fanny said, glancing up the grand staircase—marble, hard, unforgiving. "Is he alright?"

"Bumped and bruised. But I do think he'll respect the staircase in the future."

Fanny smiled politely but wondered if a hired nurse would be more attentive. Sometimes Harriett had the strangest ideas on parenting—as though a child could learn to avoid stairs. Better to put a chair at the top and prevent harm, Fanny thought. But it was not her place to say so.

"You received a letter from Molly today," Harriett continued as she passed Fanny in the foyer. "I had Mathew put it on your desk. She wrote to your father as well, but he won't be home until dinner."

That Harriett had not opened Molly's letter meant that it had not been addressed to her. Fanny wondered if Molly had intended the slight—it was not like her.

"Do you remember that I won't be home for dinner?" Fanny said when Harriet reached the first stair.

Harriet turned back to her. "That's right, tonight is your lecture at the college."

"Jewett and I will get dinner beforehand."

"Very good," Harriet said, moving up the stairs. "I believe I will lie down while the nurse keeps William occupied. I daresay I would probably be better served if the nurse stayed overnight so I might get a full night's sleep."

"Father would be glad to arrange it," Fanny said, reminding her stepmother that not having a nurse during the night was her own choice.

"I'm sure he would," Harriett said, smiling softly. "Only I am far too selfish. I want my face to be the one William sees when the tremors of night wake him from his rest. I am unwilling to share."

She really was the most peculiar mother. Harriet continued up the stairs, and a minute later, Fanny climbed the stairs to her own room.

She spotted Molly's letter on her writing desk and hurried across the room, eager to hear from the sister she missed so very much.

Fanny had been so tempted to go to England with Molly when she'd issued the invitation back in March, but she did not want to encroach on the couple's time to set up a household together. Molly had written faithfully twice a month, and Fanny drank down every word like it was fine wine. They had celebrated their birthdays together every year, until this one, and the ache of longing Fanny had felt was more than she'd dared admit to anyone. She settled at her desk and opened the letter, letting the words take on Molly's voice in her head. When she reached the second line, she gasped.

"I am an aunt," she said quietly and read the announcement a second time.

It was not unexpected. Molly had written of her pregnancy for months now, but it was fantastic all the same. And perhaps a bit of a sharp reminder. In the time it had taken Molly to move into two new life-roles, Fanny had stayed the same. There were a few suitors who had come calling, but her interest was not sparked by any of them. Because Molly was not with her, Fanny hadn't gone to Lenox for the summer and instead attended Harriett and William to Newport. It had been a nice trip, the sea was lovely and Fanny had enjoyed the countryside, but when she remembered the prior summers with Molly, she'd found Newport wanting.

The one accomplishment she could claim over the last months was that she'd become a great reader. She'd enjoyed everything from Balzac to novels and read all manner of essays and commentary that had once seemed uninteresting. Perhaps words had become her new friends now that Molly was gone.

Fanny returned to the letter and read about her new nephew,

Ronald Mackintosh, who had been born on Molly's birthday. A Scotsman like his father, he was healthy and fat and "always hungry."

Fanny wondered at a line about the difficulties with his birth, but Molly did not expound, and Fanny knew enough about childbirth to know it was never without hardship. She hoped Molly was improving and immediately began wondering when she might make a trip to England to meet her nephew. She would not be encroaching now that there was a child. Rather, she would be helping her sister while soaking up the magic of her new nephew.

There was little keeping her in Boston as more and more friends married or sought their fortunes in other cities or even other continents. Everyone seemed on the move—everyone but Fanny.

After Molly's letter, Fanny immediately began to pen her response, using her most flowery words to share with her sister how truly happy she was for her and Robert. She expressed how eager she was to meet her "Cockney nephew" and wished them every happiness.

By the time she finished the letter, it was time to prepare for the lecture. Fanny moved to her vanity and repaired her hair for the event.

Richard Henry Dana was a fine poet, and Fanny found his commentaries fascinating as they distracted her from all the ugly politics that bogged down her mind. Locofocoism, abolitionism, and Harrisonism had become the topic of nearly every dinner party and drawing room. Fanny had had enough of it. Literature was a much kinder place to center her attention, and Mr. Dana provided a welcome playground for her thoughts. She had just placed her new hat upon her head when Mathew announced that Jewett had arrived with his carriage.

Fanny pinned her hat into place and hurried down to the foyer where her cousin bowed elegantly over her hand. He complimented her new hat when she preened and posed for him, and they spoke of all manner of things during dinner at Jewett's favorite pub as well as on the ride to Cambridge, where the driver let them off in front of the lecture hall.

It was cold, and Fanny was glad she'd worn her wool petticoat and thicker boots. The doors to the hall were open, and Jewett walked behind her with his hand at her back so they would not lose one another in the stream of attendees filtering in.

"I do think you are quite outnumbered," Jewett said from behind her. "I haven't seen another woman here yet."

"Truly?" Fanny was relieved when they reached the hall and she could pick out half a dozen colored hats and coats amid the determinedly black and gray sea of men's clothing. She was glad not to be the sole representative of her sex and a little proud that she was one of only a handful of women reaching beyond what was expected of them. She liked to think she and her scholarly sisters in attendance tonight were doing their part to prove that a woman's mind was equal to that of a man's.

Jewett found two seats only a few rows from the front and led Fanny toward them. She took her seat and unwrapped the scarf from her neck. She had nearly settled into her seat when a familiar form on the platform at the front of the room made her pause.

She had not seen Mr. Longfellow for months, not since Tom's birthday party in March. She hadn't sought out Mr. Longfellow's company that night, but during a brief encounter with him toward the end of the night, he had recommended that she might like to read Macaulay's essay on Milton. He knew of her love of Milton from their time in Germany. She had thanked him for the recommendation and then thought little of it until Newport, where she happened to find a copy of the *Edinburgh Review,* which had featured the essay back in 1825.

Even standing with the periodical in hand, she'd hesitated; she wanted no more connection to Mr. Longfellow than that of an acquaintance and was proud of herself for having overcome the most intense reactions toward *Hyperion* to allow even that. To read what he'd recommended—obviously referencing their connection in Europe so many years ago—made her feel as though she were inviting him in somehow. She nearly ignored the essay completely, but then her love of Milton swayed her and she gave in.

She'd found Macaulay's insights quite fascinating, enough that she'd considered for one crazy moment writing Mr. Longfellow her thoughts. There were not many people of her acquaintance with whom she could discuss literature at depth. The idea to write him was dismissed as soon as it had come, of course, but seeing him now renewed her wish that their friendship had been sustained. She would like to have discussions with him without worrying she would give him the wrong impression. It was too bad he had ruined whatever chances they had for *that* kind of friendship. It had been over a year since *Hyperion* had made her a topic of gossips and speculators, and though the fervor had died down, the impressions had not.

"Ah, your beau is here," Jewett said as he unbuttoned his coat. He nodded toward Longfellow conversing comfortably with Mr. Dana as they waited for the lecture to begin. Jewett gave her a sideways look. "Please don't tell me that's the true reason we are here."

"As though I would cross the river for him," Fanny said, then winced at how rude it was. Why was it so easy for her to be caustic with Jewett?

"Better to throw yourself into it," Jewett said with a merry grin. He put his hands together and pantomimed diving into the very river he referenced.

Fanny could not keep from smiling, despite how terribly

inappropriate his comment was, but she shook her head. "You are bringing out the worst in me." She lifted her chin. "And I am trying very hard to appear as dignified as my company."

Jewett looked around the audience—the hall was nearly full—and then back at her. "If dignified means tattered coats and ill-fitting hats, then I suppose I shall have to agree. I feel like a rose among thorns. It was a waste to wear my new shoes." He lifted his pant leg so she could see his new leather shoes, shined to a gleam. It was the second time he'd drawn her attention to them. The first time was in the carriage ride, and then, like now, she rolled her eyes at his vanity.

"If you are the rose, what am I?" she asked, acting affronted. As though he would be noticed before she would.

Jewett shrugged. "You're the one who called the company distinguished."

She was phrasing an appropriate response when the sound of someone clearing his throat drew her attention, along with the attention of the audience.

Mr. Longfellow stood at the podium, awaiting the crowd to quiet down so that he might, apparently, begin the lecture. While he waited, he scanned the crowd rather languidly until he saw her. His gaze instantly stopped for one count. Two. Three. She felt her face heating up as people around her began turning to see what had captured the attention of the man on the stand.

Finally, Mr. Longfellow seemed to collect himself and looked up, but his demeanor, which had been comfortable before, was now rigid and tense.

Fanny sunk lower in her chair. She heard someone behind her whisper her name to someone else.

"Oh, from the book?" came the whispered reply.

Fanny closed her eyes, mortified. Would *Hyperion* ever go away?

She was slinking even lower in her chair when Jewett put his hand on her arm and leaned toward her.

"Don't give them reason to think less of you," he whispered. "Your embarrassment will only give them permission to think ill."

She nodded and straightened in her chair, lifting her chin and keeping her eyes on Mr. Longfellow as though it did not take every bit of her focus to appear unaffected. He did not look at her again, skipping over her when he took in different portions of the room.

She was glad he did not risk noticing her again, but she could see that his own neck was red and could tell by the way he fumbled through his introduction that her presence had unnerved him. She hated causing him discomfort but was also irritated that he was putting a blemish over what was supposed to be a very fine evening. He had not been present at Mr. Dana's last lecture. She hoped he didn't think she'd come to see him.

" . . . and so it is my pleasure to introduce you to the estimable Mr. Richard Henry Dana."

Fanny applauded with the crowd while Mr. Longfellow and Mr. Dana traded places at the podium. Fanny was soon captured by Mr. Dana's beautiful interpretations of culture and history. She was glad she had come, despite the initial discomfort. At one point she shifted her attention from the podium and saw that Mr. Longfellow was not there. She took a longer look, focusing on each face on the stand until she was certain he was not among the other faculty members.

He hadn't left because of her, had he?

She chided herself for the wave of guilt that washed over her. Mr. Longfellow could have left for any number of reasons, why should she flatter herself into thinking she was the cause? He was a busy man—a professor, a writer—and he was responsible, in part, for the growing support of the public lectures that were becoming more and more common at the college.

He'd spoken of his vision of this very thing in Switzerland, she remembered. And here was a lecture hall packed with all manner of people drawn to the campus to listen to a great mind. It was progressive, and she was here because of his vision. But he was not, and it bothered her.

Fanny kept her chin up but hoped her presence hadn't chased him away. Then she wondered at her regret if it had.

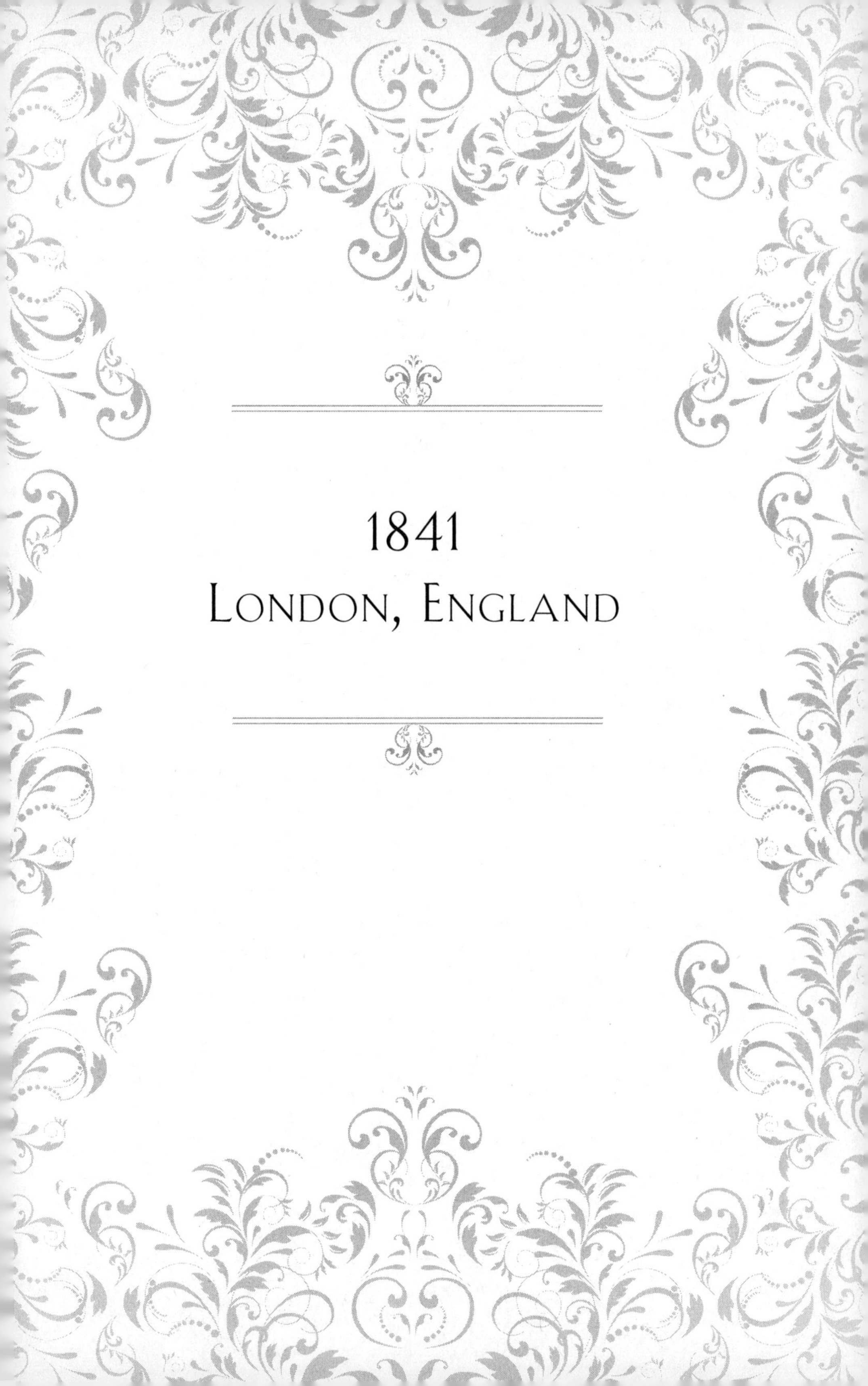

1841
London, England

Twenty-Seven

To England

Fanny stood on the deck of the ship, using every bit of restraint to keep from jumping over the railing onto shore. They had been docked for nearly thirty minutes, but the gangplank had not yet been lowered to allow the passengers to disembark.

"Oh, Tom, my heart is about to burst from my chest!" Fanny said. It had taken two weeks to cross the Atlantic by way of the new Cunarder, SS *Columbia*, and now they were delayed in getting off the ship.

Tom laughed and shook his head. "You are eighteen years old all over again and seeing Europe for the first time."

"I feel almost as giddy now as I did then." She scanned the crowd for a familiar face. She did not know if Molly would be able to come to the pier to collect them, but Robert would be there. To see him would mean seeing Molly was close at hand and Fanny could hardly wait. "I cannot believe it has been a year."

"A year and two months, to be exact," Tom said. "But now—"

He was cut off by the bell announcing that the passengers could now leave the ship. Tom grabbed Fanny's hand and used his larger frame to push his way into the line, which moved agonizingly slowly. It was ironic that the combined enthusiasm to be off the ship slowed the very attainment of the goal.

Finally, Fanny's feet hit the wooden dock, and she could have kissed it. Not because the voyage had been miserable—crossing by steamship was remarkably fast and smooth—but because she was here. And Molly was here. And she could not wait to see her sister and Ronald, who was seven months old already.

Tom led Fanny to an area somewhat removed from the crowded portion of the dock and told her to wait while he found a lackey for their trunks. She could watch for Robert but was forbidden to leave the place Tom left her in for fear they would get separated. Fanny agreed and told him for the hundredth time how much she appreciated his help. She could never have come to England alone, and Father could certainly not leave his young family to come with her.

It took nearly an hour before Tom had retrieved their luggage, and still Robert had not appeared. Fanny had Molly's address, and they had just decided to hire a hackney to take them to the cottage when they heard Tom's name called out in that endearing brogue that could only belong to their dear brother-in-law.

It was a joyful reunion when Robert reached them, then it was back to the business of having the lackey bring their trunks to Robert's carriage and get all the passengers and trunks situated. Finally, after what felt like half a day, the three of them were in the open carriage as it bumped and hopped down the road toward the cottage located just off Regent Park, something Molly was quite proud of.

"I am so glad to be here," Fanny said again, her cheeks hurting from all the smiling. "And I can hardly wait to see my dear sister."

Robert smiled, but something about it seemed hesitant. He looked outside the carriage and said nothing.

"Is everything well, Robert?" Fanny asked with concern. "Is Molly all right? Ronald?"

"They are both well," Robert said, but still hesitant. "An' Molly was in fits about being unable ta meet you at the pier. She was so excited . . ."

"But," Fanny added when he did not, watching a struggle take place behind his eyes. "What should we know before we arrive?"

"Molly told you she's 'ad a difficult time of things since Ronald's birth," Robert began. "Only, I know she wishes she were more recovered."

"It has been months," Fanny said carefully.

Robert nodded gravely. "It was a difficult birth. There were moments when . . . Well, I need not speak of that now. They both came through an' I cood not be more grateful. Only, Molly still struggles with her 'ealth and with her legs especially. She can only walk short distances an' complains of a great deal of lingerin' pain."

"She's seen a doctor, surely," Tom said.

"She has," Robert assured him, nodding for emphasis. "Three of 'em, in fact, but nae of 'em can explain her difficulty, though they 'ave given her medication to ease the pain. She will have times when she is much better, but then a week'll pass an' she'll spend days in bed again." He focused his attention on Fanny. "She is worried you will be disappointed."

"Disappointed?" Fanny said, offended at the notion. "That she is ill? Whatever would make her think such a thing?"

"Disappointed that the two of you canna enjoy long walks an' visit the shops as you expect to."

Such excursions were exactly what Fanny had hoped for, but that was not why she had come. "I'm here to be with her and help her. Not judge her or cause her worry."

"That's what I've told 'er," Robert said. "Only, with 'er discomfort comes some melancholia, an' she is not always herself."

Tom and Fanny exchanged a look of concern. Not herself? What exactly did Robert mean by that?

"I have noticed her letters have not been as enthusiastic as they once were," Fanny said. "I assumed she simply missed her family. I had hoped Tom and I would be a remedy."

"An' I do believe you will both be exactly that." Robert attempted a smile, but it did not reach his eyes nor soften his expression. "In fact, I hope an' pray most fervently that you will be." He swallowed what Fanny thought might be some emotion he did not want to express.

When the carriage arrived at the house in St. Catherine's, Fanny forced a smile and said—for the second time—that all would be well. There could be no better medicine than a brother and sister to help one through difficult times.

The men and the driver set about unloading the carriage, while Fanny headed up the walk. She knew Molly had a nurse to help with Ronald, and a cook, but she was unsure if there was a servant to open the door or if she should let herself in. She kept thinking of what Robert had said about Molly's difficulty with her legs. She was anxious about seeing Molly in such a state, afraid she would not be able to school her reaction.

Fanny had just stepped onto the porch when the door was thrown open to reveal Molly so changed that Fanny gasped at the sight of her. It had been only a year since Fanny had last seen her sister, but there was gray in Molly's hair and her eyes were red as though she'd been crying. Her face was swollen, but the rest of her frame was very thin.

"Oh, Fanny," Molly said with a sob. She nearly fell forward and Fanny had to hurry in order to catch her sister. "I'm *so* glad you've come." The words were slurred and wet.

Tears came to Fanny's eyes as she realized just how serious things were for her sister. She struggled to lift Molly into an embrace, holding her tight against her own body and leaning against the doorframe to keep them both upright since Molly was not fully supporting her weight.

"I'm so glad to be here," Fanny said with forced brightness while Molly cried into her shoulder. *Thank heavens we came,* she thought as she turned Molly toward the inside of the house. Before she shut the door, she looked over her shoulder at Tom. He watched her with a fearful expression. She did not smile, rather she sent him a look of pleading. What had happened to their sister?

"I told you she was not well," Robert said, defensive. It was past ten o'clock on the evening of Fanny and Tom's arrival, but there had not been time to talk privately until now. Ronald and Mary had gone to bed—Mary with a heavy dose of opium that she'd seemed rather too eager to take.

"'Not well' is a bit of an understatement," Tom said without a touch of humor.

"I 'ave done all I can," Robert said, bristling. "I 'ave brought in doctors, nurses, staff I can nae afford. Nothing 'as helped."

"You should have *told* us," Tom said. "My father would have helped."

"With money," Robert said as though that were a paltry offering. "This is nae about money."

"You just said you couldn't afford her care," Tom spat.

"Enough," Fanny said with a calmness she did not feel. She raised a hand to her head that had been pounding for hours. She put her other hand over Tom's and gave him a look she hoped he would understand. They needed to work *with* Robert, not against him. She smiled at her brother-in-law. "We are here now. And the three of us can work together toward her good."

"I 'ave tried everything."

"Don't say that," Fanny said, sharper than she intended. She paused for a breath. "What I mean is, don't turn away from solutions only because the first attempt did not work at the time you made it."

He seemed to understand and nodded, though she could tell he needed encouragement. What must it have been like for him these last months, managing his wife and child? Her heart went out to him, and she moved her hand from Tom's to his, smiling with more feeling when he met her eye. "We all love Molly," she said. "That is what we need to remember."

"How can we help?" Tom asked, apparently willing to give up his ire.

Fanny smiled at him with gratitude. "First, we need to assess how much medication she is taking."

"She is in so much pain," Robert said.

"I have no doubt about that. But in watching her today, she takes laudanum more often than she should." She met Tom's eye. "More often than cousin William did when he was in distress."

Tom's look became even more serious. William had been taking the medication around the clock, but he was dying. His pain had been excruciating.

"And she is nervous about s' many things," Robert added. "The medication 'elps to calm her."

Fanny nodded. "Well, we are here to calm her now."

Robert looked doubtful, but Fanny pushed forward. "Tom, I deem you the entertainment committee. It is up to you to find places

Molly will feel well enough to visit with us so there is more to discuss than her pain and the four walls of her house." She turned to Robert. "Has she made any friends here?"

"Oh, yes," Robert said, his eyes lighting up at the chance to say something positive. "My two sisters live nearby and visit 'er weekly. They genuinely enjoy one another's company, an' they know . . . *some* of what Molly is dealing with. There are a handful of neighbors, too, who visit every few days. They are not aware of how bad things are 'owever. I try to keep those visits short."

That Robert's position had ended a few months ago and he was now unemployed had not been spoken of directly, but Fanny wondered if perhaps that were a blessing. Without the need for him to leave home every day, there was someone to care for Molly. At the same time, Fanny had never known a man—except perhaps Tom—who was content without a career. She wondered at the toll Robert's enforced idleness had taken on his own health, and how much his lack of employment might be affecting Molly. She may very well be taking advantage of her husband's accessibility, and Fanny could understand why Robert had not found a new position when he was needed at home.

At least there was still money from Molly's inheritance as well as some belonging to Robert. They were still able to maintain their lifestyle, though it was far simpler than what Molly was used to in Boston.

Fanny turned back to Tom. "I would like you to pay special attention to her friends."

Tom's eyebrows lifted, and Fanny could not help but smile.

"Not *undue* attention," she said. "I'm not asking you to entertain them, only be attentive to those who are a more positive influence on

Molly when they are here. We shall encourage those relationships and not invite anyone who might not improve Molly's mood."

"Ah, I see. I can certainly take charge of that. I'm an excellent judge of character, if I do say so myself."

Fanny smiled, grateful for his lightness. She turned to Robert. "I would like you to ask around after the best surgeon in London."

He opened his mouth to protest, and Fanny cut him off. "I know you have had doctors attend her already, but there must be someone of great renown, someone with a reputation of excellence that could give her a fresh perspective. You know enough people that if you were to ask, I'm sure you could find such a man. I am equally sure that if his fee is too severe, Father would be happy to cover the expense, for Molly's sake."

Fanny's confidence seemed to lift his own, and he did not even argue Father covering the expense, for which Fanny was grateful. She did not intend to be the least bit economical when it came to Molly's health, and she was grateful not to have to argue her point too intently.

"I shall ask after it," he finally said. "Only I don't want to embarrass Molly by making 'er struggles too public. She is very anxious about people knowing 'ow ill she is."

"Then I suggest you ask carefully," Fanny said with an encouraging smile. "Perhaps begin with your sisters, as they are already aware of some difficulty. They may be able to ask without revealing too much information."

He nodded.

"And what is your task, Fanny?" Tom said, leaning back in his chair. "I'm to be entertainment master, and Robert is the medical liaison. What is your position in this little militia of ours?"

"I am to be her sister," Fanny said, pushing up from the table to look between the two men. “I will help her run her household and enjoy her child. We shall go for a walk—albeit a short one—in this pretty park out front every morning, and I’ll make sure she takes in nourishing food. I will encourage her and support her and love her as only a sister can.” She paused a moment. “No offense to either of you, of course,” she said, her cheeks heating at the inadvertent insult she had offered.

“None taken,” Tom said while Robert nodded. “It may very well be the most important job of them all.”

Twenty-Eight

Mrs. Craigie

Henry finished reading "The Wreck of the Hesperus," included in his most recently published book, *Ballads and Other Poems,* and closed the slim volume while looking at his audience of one.

Mrs. Craigie lay against the pillows, breathing evenly with a slight smile on her face. It was a few seconds before she fluttered open her papery eyelids. "It is a lovely work, Mr. Longfellow," she said in a voice raspy with age and illness. "Thank you for reading it to me, drat these eyes of mine." She blinked up at the ceiling as though that might help her focus, then spoke as if she were looking at him, though she was not. "I shall be eternally glad to have known a man such as yourself, Mr. Longfellow, and I take great pride in the fact that you produced such great work while living under my roof." She reached a thin hand toward him, and he took it, feeling his heart swell with emotion.

"I shall be eternally grateful to you for housing me under said roof," he said. "You nearly turned me away, you know."

Mrs. Craigie closed her eyes and smiled. "I'd had my fill of students and was certain this skinny young man was yet one more of them."

Henry laughed, though his throat was thick. "Skinny, yes, but not young. Why, I'm not sure I have ever been young."

"Ah, life does age us at different rates," she said, her smile fading. "I do hope, however, that you take advantage of the life ahead of you. You may feel old, but you are too young a man to carry such weight, and as a dying woman, I have the right to say as much."

Henry let his smile fall, she could not see it anyway, and looked at his hand holding hers. He rubbed his finger over the paper-thin skin, corded with blue veins and rounded bones. "I am trying to live above the burdens I carry, Mrs. Craigie," he said. "I assure you."

With her other hand, she fumbled around until she could place it over his. "I know that you are, but you have spent far too many years pining for that woman. It is time to let her go."

How many times had he been told that very thing? How many times had he believed he was done with Fanny Appleton, that she no longer held his heart hostage, only to see her or hear of her or think of her and have every ounce of energy he had ever felt flood back to him? When others gave him the same advice as Mrs. Craigie, he made a joke on good days and ignored it on bad ones. There was no reason not to be entirely truthful with Mrs. Craigie, however. She had watched the tragedy from the sidelines for all these years.

"If it were decision enough that would ease my heart, I would have chosen such a course long ago."

She patted his hand and closed her eyes though she remained alert. They had begun as landlord and patron, eased into an odd friendship, and now he felt as close to her as his own family. "I only want you to be happy, Henry." She didn't often call him by his given name, and the familiarity touched him.

"I thank you for that," he said. "It is not that I am unhappy, just not wholly so."

"And you will never be wholly happy until Fanny Appleton loves you as well as you love her?"

Henry considered that a moment and then continued on the course of honesty he had already chosen. "I fear that is exactly what it would take."

"Will you try to find another way?" She turned toward him and opened her eyes. She almost looked as though she were focused on his face, though he knew the best she might see is an outline. "Will you promise me, a dying woman with few wants left in mortality, that you will try to find happiness without her? You are not a better poet because your love is refused, and after all this time, I fear Fanny Appleton's heart will never change. Promise me you will try to let her go?"

Henry took a deep breath. He did not take promises lightly and would not be dishonest to her, but he was thirty-five years old. Would he give Fanny his heart and his hope forever? He felt something crack within him, just enough to imagine a thin line snaking through his resolve to love Fanny all the days of his life. It frightened him, but perhaps like a chick breaking out from its egg, or a walnut in need opening, this crack would lead to something good. Something better. "I will try to find happiness."

"Without Fanny Appleton," Mrs. Craigie said. Even in her final days, she had not missed his omission.

"Without Fanny Appleton," he repeated and wondered—perhaps even hoped—it might possible.

"Did you not say she is in England?"

"Yes, until the fall sometime. She and Tom went to visit their sister. I received a letter from Tom a few weeks ago. They met Carlyle and saw the actress Rachel on the stage."

"Ah, two of your greatest loves."

"Rachel, perhaps," Henry said. "But I would not call Carlyle a great love."

Mrs. Craigie laughed only enough that he could hear it and patted his hand again. "The house is settled. Worcester has agreed to rent you the eastern half indefinitely. It will be strange to have a husband and wife living here again."

Henry ignored the stab of painful memory. Three years ago he had thought Fanny would accept his proposal and be the first wife to live in the house since Andrew Craigie had left his wife a widow in 1821. It was not to be, and now John Worcester would be the one to change the occupancy.

"They will love the house and care for it well."

"I'm not sure they love it like you do, Henry," Mrs. Craigie said. "I did not *sell* it to him as I hope that one day you might be able to purchase it. Of anyone who has lived here, other than myself, you have loved it best."

That Henry would one day own Craigie House was his own dream as well, and if his writing continued on the same course it was on, he might be able to do so in a few years' time. Worcester had already told Henry he hoped to build a home of his own so he did not have designs on keeping the house for himself. Only, it would be strange to live here alone.

"I appreciate the consideration," Henry said. "I hope it will come to pass."

"You must promise me something else," Mrs. Craigie said, closing her eyes again.

"Yes?" Henry said when she did not expound immediately.

"You must promise me that seeing an old woman in bed will not turn you away from marriage completely."

For an instant Henry was shocked by her joke, and then he

laughed, loud and rich and heartfelt until tears streamed down his face in both mirth and mourning. Mrs. Craigie laughed too, as much as she could, and soon tears were leaking from her eyes as well. Henry got control of himself and handed her his handkerchief, not bothering to dry his own eyes.

"I shall miss you, Elizabeth," he said in a trembling voice.

"Oh, Henry," she said, her own chin quivering. "I shall miss you too. Please come read to me again before I go. If you can."

"As often as I am able." He rose from the chair and leaned forward to plant a soft kiss on the old woman's forehead. "God bless you."

She answered with a squeeze of his hand.

He didn't bother to turn down the light as he left; her nurse would check on her throughout the night, and the light would not pierce the darkness of Mrs. Craigie's eyes. He closed the door softly behind him and paused a moment, reflecting on the gift of her life. He hoped that in some way the house would always stand as a legacy to her kind heart and good will.

He thought back to a day when he'd come home from teaching to find Mrs. Craigie on the front porch, the canker worms from the trees she would not allow treated crawling all over her face and hands and turban. It was an appalling sight, and Henry had tried to help her in the house, but she'd refused. "They are God's creatures," she said, watching a worm inch its way up her arm. "They've as much right here as we do."

"Indeed," he said to the darkened hallway as he turned toward the stairs. "Indeed."

Twenty-Nine

A Changing Heart

Fanny and Molly walked arm in arm along the pathway of Regent's Park, located across from the court where Molly lived. It was early fall—Fanny's favorite time of year—and the scent of wood smoke was in the air. Though it was not cold, there was a welcome coolness that tickled Fanny's nose and made her think longingly of Boston, which heralded the seasons with more dramatic presentation than London did.

Fanny wished she could use the splendors of Boston in the fall as greater inducement in her plea for Molly to return to America for a time, but they would never make it back to America in time to see the season change.

"Harriet will have the baby in November," Fanny said, trying yet another avenue to tempt her sister home. "And Ronald would have a playmate in William."

Molly looked at the path in front of them while they took slow, careful steps. "Robert's family is here," she said.

"And your family is *there.* I know it would be hard to leave his family, especially his sisters, who have been so kind and attentive."

Molly nodded.

"But you would not have to stay forever, just until Robert can shore up some connections and find another post. Just until after the baby is born and you are in good health again." That was Fanny's biggest reason to encourage a return home—Molly was pregnant again.

After all Molly had suffered with Ronald's birth, Fanny could not bear to think of her sister experiencing such trauma again without her family, and good doctors, to attend her. True, the doctor Ronald had found through his inquiries had been excellent and had helped them all through the months that followed, both with increasing Molly's strength and decreasing her dependence on the medications, but Fanny could not help but think better care earlier on in Molly's struggles would have avoided a great deal of difficulty. Though she did not fault Ronald, she was also quite sure if *she* had been present, things would not have gotten so out of hand.

"The idea of traveling by boat when I feel so wretched makes me want to cry," Molly said. "I am not as good at sea as you are."

"But you have not yet traveled by Cunarder," Fanny said. "It is a remarkably smooth ride and only two weeks of travel."

Molly didn't respond directly. After a few moments her mouth pulled down into a frown. "I know we can't keep the house much longer."

Fanny took a quick sidelong glance at her sister. She had made the same determination but was surprised that Molly had realized the severity of her and Robert's financial situation. Fanny thought it wise not to comment.

"And there is talk of a post in India," Molly said. "Mr. Rich was telling Robert about it the other night when they came for dinner."

Fanny took a calming breath before she spoke. The idea of her pregnant sister traveling to India made her chest catch on fire. But

Molly was not a child, and Robert needed a job. "Would you *like* to go to India?"

Molly looked at the ground. "I don't think I would," she said quietly. "But I support Robert in his career. It is not my place to make the decisions."

"You can certainly have an opinion, though," Fanny said carefully. "Especially regarding the child you are carrying."

Molly said nothing, and they walked in silence until the path broke off toward the house.

"You go on," Fanny said, releasing Molly's arm and keeping her expression soft. "I'm going to take one more round. The weather is so fine today."

Molly gave her a quick kiss on the cheek and moved toward home, while Fanny began walking again, this time at a more comfortable pace. Molly had to walk slowly, which at times made Fanny feel the need to run.

She was grateful for her health, for the chance she had to come to London when she did, for Tom and Robert and how committed both of them were to Molly's improvement. She smiled when she thought of her nephew, nearly a year old now and beginning to pull himself up on the furniture. She thought about Harriet having another half sister or brother to add to the Appleton family.

Family.

Though Fanny would not say she had outgrown friendships—she had a number of people she was excited to see once she returned to Boston—aside from perhaps Emmeline, none of her friends inspired the same feelings of belonging and connection as her family did. She had seen that connection more than once during this trip as she watched the closeness between Robert, Molly, and Ronald during the day. The way Robert stood a little taller when Molly entered the room, the way her hand lingered on his when they parted company, and the way Ronald gazed at Molly with such abject adoration. It was beautiful. And a bit painful too.

Fanny was nearly twenty-four years old. Not on the shelf, but she had proclaimed her desire not to marry loudly enough that there were few men who attempted to talk her out of it. She could enjoy their company, even flirt now and again, but she felt nothing like what she saw between Molly and Robert. Between Father and Harriet. Between her aunts and uncles. All around her were married couples who enjoyed such accord. Until this trip she would have said she admired it, but now she wondered if she envied it. Did she want such a connection for herself?

She thought of Molly and could not imagine that her sister would ever feel complete without little Ronald. In fact, it was increasingly difficult for Fanny to remember what Molly had been like before she married Robert, before Fanny had seen her care for her son with such tenderness. There was something inspiring about that connection.

But Fanny was not Molly. They had different temperaments, different expectations. Molly's opinion regarding a post in India was the perfect example. Fanny couldn't imagine living in such a wild place as India, but more she couldn't imagine *not* having an opinion about it. Or not expecting her husband to regard her opinion.

Should she marry, would she and her husband argue about everything? Would he expect her acquiescence, and she withhold it to her dying breath? What a pretty marriage that would make.

And that was assuming there was anyone she wanted to marry. She'd had some *tendrés* in the past, a few that felt serious, but they had come to nothing and made her distrust her own interest. Was it the want of a child that had her considering the necessity of a husband?

She grunted, frustrated with her thoughts, then looked around to make sure no one had heard her. None of the people strolling the park paid her any attention, and for a moment, she felt inexplicably lonely. Tom was in Paris for a few weeks, Molly was in her home, and Fanny had the strangest sensation that if she disappeared, nothing in the world would change. No one needed her. No one turned to her for particular comfort. She had no legacy to leave behind and had made no mark upon the world. Until that moment, she had not thought those things important to her, but suddenly they were.

Family.

There were no more dear people to her in all the world than her own family, so why was she so resistant to a family of her own? She pondered a moment and then sighed when Mr. Longfellow came to mind. Oh, that cursed man! Not for the first time, she wondered if her displeasure with him had created a displeasure with all of his sex. She could flirt and dance and enjoy a man's arm around her shoulder, but she didn't long for it. She didn't want to deepen those relationships. Could that be because she worried such depth would come with that same discomfort Mr. Longfellow's attention bore in her?

She shook her head. Longfellow, Longfellow, Longfellow. Would she ever be free of that man? If not, whose fault would that be—hers or his? She was a grown woman after all. Why should she let him affect her like he did? Why should she care so much?

She turned around on the path, determined to return home earlier than planned and help Molly with Ronald before supper was served.

It did not escape her notice, however, that, while wondering at her future and questioning whether she was set against a family of her own after all, it was Henry Longfellow who came to mind. Surely that was because his was an open offer. She had no doubt that if she appeared on his doorstep and announced her heart changed, he would accept her without hesitation.

But her heart was not changed. She was only thinking of things differently, and, of course a desperate suitor such as himself who made no attempt to school his affection would come to mind. Of course he would.

Wouldn't he?

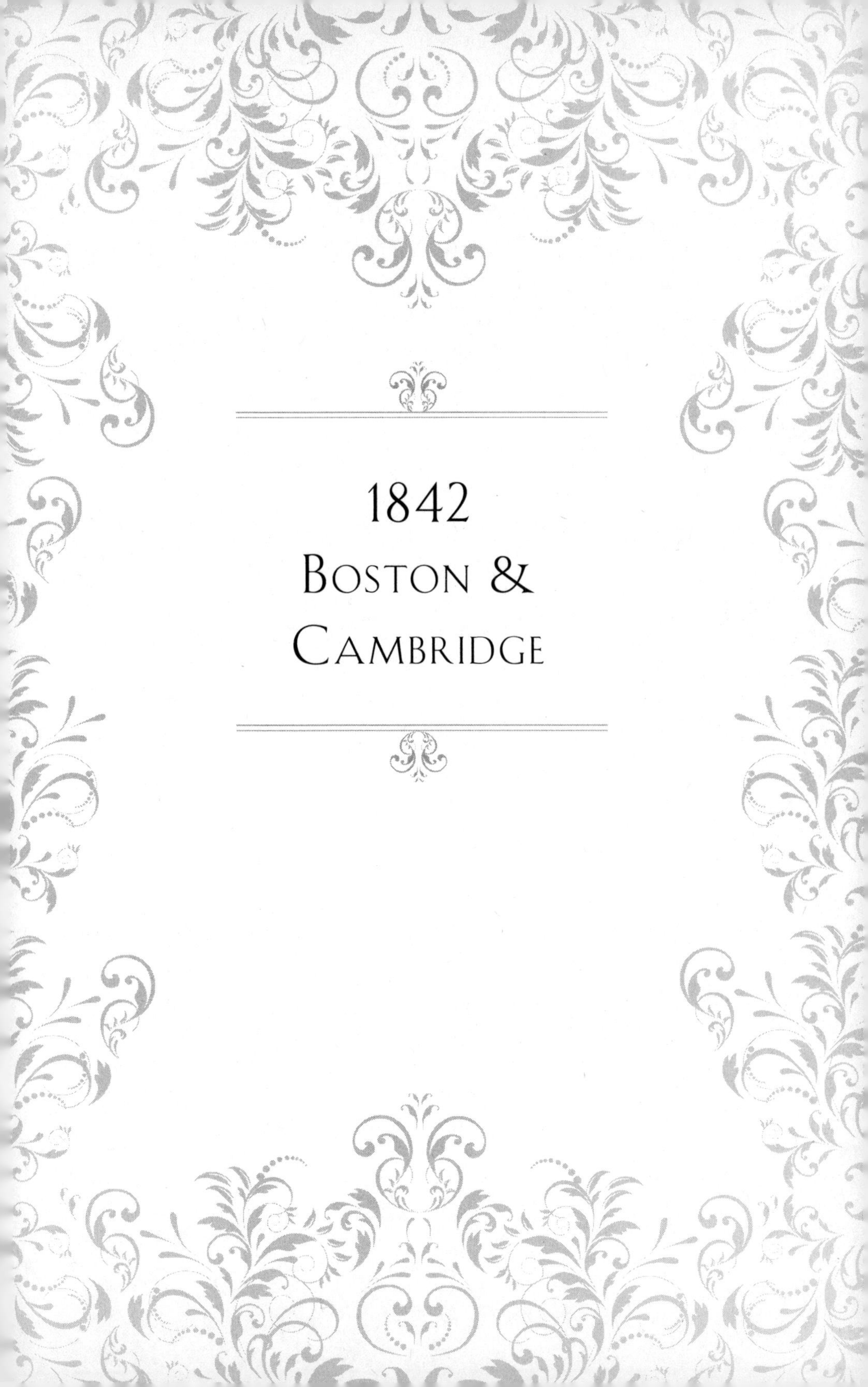

1842
Boston & Cambridge

Thirty

A New Year

Fanny read the name on the card and took a deep breath—Professor Henry Longfellow. "He knows I am the only one receiving today?" Fanny asked Mathews, who awaited her response.

"Yes, ma'am."

Well then, there would be no avoiding him. "Show him in, and send up fresh tea and cake."

"Yes, ma'am."

Mathews exited the room, and Fanny used the next few seconds to sit up a bit straighter and put a polite smile on her face. It was New Year's Day, 1842, and despite all the changes to the Appleton family of Beacon Hill, Fanny had let it be known that she would be accepting the expected New Year's visitors on behalf of the family.

Tom had accompanied Father to Washington—Father was contemplating serving in Congress again—and Harriet had gone to stay with her sister in Cambridge for a few days with William and the new baby, Harriett. Molly and Robert had taken Ronald to the Sedgwicks' home in Pittsville. Fanny had been invited, but, though she didn't say so, she had looked forward to a quiet house. With three children beneath the age of two in the house that was also brimming with adults, it had not been a quiet winter.

Fanny had offered to stay home and keep house, supervise the removal of the holiday decorations, and receive any callers. She had also enjoyed parties with friends and even a dance where she'd been reacquainted with Malcolm Pace. He was a nice young man she had known for many years, but a bit too eager for her tastes. She'd had enough of eager suitors.

She had wondered, as the day went on, whether Mr. Longfellow would call as he usually did. That he had did not surprise Fanny—he had already proven how determined he was to remain on good terms with the family—what did surprise her was how mild she felt toward the visit. She had not seen him for months, not since before leaving for England in the spring, and she wondered if all that had happened since then had helped her grow out of her determination to feel insulted by the man.

Mr. Longfellow entered the room, and Fanny was immediately struck by how thin he was. His face was gaunt, and there were shadows under his eyes—similar to how he looked when they had first met in Interlaken. Any lingering defensiveness she felt drained away out of concern for his health. He approached her chair and bowed, but without reaching for her hand. She had the impression he didn't want to touch her. She was oddly hurt by it.

"Please, have a seat," Fanny said.

He did so, sitting rather primly on a chair across from her. His trousers pooled upon the tops of his shoes, and his coat betrayed the thinness of his shoulders underneath. In her appraisal of his appearance, she had not noticed he held a parcel. He set it on his lap and stared at it a moment as though trying to remember what was inside the box.

"I won't take much of your time," he said.

Fanny's heart pricked with conscience at how despondent he sounded. He would not meet her eye. "Don't be silly," Fanny said brightly. "You are always welcome here, Mr. Longfellow."

He glanced up, but then back to the floor. "Your butler said you are the only one home."

"Yes, but we are friends, are we not?" She hoped he understood her emphasis; she did not want him to misconstrue her kindness as an invitation for something more. But she had no desire to be unkind, especially when he struck such a sorrowful figure.

"*Are* we friends?" he asked, taking Fanny off guard with his boldness. He lifted his head and met her eyes.

She felt the look move through her, as it had on the first day they met, and she looked away. "Of course we are," she said, wondering if perhaps she should have refused his visit after all. She gathered her confidence and offered him a broad smile, trying desperately to hide her feelings though somehow she doubted that was possible.

"I am glad to hear that."

His calm, soft, and heartfelt voice pricked her heart in a different way. She had come to terms with the whispers regarding her connection to *Hyperion,* and she tried to forgive herself for the caustic gossip she'd made to Jewett, but until this moment, she had not considered Mr. Longfellow's feelings about her anger. She felt shame for having hurt him; he looked like a dog expecting to be kicked. The image wasn't a pathetic one, as it may have been a year ago, rather she recognized that for him to meet with her today took a great deal of courage.

A maid brought in the tea tray, and Fanny busied herself with pouring.

"How was England?" he asked when she handed him his cup and saucer.

"It was lovely," she said sincerely. "Though next time I shall go in the fall and be spared a New England winter. That was not the best welcome to return to."

He smiled. "And Molly has come back to Boston?"

"For a little while. They went to Pittsville for the holiday." Molly was doing much better, well enough to want to see family and friends. "I know she'd have been delighted to see you."

"And your father and Mrs. Appleton have had another child?"

"Yes, a girl. Little Harriet." Fanny smiled at the thought of her half sister. "She is a delight."

"Please share my greetings and congratulations with both Mr. and Mrs. Mackintosh and Mr. and Mrs. Appleton. I am very glad for their happiness."

"I shall certainly do so," Fanny said, then paused. "And you, Mr. Longfellow, are you well?"

She could not tell if he avoided her eye from embarrassment or not. "I am well enough, Miss Appleton."

Mr. Longfellow had called her by name since their European tour, though she had not invited him to. She had been both irritated and unaffected by his familiarity, depending on her mood. She felt the distance of his more formal address today, and she didn't like it, though she wondered why she had noticed at all.

"'Well enough' does not sound all that well, Mr. Longfellow." She did not fully understand why she was being so bold, but then many aspects of her relationship with Mr. Longfellow were strange. "Is everything all right? Have you been ill?"

He shook his head, avoiding the question, and looked at the

package in his lap a few moments longer before holding it out to her. "I brought this for you and your family."

Fanny took the box from him. "Thank you," she said. The parcel was wrapped in paper, and she tugged at the string holding it together. When she pulled back the paper, she lifted her eyebrows and stared at a very familiar presentation—a book and a wedge of cheese. It took her back to the first time she'd received such items in this very room two and a half years ago, but with Jewett as the presenter instead of Mr. Longfellow. The reminder of her conclusions from that time—of his nostalgic gift—left her speechless. She lifted her gaze to meet his.

"This cheese is from Interlaken," Mr. Longfellow said, with more energy than he had shown to this point. "I ordered it from a man in New York."

"Interlaken?" Fanny repeated, pretending she didn't understand the significance since she had never admitted her conclusion to anyone.

Mr. Longfellow nodded. "The last cheese I sent was from Zurich, which pleased me, but this is even more specific to very happy memories for me."

"The cheese represents our time in Switzerland," Fanny said as though only now discovering the connection.

"Of course," Mr. Longfellow said. "We had many wonderful conversations over afternoon tea, complete with a selection of cheeses." He scanned her careful expression. After a moment, Mr. Longfellow's forehead wrinkled. "As I explained in my note when I sent you my first book of poetry."

"I'm afraid whatever note you sent did not make the journey," Fanny said, smiling sympathetically and wishing she dared admit that she knew from the start. But it was too much risk. "Just the book and the cheese."

He blinked and then let out a breath. "So you received an offensive book and a confusing parcel of cheese."

Fanny felt her cheeks heat up with how perfectly he had articulated her feelings toward *Hyperion,* and then she felt even worse when his neck began to turn red with his own embarrassment. She could remedy that if she felt strong enough to resist the consequence. She leaned forward without thought and placed her hand on his knee.

"Don't feel bad," she said. "I had felt sure you had sent a note, and . . . and the gift was very kind and very thoughtful."

Mr. Longfellow stared at her hand, causing her to pull it back, drawing with it his gaze as she straightened in her chair. "Without an explanation you must have thought I was making some kind of joke."

"No," Fanny said sincerely. She had never jumped to *that* conclusion. His discomfort felt like a heavy beam across her shoulders, and she felt a growing desperation to be free of the responsibility. But not enough to tell him the truth. What kind of woman had she become?

"Then you must have thought I was insane," Mr. Longfellow said.

Fanny did not comment on that since she *had* wondered if he'd lost his mind—if only for a few moments. "It was very thoughtful," she repeated, meaning it. "As this is, thank you."

"You're welcome," he said, a note of dejection in his voice.

Mathew came to the door. "Miss Austin to see you, Miss Appleton."

Mr. Longfellow stood quickly, prompting Fanny to stand as well.

"Thank you for your visit today, Mr. Longfellow, and for your kind gift." It bothered her that he might not know she meant what she said. He was used to her polite commentary and this was no different, except that she was not simply being polite. She wanted to offer remedy she could not give.

He bowed slightly, but she could feel his urgency to leave and it pricked her conscience.

"I wish you many happy returns in the new year, Miss Appleton. Please give my best to your family."

"I will," Fanny said. "And many happy returns to you too."

He bowed again and exited the room.

Fanny watched him go and then looked at the cheese she held in one hand and the book of poetry she held in the other. She read the title—*Ballads and Other Poems.* It was Mr. Longfellow's newest book, and in Fanny's opinion, his best work to date. Tom had purchased a copy and she'd read it almost as soon as she had returned to Boston, so why hadn't she told Mr. Longfellow she'd admired it? Why had she withheld a sincere compliment? She would have said as much to anyone else of her acquaintance under a similar circumstance—why not him?

The sound of footsteps caused her to look up.

Emmeline stood in the doorway of the parlor, her dark eyes framed by round spectacles. She cocked her head to the side. "Not more cheese," she said, then let out a heavy breath.

"And another book," Fanny said, lifting the volume before waving her dear friend to the chair Mr. Longfellow had recently vacated. She returned to her own seat and put the book on the table. "Have you read it?"

Emmeline shrugged and pulled off her gloves. Mathew came to the door, and Fanny ordered a fresh pot of tea.

"I read it," Emmeline said once they were alone again. "'The Village Blacksmith' was well enough, but the rest is *peu de chose.* What more can one expect from such a *mocking-bird,* though?"

Fanny smiled, but was not comfortable with the remark, which was based on comments Fanny had made over the years. "He seemed so . . . sad, Emmeline. As though he has no joy in his life at all."

"He always seems that way," Emmeline said with a dismissive wave. "If he is unhappy, it is of his own making."

"I fear he is unhappy because he has set his sights on a woman who does not want him."

Emmeline regarded Fanny a few moments. "I hope that this woman will not pretend otherwise simply to remedy his poor mood."

"Of course not," Fanny said, as frustrated with her inability to put her feelings into words as she was with his inability to hide his feelings. "I just hate feeling . . . responsible, I suppose."

"Well, you *aren't* responsible," Emmeline said. "He is. And you received him with kindness today, which I think was generous of you after how he's treated you. You should not waste one more minute worrying over *his* thoughts and feelings when he has spent nary a one pondering on yours."

"He explained the purpose of the cheese," Fanny said, waving toward the wedge. "It was a thoughtful connection to our time in Switzerland." Poetic. Romantic even.

"Well," Emmeline said, raising her eyebrows from behind her spectacles. "I'm glad to know he is not fit for Bedlam, but it is still cheese of all things. *Cheese,* Fanny."

Mathew delivered a fresh pot of tea, and Fanny considered telling Emmeline of the day she and Mr. Longfellow had bought cheese in Zurich, how she'd watched him converse with the shop owner and felt such admiration. She had found him so interesting then, full of ideas and opinions that had dazzled her. He'd told her that she had a quick mind, that she was smart and capable. To think of that memory and then picture him as he'd been today left her feeling even heavier.

Perhaps her rejection wasn't simply that she didn't want him. Maybe she knew she didn't deserve him.

"Now," Emmeline said, "enough about *the prof.* Tell me all about the dress you shall wear to the Rangeys' party tonight—every splendid detail. I do so love New Year's celebrations, they seem to set the tone for the entire year."

Thirty-One

Valley of the Soul

The wind was bracing as Henry stepped out of the house onto Beacon Street, the smirking expression on Miss Emmeline Austin's face hovering in his memory. No doubt she and Fanny would laugh over his pathetic visit as they likely had his other calls over the years. As much as he wanted to think Fanny above such gossip, he knew of her sharp tongue and hated to think of it turned on him. He could not bear the thought.

Henry pulled his shoulders toward his ears, hunching against the cold, and stuffed his hands deeper into his pockets as he descended the front steps and turned on the cobbled sidewalk. He had planned to make other New Year visits in Beacon Hill, to Samuel Appleton and his wife and the Andrew Norton family specifically, but had chosen Nathan Appleton's house to be his first call so he wouldn't be carrying the parcel around to the other homes.

He had reconsidered the visit entirely when he realized only Fanny was home, but Mrs. Craigie's words—spoken when his mind was clearer than it was today—had come back to him, and he decided not to avoid the meeting.

Once again, things had gone horribly wrong instead of the way he had pictured in his mind.

Henry groaned into his scarf as Fanny's words rang back to him: "Whatever note you sent did not make the journey."

Isaac Jewett had presented her with a book and a Swiss cheese all those years ago with no explanation for either item, no shared experience that would draw the significance together in her mind. Fanny had said she did not think his gift of *cheese* was a joke, but he'd seen the relief in her eyes when he'd explained the purpose. Her relief spoke volumes of how confused the Appletons must have been, how confused they must have thought *he* was to have sent it. And that was *before* she'd actually read *Hyperion* and seen herself in its pages. Why hadn't Tom ever told him of the confusion? Why had Henry come again today after never having heard how the first gift was received?

Henry had gone to Portland for Christmas, enjoyed his family, and returned to Cambridge determined to see Fanny again and present the Appletons with his newest book. It made no sense now, but he supposed the renewing spirit of Christmas had left him drunk and once again overly hopeful. It was the wrong decision. He should give Fanny the distance she obviously wanted rather than continually put himself before her. Each meeting seemed more awkward than the last.

"You are a fool," he said into his scarf. Why had he gone? What did he hope to gain?

Hope was wearing him out. That he was at a low part in his own mind made it all the worse. Christmas with his family had helped, but he'd come back to a gray Boston, an upcoming term, and now a visit that assured him Fanny Appleton thought him a fool. An idiot. An old, broken man with no merit at all.

I must give it up, he said to himself, hunkering even further against the wind. Mrs. Craigie had hoped he would find happiness. If he did not give Fanny up, would he waste the rest of his life? Was there any point to living at all if he pinned all his hopes on a fantasy that was only getting further and further away from him?

He could not bring himself to make the other calls now. He was too overwrought, too embarrassed and low to be good company. Was he ever good company for anyone? He was tired of himself, and he felt sure his friends were weary of his moods as well. All of them were too busy to find time for the evenings they had all once enjoyed so much. Sumner and Tom were abroad more often than they were in Boston. The other men had responsibilities—courtship for Felton, a family for Cleveland. Sparks's aspirations toward school administration kept him busy. Henry could not ignore the possibility, however, that his friends were avoiding his company. And why not?

His publisher wanted another book, but Henry had written very little in the last few months. He could not seem to concentrate, and when he did, only words of pain and sorrow and longing filled the pages. At times he felt as though he were suffocating in a misery that seemed to creep over him from all sides.

Some part of him had thought seeing Fanny today would draw him up from the depths, like a light in the shadows, but he wondered now what made him even hope for such a thing. After *Hyperion*? He growled deep in his throat and wished he might go home, crawl into bed, and let sleep take him forever. The alternative—the life he lived day in and day out—was devoid of joy and meaning.

Fanny Appleton's image remained ethereal, like a spirit hovering just out of reach. The more he moved toward her, the faster she retreated. There was nothing solid for him to pin his hopes on, no reason at all for him to expect any return of feeling from her. Yet he kept visiting. Kept hoping. Kept making himself a nuisance to her and her family.

Snow began to fall, lightly at first, but nearly blinding by the time Henry reached Craigie Castle, his feet frozen. He took the back stairs and did not remove his wet coat until he reached his room. He was angry and tired and disillusioned to the point that all he could do was sit in front of the fire and let every miserable aspect of his life promenade through his mind.

What was it all for?

Why was he here?

What was the purpose of so much unhappiness?

Over and over his thoughts went back to Fanny and Mrs. Craigie's parting advice until he felt sure he would go mad. "I *must* be finished with her," he said to the crackling flames. "I must accept what is and chase her from my thoughts." He felt tears rise in his eyes. "Oh, dear God, draw this poison from my veins. Free me of my path to purgatory and bathe me with Thy light and glory." The tears began to fall, and he did not try to stop them. "Spare me," he whispered. "Save me. Let me go."

Thirty-two

New Eyes

It was late, and Fanny had already retired to her room when she remembered Mr. Longfellow's book. She'd left it in the drawing room after his visit earlier in the week and every night had wished she'd brought it to bed so that she might read his poems as her mind let go of the daily cares.

For a few moments she argued with herself as to whether or not it was worth a return to the drawing room in the dark before giving in. She picked up the lamp from beside her bed. She walked carefully and quietly downstairs and then turned up the lamp once she was in the drawing room.

She checked the table where she felt sure she had left it, but it wasn't there. For the next few minutes, she skirted the room in case her memory was wrong, but after looking through the whole room she was forced to admit that the book was gone. She frowned in the darkness and was contemplating where else the book could be when the squeak of a door hinge made her jump. She nearly dropped the lamp.

"Miss Appleton?"

Fanny put a hand to her chest. "Mathews," she said with relief. "I'm sorry if I woke you."

"You didn't wake me, ma'am," he said. His coat was not square on his shoulders and one pant leg was tucked into his sock. He'd obviously heard someone up and about and hurried to dress in order to find what was the matter. "Is everything all right?"

"Yes," Fanny said. "Only I am looking for a book I left here a few days ago." She cast another glance around the room as if the book may have suddenly appeared.

"Was it Mr. Longfellow's book, by chance?"

"Yes, a book of poetry."

"Mrs. Appleton was reading it this evening, ma'am. I believe she took it to bed with her."

Harriet had returned that evening from her holiday visit with her sister; she'd had dinner with Fanny before Fanny went to Emmeline's to play bridge with some other friends. "Oh, well, I'm glad to know it's in safekeeping." She smiled and moved toward the door. "I apologize again for waking you."

"No apology necessary," Mathews said as he held the door for her. "Is there anything else I can help you with?"

"No, thank you. Good night."

It was nearly lunchtime when Fanny went upstairs to the nursery. She knocked on the door and then let herself in. As soon as Fanny realized Harriet was nursing little Harriet she stopped, embarrassed. "I beg your pardon," she said, backing out the way she'd come.

"You may come in, Fanny," Harriet said. "I am almost finished."

Still mortified to have intruded on such a private moment, Fanny came into the room and moved immediately toward William, who was making a tower of blocks. She kept her back to Harriet and the baby while she played with her brother for a few minutes.

When Harriett said she was finished, Fanny turned without getting up from where she sat on the floor. Harriet put the baby over her shoulder and began patting the tiny back.

"Can I help you with something, Fanny?"

"I just wondered if you were finished with Mr. Longfellow's book."

"Oh," Harriet said. "I'm sorry, I had thought you had already read it."

"I have," Fanny said, wishing she didn't sound so guilty. "But Tom took his copy with him. Mr. Longfellow brought a new one for the family, only I left it in the drawing room and Mathews said you had picked it up."

"I wouldn't have if I'd known you'd wanted it."

The baby's body suddenly bounced in connection with a burp that seemed too loud to come from such a tiny thing. Harriet chuckled and Fanny smiled. "Would you like to hold her?" Harriet asked, gently lifting the infant from where she rested so perfectly against her shoulder.

"Certainly," Fanny said. She rose from the floor and sat in a chair near Harriet's rocking chair. Harriet laid the baby on her lap and wrapped the baby in a blanket so only her face peeked out. Then she handed the bundle to Fanny, who was rather well practiced with baby-holding these days. The baby molded into her arms, and Fanny curled round her, tapping her perfect chin, complete with a divot in the center like Father and Tom had. She began gently swaying, and little Harriet's eyes closed.

"Would you like me to fetch the book?" Harriet asked.

Fanny noted how content her stepmother looked, though her eyes were tired. She thought of all the nursemaids she'd seen in England, how attentive they were to their charges, freeing up the mothers to rest, visit with friends, and pursue their own interests. Harriet's interests, however, were her children, and although it appeared to be a taxing endeavor, there was no doubt Harriet adored the responsibility and her children thrived beneath her attention.

William—soon to be two years old—seeming to realize his mother's lap was free, pushed himself up from his blocks and toddled to her with his arms raised. Harriet smiled and lifted him into her lap before she began rocking gently back and forth, stroking his hair.

"You're a wonderful mother," Fanny said, surprising herself.

Harriet looked up, seeming as surprised to hear the compliment as Fanny was to say it. "Why, thank you, Fanny. What a kind thing to say."

The mood of the room seemed to unlock Fanny's usually guarded demeanor with her stepmother. She looked into the face of her little sister when she spoke so as to avoid any scrutinizing look Harriet might direct her way. "Is it everything you hoped it would be?" she asked carefully. "Motherhood, I mean."

"Yes and no, I suppose," Harriet said. The gentle creaks of the rocking chair were comforting, adding to the soothing atmosphere of the room. "I'm not sure it's possible to comprehend the investment of such a thing, but it's equally impossible to describe the joy of it."

Though she didn't say the words, Fanny felt sure Harriet heard them. *Please try to describe it.*

Harriet smiled and looked at William, who was settled against her, his eyes closed as though heading toward the oblivion of sleep.

Harriet began talking about the difficulties—not enough time, questioning herself, and feeling run ragged from lack of sleep. She missed her friends and the endless days where she could choose all her activities. It was lonely, she said, and exhausting, and some nights she would go to bed and cry herself to sleep for any number of things that had not gone right that day.

Fanny was rather horrified. Why would anyone want such a thing? Why hadn't Harriet hired a nurse to do the work for her so she wasn't so miserable?

But then Harriet began to talk about the reflection of Father in her children's faces, the absolute adoration in their eyes when they saw her, and what she called a spiritual calling that reminded her of how eternally connected they all were. She talked about feeling them move within her for the first time, the fear that all would not go well, and the ecstasy of holding a child—flesh of her flesh—in her arms.

She spoke of other nights when she didn't fall asleep in tears, where she felt filled with a sense of purpose, where knowing how needed she was by these children who could not do without her made every regret seem paltry and inconsequential.

"Perhaps it was a good thing I didn't know the whole of the splendor before William was placed in my arms, otherwise I may have gone to great lengths to achieve it any way I could." She smiled. "As it is, my blissful ignorance allowed me to wait until your father came along. I am grateful every day that my children have such a man to guide them through this life. I feel as though I found a great treasure in him, and because of him all the bounty of earth and heaven is available for me."

Fanny had never—not once—heard her stepmother talk so openly and was mesmerized not only by the words but also by Harriet's sincerity. Fanny was reminded of the day Harriet had married her father, of the tears Fanny had spent most of the day holding back, of the resentment and embarrassment she'd felt. She did not feel those things any more save for the memory that she once had had them. If not for that marriage, there would be no little William or little Harriet. Fanny could not imagine life without them.

"That is a beautiful testimony," Fanny said.

Harriet smiled and looked to her namesake still nestled in Fanny's arms. "You're very good with children, you know. Not too soft but not too hard either."

Fanny chuckled. "There are not many people who would say I am soft at all."

"You are with Ronald, and with your brother and sister. You connect with them, and they feel that you love them."

Fanny met her stepmother's eyes with a questioning look.

"It's true," Harriet said, still rocking back and forth. William was asleep on her lap, and Fanny wondered if Harriet would hold him for the duration of his nap. "I think it's because they know they can trust you. You watch out for them, but you are kind—a perfect combination of security and love."

"I've never had much time around children until these last few years," Fanny admitted. "I do find time with them more enjoyable than I would have expected. So many women seem to continue life after having children the way they did before. As though their children are of little consequence, especially when they are young." She shook her head. "To listen to me you would think I spend a great deal of time with them when I do not." She gave an embarrassed shrug. "It's not as if I am a caretaker of any kind. I simply get to play with them on my own schedule. That is hardly the investment a mother would make."

"Do you want to have children, Fanny?"

The question surprised her, and she looked down at the baby in her arms. The instant answer that came to mind was that without a husband it was not worth considering, but in that moment she knew she very much wanted children. She wanted to feel what Harriet had described; she wanted that kind of connection and sense of purpose. But she was hesitant to let the fantasy take root when she felt such little control over her future.

"Not every woman is meant to be a mother," Fanny said. "I believe God does not expect it from every woman, nor should every woman feel it is the only road to happiness."

"I agree," Harriet said, again surprising Fanny. She thought her stepmother might argue the point. "But for many women, motherhood *is* that very road."

Fanny nodded as though they were agreeing, though she was unsure that they were. She felt anxious about the direction the conversation had taken and unsure what to say. Most women she knew viewed their role and position as the only one worth pursuing, shoring up their own confidence by making it seem it was the only way to find true happiness.

"There is one other point I would like to make," Harriet said.

Fanny felt herself tense. She did not like it when people made points with her. As though they were delivering a reprimand. She looked at Harriet with controlled expectation.

"God can help you find the path that is uniquely yours," Harriet said. "I was older than you are when I decided to ask the Lord what he wanted of me. I served, of course, and helped others, especially my family. I was content with my life of independence and society. But in my study of the Bible, I began to feel that I was not on the course God wanted for me. I began to feel as though I was not doing my duty as a Christian woman.

"I spoke to Dr. Channing about my concerns, and he encouraged me to undertake a search of God's plan for me—just me, not a general ledger that gave every person the same map to follow, but the journey set apart for my feet alone. So I did, and in time, that journey led me to your father and these little ones." She jostled William in her lap and nodded at little Harriet in Fanny's arms. "Sitting here today, I have no doubt that this is exactly the course I should have taken, but the path was not laid out to me until I asked to see it. Perhaps God is unable to show us our way until we prove to Him that we truly want to follow it."

Fanny felt the truth of Harriet's words in her heart just as she had felt other truth from time to time. Strong enough that she could not deny it, but soft enough to know she was not forced to believe. But she *did* believe. Harriet's words resonated with her and gave her a great deal to think about.

If God had a path for Fanny Appleton, just for her, would it not be in her best interest to find it? She was about to ask how, exactly, one would search for such understanding when Harriet stood from the rocking chair and gently carried William to a pallet set in the corner of the nursery. She pulled a blanket over her sleeping son.

"I'll fetch you Mr. Longfellow's book, Fanny," she said. "And then I will stop bending your ear. I do go on sometimes."

She left the room and a few minutes later returned and traded Fanny the book for the baby.

"Thank you," Fanny said, feeling conspicuous as she stood there with the book in the middle of the nursery. She took the book to her room, though she didn't intend to read it until that night. But then she noticed a pink tassel of silk hanging out of the pages.

She opened the book to the page Harriet marked and read the title of the poem that began on that page—"The Bridge." Fanny recognized the poem. It was about a man finding solace on a bridge, but as she read it again, she saw the man as Mr. Longfellow and the bridge as the West Bridge that connected Boston to Cambridge. She had not been particularly struck by the poem the first time she'd read it, but the words sounded different to her now as images and memories swam through her mind, connecting to real people and places.

And forever and forever,
As long as the river flows,
As long as the heart has passions,
As long as life has woes;

The moon and its broken reflection
And its shadows shall appear,
As the symbol of love in heaven,
And its wavering image here.

Have you missed something? The same gentle softness she'd felt in the nursery seemed to ask the question. She lowered herself into the chair beside her bed and felt anxiety flutter in her chest that she could not explain.

Fanny turned to the front of the book, planning to read from the first page to the last without the prejudices she had long since held around herself when anything regarding Mr. Longfellow came too close. In the very front of the book was an inscription written in Mr. Longfellow's elegant hand. It was not written to anyone in particular, not to "The Appleton Family" or even to her specifically, but somehow she knew it was meant for her.

Forever and Forever
—Henry Wadsworth Longfellow, 1842

Have you missed something? the voice said again. Fanny didn't know the answer. She turned to the first page of the book she suspected she had not understood as she ought and began to read with new eyes.

Thirty-Three

The Water Cure

"Germany?" Sumner said, scowling from across the table.

If Henry didn't know his friend so well he would assume his friend was angry. "Near Boppard. There is an old convent there that applies the treatment. I feel it the best hope of regaining my health. Dickens mentioned the place to me during his visit, and while I admit he may have meant it in jest, I have looked into the procedure and found that it does seem to have merit."

Sumner's eyebrows remained drawn together. "And you were awarded leave?"

Henry nodded. "I received the notice just yesterday. Felton had already agreed to take over my supervisory duties if the leave was granted."

"How long?"

"Six months. I leave in May, and I wanted to be sure I told you myself."

Sumner huffed and sat back in his chair, turning to look at the darkened windows of the pub where they had met for drinks. "What is this treatment? You say Dickens mentioned it in jest?"

He and Sumner had met Charles Dickens a few months earlier, and the three of them got on very well. It was incredibly flattering to Henry to be accepted by a man who was known to select his friends with care.

Henry doubted Dickens had thought he would be intrigued when he said that what Henry needed was to spend enough time bathing in a convent on the Rhine that he became web-footed; but the idea hadn't left his mind. A logical man like Sumner would find it difficult to put any stock in something of this nature, but that was why Henry had requested they meet, so he could adequately explain the situation. No one understood the level of desperation Henry felt to find healing for his body and his mind, both of which seemed to be failing him.

"It is called the Water Cure and consists of taking baths and tonics of water with a high mineral content. It's supplemented with gentle country walks, a minimal diet, and a great deal of rest."

"It sounds like horse dung," Sumner said forcefully. A few people at the nearby tables looked their way. Henry would have been embarrassed if he had not anticipated this very reaction. He remained quiet and Sumner continued. "They are charging you a pretty penny for it, I'd wager, and you will be cut off from all who love you and forced to follow a regimen that may very well make your health worse, not better. They probably mix whiskey with the water and tell you it's minerals. You'll be stuck in some ruin of a building and catch your death."

Henry smiled even as Sumner's scowl deepened. "Oh, my dearest friend, how I shall miss you."

Sumner huffed. "You are going then."

"I have decided." Henry looked at his thin hand holding his glass. He was desperate. For months he had been losing weight, suffering headaches, skin discomfort, and insomnia. There had to be relief for him in Europe, there had to be. "And I am eager to go. I need a new place, a new sky to look upon, new thoughts in this soggy brain of mine. This most recent black mood has not broken except for a few days of light here and there, but I never find the restitution I need. I don't sleep, I barely eat, and I find myself in front of my students with my mind blank. I cannot write, I cannot focus on happy things nor believe they exist. I find myself thinking that perhaps death would be a haven and that frightens me."

Sumner's expression relaxed into acceptance, telling Henry that his honesty was not misplaced.

"I am trying, Sumner. I swear I am trying to rise above this, but I cannot seem to keep the air in my lungs, and I fear that one day I shall just stop breathing all together. I am desperate for relief, and I feel this might be my only chance."

"And Miss Appleton? Are you not simply running from her?"

"Yes, I am running from her," Henry said, looking at the tabletop, waiting for a reaction at hearing her name. It came, but it was as muted as was every other thing that had once brought passionate energy to his mind. "But not simply her. I am running from all of it, school and writing and associations and responsibility, in hopes that I shall return prepared to see things for their true color and shape—things that are lost to me within the bleakness of my thoughts."

"You are certain you cannot find solace here?" Sumner leaned forward. "Perhaps a trip to the south? The coastal towns there are very fine—you could drink the waters there."

"I am going to Germany," Henry said. "I must tell you that when I received the administration's letter approving my leave, I felt more lifted than I have in a long time. It was as though the clouds parted and a voice said 'This is hope.'"

"Are you expecting to come home cured enough that Miss Appleton will see a new man?"

Henry shook his head, not surprised that Sumner had looped back to that topic. Sumner had seen Henry suffer for want of Fanny for many years and was particularly irritated by it.

"I am hoping to return home free of the hold she has upon me." He lifted his glass and swirled the wine within it until it created a small tornado of red liquid. "I know she is lost to me, Sumner, and that she was never truly mine for the asking. I know it in here"—he tapped his free hand against his head—"but my heart won't yet accept it. I cannot survive with my mind and heart so separated. I go to Germany with the belief that I can connect my head to my heart once again and exorcise Fanny Appleton from both of them completely. It is my intention to return home a new man, free of Fanny, free of the fantasy that has hung like a millstone around my neck all these years. I want a family, I want a woman to love and who will love me back, and I am running out of time. I must separate Fanny from that expectation, and I feel sure that Germany is where that will happen."

Sumner took a deep breath and then let it out slowly. "Then I shall wish you well. I want you to know how greatly you shall be missed. You are my dearest friend, Longfellow, the best I have ever had. I shall count the days until your return, and while I will sorrow for myself, I wish you the treasure of your health and, above all, hope you will be happy."

Henry blinked back tears, surprised at the depth of feeling from this man who appeared so hard on the outside. He reached across the table and Sumner took his hand in a symbolic embrace. "Without the love and support of my friends, Sumner, I would not have made it so well and so long. I thank you from the depth of my soul for your faith and your care."

"God speed to you," Sumner whispered, his own eyes glassy. "Find that happiness. Be well."

Thirty-Four

New Life

Henry trudged up the hillside, sketchbook in hand, lungs heaving, and muscles burning until he reached the crest which afforded a view of the smoking chimneys and bell towers of Marienberg, the village just outside the convent where he had been taking the Water Cure since June.

Am I cured? he wondered, and then smiled at the paper in his hand. Three months ago he was not writing, and now he was. He had gained back some of the weight he'd lost, and his sleep and digestive struggles had evened out. He walked for hours every day without pain in his joints, and his headaches were far less frequent than they had been. Though he was hesitant to proclaim himself completely cured, he had not felt this good in years.

He settled himself on the hillside and let the color and shapes of the view surround him. The landscape was beautiful: quaint, rustic, and free. After months of baths, drinks, bland food, and long walks, he had come to realize that while he may never be *cured* of what distressed him, he *could* rise above it.

Here in Marienberg there was no one to complain to and, after looking around at the company he shared his time with, he realized many people suffered from ailments of every kind, making him oddly grateful for his own. Some of the residents were in far greater distress than he, dealing with all manner of physical and psychological impairments that tugged at Henry's sympathy. Some seemed to regard their time at the convent as an excuse to be idle, and yet others seemed to enjoy the attention, often making up new ailments and complaints, then watching with bright eyes the way their attendants rallied around them.

Henry was unsure which category he would place himself in, but he knew one thing—he had more power over his moods than he had thought. What's more, he'd come to take a certain comfort in his ability to feel things so deeply. Perhaps because his mind could go to dark places, he had the perception and ability to recreate such ethereal concepts in his writing. Perhaps his weakness was also his strength.

He had even come to terms with Fanny and the role she played in his life. He loved her and accepted that he would love her all the days of his life, but he would never have her. Not the way he wanted, not the way he hoped.

There was something in his mind, some pull toward depression that had brought him to the depths of despair on many occasions. In those moments, he often wondered if death was the only respite he could hope for, the only relief at hand. Each time, however, when he was dragging upon the seabed of his misery, thoughts of Fanny and a flame of hope would bring him to the surface again. One more day. One more month. One more chance to be in her company and feel the light she brought into a room even when he knew she was angry with him.

That light had been enough—so many times it had been enough—that he could acknowledge her influence in keeping him from the ultimate despair. Without the hope that one day she would love him back, he would have had no purpose. God's ways were most certainly mysterious, and Henry could not pretend to know all the reasons why Fanny was so important to him, but he felt certain she had given him reason to live when he could find no other.

But now he would move on. Now that he better understood his mind and its limitations, he would find other reasons to live. Other sonnets to sing and other purposes to fulfill. Fanny had played her part, and he would always love her for that, but he would no longer put aside all other beauty for the sake of wanting to capture hers.

Another thing had become clear to him these last months, creating a new confidence within him that was exciting. Henry was not a writer—he was a *poet.* The beauty of words seduced him, and the ability to choose the right one with the right tone and structure to express what he wanted to say with absolute perfection was both a gift and a salvation. He had begun writing again, prose within his journal and poetry within the pages of his sketchbook, and the words had become living things. Creations all his own. He did not think of any audience but himself and his God, whom he felt more clearly than he had before. He felt sure that He was pleased with Henry's work so far.

Early on his way to the Rhine, Henry had the chance to spend more time with Charles Dickens in London, and he had felt ignited—as much as he could, given the state he had been in—by the social awareness that Dickens wore like a second skin. Dickens told stories with great teachings disguised within his characters. But not so disguised as not to be recognized. His position had not made him popular with everyone, and yet he did not allow the people's opinion to dissuade him. Dickens had said he believed that God had given him permission to preach within the pages of his books, but to the denomination of humanity rather than any one sect.

Henry had found Dickens's determination inspiring then, but as the days and weeks had turned brighter, he had found even greater value. That same devotion had come alive in Henry, and the light had poured out from his pencil in the form of new work, different work—work that would be hated by some and raised like a banner by others.

Henry's time in Germany was coming to an end, and he was determined to do all he could to secure the foundation he planned to stand upon once he returned to Boston. Not broken, decrepit, and nursing his wounds, but confident, determined, and willing to accept the fullness of the thing that had been so far away for so long—himself.

Henry lifted his gaze to take in the view around him and then wrote the date on the top of the page. The words had been marching through his mind for days, waiting for him to write them down. He could feel the eagerness of the pencil in his hand to birth this idea and give it wings. *Mezzo Cammin* was part of the first line of *The Divine Comedy,* but it was fitting since he was at his own midpoint—"Mezzo" meaning middle—not only in years, but in regard to the change that had taken place. That "Cammin" was a city in Germany was equally fitting for the tribute he was eager to pour upon the paper from the beautiful perch above the city.

He was not sure the poem would be something he would share, but he needed to write it. He needed to mark this point in his life.

Half of my life is gone, and I have let
The years slip from me and have not fulfilled
The aspirations of my youth, to build

Some tower of song with lofty parapet.
Not indolence, nor pleasure, nor fret
Of restless passions that would not be stilled,
But sorrow, and a care that almost killed,
Kept me from what I may accomplish yet;
Though, half-way up the hill, I see the Past
Lying beneath me with its sounds and sights,—
A city in the twilight dim and vast,
With smoking roofs, soft bells, and gleaming lights,—
And hear above me on the autumnal blast
The cataract of Death far thundering from the heights.

Thirty-Five

SHIFTING WIND

Fanny pulled back the drapes and looked at the full moon that bathed Beacon Hill in silvery light. She let the drapery fall, took a breath to calm the butterflies in her stomach, and moved toward the wardrobe where she had put the old coat of Tom's and the hat of her father's that she'd taken two days before. Neither men wore the items often, they would not be missed, but Fanny was anxious about someone finding the items in her room.

She put the hat on her head and the coat over her riding breeches and boots. She hoped the disguise would hide her gender in the dark. As she rolled up the sleeves of Tom's old coat, she shook her head at her foolishness. Twenty-five years old and she was embarking on such a childish caper.

She scowled at her reflection in the glass—she did not a handsome man make—and then turned up the collar and moved to the door of her bedchamber. She had oiled the hinges herself earlier in the week, and the door eased open without a sound. She closed it just as silently and tiptoed carefully down the hall, the stairs, and to the back door that led to the alley behind the house.

She remained ever watchful for servants—especially Mathews since he had caught her the last time she was bumping around the house in the middle of the night. Only she wasn't bumping this time, she was merely a whisper. When she shut the back door behind her, she dared feel the first sense of victory. Her pride did not last long, however; there was still the matter of crossing Beacon Hill and making her way to the river undetected.

Her chest was hot with the possibility of discovery, and as she walked, scanning from side to side, she imagined the write-up in the paper if Frances Appleton, daughter of industrialist and Congressman Nathan Appleton were found dressed like a man wandering the city at night. How would she explain herself if she were caught? Would claiming poetry as her reason help her to claim insanity?

The further she got from home, the more complex her feelings became. She hadn't been caught, but every nervous step she took made it less likely that she could run for the safety of home. Yet she kept taking those nervous steps, her hands sweating in her pockets, and her mind spinning with horrible scenarios that would result from her discovery. However, it was nearly two o'clock in the morning, and Boston, it seemed, was sleeping.

Movement caught her eye, and she startled, taking in the hunched figure of a man walking the opposite direction on the other side of the street. She looked down and moved forward as though she too had purpose.

Finally, after what felt like the longest walk she'd ever taken, she saw the bridge and her anxiety turned to anticipation. She fingered the book she'd stuffed into the pocket of the coat and smiled. What an adventurous woman she was! If only there was someone she could tell of this brazen act who would not reprimand her for it.

Fanny reached the bridge but did not stop until she had crossed it and turned back to face Boston from the Cambridge side. That is how Mr. Longfellow would have approached.

She allowed her thoughts to still and her breathing to slow while she took in the scene before her. The West Boston Bridge, illuminated by the light of a full moon, stretched across the Charles River, both connecting the two cities and keeping them separate. She began to walk in slow, calculated steps, imagining the burden Mr. Longfellow had carried the night he had taken this same route.

She reached the center of the bridge and moved to the railing where she could look over the side. The black water moved inland with the fluidity of light and the stillness of a serpent. She allowed the mood to fall upon her—the air, the moonlight, the smells, and the warmth that rose from the bridge itself. Then she reached carefully into her pocket, removed the book, and turned to the same page that had been marked when Harriet had returned the book to her months earlier.

"The Bridge" was the first poem Fanny had read from her new perspective of trying to better understand the writer. Until that day, everything she had read of Mr. Longfellow's was with a critical eye and, even more shamefully, a predisposition to find the work poor. That was not to say she didn't still find merit, but she had not been looking for merit. She had been looking for flaws.

Since her discussion with Harriet in the nursery, however, Fanny had not been so intent upon the weaknesses of Mr. Longfellow's work. And what she had found was beauty. Great beauty, awesome depth and goodness that she had not seen before. She had reread *Ballads and Other Poems, Voices of Night,* and *Outré Mer,* and her impressions of Mr. Longfellow's work was very different than it had been.

Even *Outré Mer,* which she had liked upon first reading, had gained depth, likely because of her own maturity. She could hear Mr.

Longfellow's youth in the pages; but rather than it being a distraction, she found it endearing. Of everything she'd reread and better understood, however, Fanny's favorite was "The Bridge."

She could see Mr. Longfellow there—here—taking in the moment and translating the experience into a poem of both hope and sorrow. She could not help but wonder how many of the cares and sorrows that inspired the poem might be related to her.

She brushed her hand over the book and tilted it so the white page caught the moonlight well enough to allow her to read, though she nearly had the piece memorized. She licked her lips, fixed the image of Mr. Longfellow standing in this very same place, and began to read.

I stood on the bridge at midnight,
As the clocks were striking the hour,
And the moon rose o'er the city,
Behind the dark church-tower.

It was not midnight. She had feared too many people would be about at that time of night, but Fanny looked around her, identifying the moon above the city and even finding the church tower. She smiled and turned back to the words of the poem.

I saw her bright reflection
In the waters under me,
Like a golden goblet falling
And sinking into the sea.

Fanny leaned forward to see the wavering reflection of the moon on the surface of the water, just like a golden goblet sinking into the sea.

And far in the hazy distance
Of that lovely night in June,
The blaze of the flaming furnace
Gleamed redder than the moon.

It wasn't June—it was August—and she wasn't sure what Mr. Longfellow meant by the flaming furnace, but she did not let it ruin the mood.

Among the long, black rafters
The wavering shadows lay,
And the current that came from the ocean
Seemed to lift and bear them away;

Them? The shadows, Fanny assumed, but she wasn't entirely certain. Perhaps shadows were a symbol, as the flaming furnace likely was.

As, sweeping and eddying through them,
Rose the belated tide,
And, streaming into the moonlight,
The seaweed floated wide.

There was vegetation on the edges of the water, waving along with the current.

And like those waters rushing
Among the wooden piers,
A flood of thoughts came o'er me
That filled my eyes with tears.

Fanny's own eyes filled with tears as the heaviness of what came next settled upon her. She had hoped she would become part of the poem if she recreated this scene, and she felt the burden he carried when he wrote these words, and the solace he hoped for.

How often, O, how often,
In the days that had gone by,
I had stood on that bridge at midnight
And gazed on that wave and sky!

How often, O, how often,
I had wished that the ebbing tide
Would bear me away on its bosom
O'er the ocean wild and wide!

For my heart was hot and restless,
And my life was full of care,
And the burden laid upon me
Seemed greater than I could bear.

But now it has fallen from me,
It is buried in the sea;
And only the sorrow of others
Throws its shadow over me.

Yet whenever I cross the river
On its bridge with wooden piers,
Like the odor of brine from the ocean
Comes the thought of other years.

And I think how many thousands
Of care-encumbered men,
Each bearing his burden of sorrow,
Have crossed the bridge since then.

I see the long procession
Still passing to and fro,
The young heart hot and restless,
And the old subdued and slow!

And forever and forever,
As long as the river flows,
As long as the heart has passions,
As long as life has woes;

The moon and its broken reflection
And its shadows shall appear,
As the symbol of love in heaven,
And its wavering image here.

Fanny finished reading, but her eyes remained fixed on the page while tears rolled down her cheeks. Such a heart. Such a burden. She wiped her eyes and then reverently closed the book. She lifted her face toward the moon, praying that its cleansing light would wash away the regrets she had felt these last months as she realized how much she had missed the man who had loved her too ardently. He was not in Boston—he'd gone to Europe to rest—and yet somewhere he was beneath the same moon. Was he thinking of her? Was it fair to hope he was?

Even now Fanny worried that what was drawing her to him was his gift of words and the ambiance he could create with them. She could not forget the unease she felt in his company. But was it unease? Or could it be something else? Something she had been too young and too stubborn to identify. The way he looked at her, as though he could see more than anyone else could see, had made her feel conspicuous, but what if it were not something to be afraid of? What if the fact that he had seen the very worst of her and loved her still was proof that, of all the people in the world, he could love her best?

The idea of seeing him once he returned still filled her with trepidation. While she was not in a hurry to experience a visit with him, something had changed within her. When he returned, and when she was ready, she *would* take the opportunity to see if that change was enough to overcome all the years that had brought her here—brought *them* here.

She had taken Harriet's suggestion to heart and had begun a new study of the Bible, a new level of pondering over the sermons she heard in church each week and what pathways God would have her take. With her increased devotion had come the sweet treasures of spirit. Awakenings. Understanding. New ideas and remedies for old laments. That she had so much time alone gave her plenty of time to explore her thoughts and feelings.

Mary and Robert had returned to England in May. Tom had come home but was gone again. Emmeline had gone to live with an aunt in New York, and Jewett was always traveling, it seemed, acting on this new idea or that one. He was a man of business, like his uncles, and did not stay in one place for long.

As Fanny had noted before, her friends were moving forward with their lives. This time, however, though it likely appeared to others that she was not doing the same, she was moving forward too. She was coming to accept God's will and was realizing more and more that His path was the better one.

His path also seemed to be leading her to Mr. Longfellow. Despite him being ten years her senior, despite him having loved before, despite the fact that his class was below what she had expected she would need to be truly happy. All the objections she had raised had been pulled out to sea like the shadows in Mr. Longfellow's poem—all but one.

Though she had read and reread his poems and *Outré Mer,* she had not yet returned to *Hyperion.* The scars held her back, as did her shameful response. She feared that, despite the awakening she had experienced these last months, *Hyperion* would breathe new life into her old complaints and eclipse all the good ground she had conquered. But she would have to read it. She had to face that demon in order to know if it, too, might look different than it had the first time she'd read with her "hot and restless heart."

Fanny closed the book of poems and stuffed it into her pocket, bidding farewell to the scene before her. "Good night, Mr. Longfellow," she said to the soft rush of the river. Then she turned toward home, turned up the collar of Tom's coat, and began her journey back.

1843
Boston & Cambridge

Thirty-Six

New Beginnings

"Good evening, Professor."

Henry's breath caught in his chest for the split second it took to recognize the voice, feel the invigoration, and then stamp it out. Each time he anticipated seeing Fanny, he felt sure he would not react in such a way. Each time he was disappointed to realize she still cast a spell over his senses.

Still, he would not give in to it. He was made of firmer stuff and had not reacted like a lovesick puppy since his return from Germany almost six months ago. He faced Fanny, who looked at him with wide brown eyes and a smile that seemed genuinely glad to see him, though he could not trust himself to properly deduce such a thing. He had been wrong so many times before, and he was determined to live beyond the fantasies he had fed himself with all these years.

"Good evening, Miss Fanny," Henry said, bowing slightly. "You look lovely this evening." She wore a blue gown, and her hair was perfectly styled. He had seen her only in passing since his return from Germany, but he'd become convinced he had overcome the power of her hold on him. Now that she was before him, however, he was not so certain.

"You have now survived another New England winter. Are you still as glad to be returned to us?"

Us? A collective pronoun would not be his undoing, but his determination to have no reaction to her began to wobble at the inclusionary word. He tried to shore up his confidence and smiled at her politely. "I am always glad to come home."

She turned her head to the side slightly. "More glad than to have remained in your beloved Germany?"

He could not help but laugh. It had been too long since she had spoken to him with such casual friendship. He ached for it. "I'm afraid it's reflective of how very boring I am. That even despite my love of Europe—and Germany specifically, as you say—nowhere is quite as comfortable as New England."

"Did you miss us very much then?"

Us again. *What does she mean by that?* He stared at her, and she did not look away or try to occupy herself with some distraction or another. What did her attentiveness mean? Could it be that she'd missed *him*? He'd no sooner thought it than he asked himself why he should not ask her that directly. He'd made his decision regarding her and had no reason to be afraid of saying something wrong. It seemed, in fact, that the more he had tried to say the right thing in the past, the more it had worked against him.

"Did *you* miss *me*?" He had never been so direct with her—at least not since his proposal all those years ago. Her cheeks turned instantly pink, and the sight quite took his breath away.

She glanced down and turned the cup of punch in her hand. "In fact, I did, Mr. Longfellow." She looked back at him. "More than I would have supposed."

Henry was rendered speechless. The silence lasted several seconds, until another guest interrupted them to ask after Henry's upcoming lecture series. Fanny lingered for a time, listening to his answer, but then a woman led her away. Henry remained engaged in his conversation but did not lose his awareness of where Fanny was in the room. She'd missed him! Did she have any idea what such a statement did to his composure? That flickering flame of hope he had nurtured over the years began to burn brighter. It was all he could do to remain attentive to the conversation at hand.

The night wore on, and Henry genuinely enjoyed the company. Eventually the attendees began to thin, and Henry took the opportunity to find Fanny, eager—though not unreasonably so, he hoped—to continue their conversation. She had responded to him differently tonight, but he had misinterpreted things so many times before that he did not trust himself. He wanted to speak with her again.

He found her talking with an older couple, but as soon as he approached, she excused herself from the conversation and faced him fully. They were in a room filled with people, and yet at that moment, Henry felt as though they were entirely alone. He had the instant desire to brush his knuckles against her cheek, but he put his hand in his pocket instead. He would not fall victim to such temptation.

"I was rather rude earlier," he said, causing her to lift her eyebrows in surprise. "You asked after my time in Germany and I did not ask after your time here in Boston. Did you travel for the autumn or winter?"

"I spent some time in Pittsville and New York," Fanny said. "It is always good to spend time with family, but I must admit I miss Molly very much when I travel."

"She and Mr. Mackintosh are abroad again?"

"Yes. Robert secured a post in England."

"I understand Tom has found his place in Europe as well?"

Fanny laughed and shook her head indulgently. "Tom has informed us that he expects to make his career as a world traveler." She shrugged. "I'm unsure what kind of salary that pays, but he seems to manage somehow, and strangely, I cannot picture him doing anything different."

"He is becoming quite a wit," Henry said. "He is well-known in England for his commentary on politics and culture, as I understand it."

"Well, then, he's done it," Fanny said, seemingly proud of her brother. "Though I hope he comes home often enough that we don't forget the look of him."

"He leaves for England next month, does he not?" Henry said. He looked around, but Tom was not in sight. "We had dinner a few weeks ago, and I believe that was his intention."

"Yes, in a few weeks' time," Fanny said. "It will be lonely without him. I can only hope that good friends will help fill the time."

She held his eyes, and for a moment Henry could not breathe. Did she mean . . .

A woman came up beside them to bid Fanny farewell. When they were alone again, Fanny faced Henry but did not continue on the same topic. "Could I trouble you for a favor, Mr. Longfellow?"

"Certainly."

"I wonder if you might walk me home. Perhaps our conversation would be less interrupted if you could. Tom is embroiled in a game of cards." She nodded toward the back of the house. "He will likely not extricate himself for some time. I'm sure he would not argue your walking me."

Henry was not about to argue and sent word with Mr. Norton that he and Fanny were leaving. They fetched their outer clothes, his traditional black wool coat and her fine velvet cape, and stepped out into the chilly night. Her house on Beacon Street was only a few blocks away, and the cobbled sidewalks were just wide enough for them to walk side by side. He offered his arm and she took it.

"It *is* cool tonight," Fanny said. "Though I suppose it is rather mild for April."

"I suppose it is," Henry said, struggling to focus on anything other than her nearness. If this were a game of some kind, if her attention was not sincere, he might very well throw himself into the Charles River come morning.

"Now, tell me of Germany and your time in Europe," Fanny said.

He entertained her with the details of his time in Germany, including the hot blankets he was wrapped in each morning and the cold baths he suffered through again and again. Fanny laughed, spurring him toward even more candor and humor.

When they turned on Beacon Street, she surprised him again by asking if he would walk the Commons with her. They were soon walking beneath the newly budded trees that in a few weeks' time would create a canopy. For the time being, the two of them were alone in the Common. It was late and the air chilled, but the gaslights glowed and the company was unmatched in Henry's opinion. They were walking as lovers would, and though he tried not to think of such a thing, the warmth of her beside him and the effect of her laugh upon his heart could not be ignored. It was the way he had always imagined it could be, but it was no longer a possibility. It was happening in the present. Just when he'd given up hope.

When the conversation dwindled into a comfortable silence, he stopped in the middle of the walkway and faced her. They did not speak for a few seconds as she gazed up at him with an expression of openness and, dare he say it, admiration? The thought came to

Henry's mind that perhaps she was waiting for him now just as he had been waiting for her all these years.

"Miss Appleton," he said softly, not wanting to shatter the dream he found himself in. "May I be candid with you?"

"Of course you may, Mr. Longfellow," she said. "I hope that you would."

"You are different tonight—different than you have ever been towards me and I am unsure how to react."

She glanced away but only for a moment. "I *am* different," she said. "But it is not only tonight. I have been waiting to see you, *wanting* to see you, for some time. You may find this silly, but I have been praying for a chance to speak with you, and tonight, when I saw you at the party, I felt sure that God had answered my prayer."

Her words both thrilled him and put him on the defensive. "I have not stopped aging, you know, and I am still a widowed man. At the risk of offending you, I must tell you that I cannot bear to be trifled with. I conquered some part of myself in Germany, denounced some demons you might say, but I have promised not to inflict misery upon myself." He felt he should say something else, he didn't want her to think he saw her as misery, but his words failed him.

Fanny raised a hand to place it against his cheek. Instant heat fired through his veins at the intimate touch. "How I regret that you know the very worst of me," she said softly. Her breath clouded before her face like a veil only to dissipate into the night a moment later. "How difficult it must be to trust me now."

He reached up and took her hand, bringing it to his lips where he pressed a kiss. He wished he could tell her all the things his heart was saying. He lowered her hand but did not release it. She stared back at him, the light of the gaslights behind him flickering in her eyes.

"I have been reading your works," she said. "You have such beauty in your heart, Mr. Longfellow, such depth and passion. I wonder why I could not see it before, or perhaps why it did not touch me as it has these last months."

Months? The word proved that her attitude tonight was not a sudden one. "Perhaps it was because of your own wounds," he said, thinking of what Tom had once said about the losses Fanny had suffered.

Instant tears sprang to her eyes, confirming that he was correct, at least in part. Had she already known her reasons, or had he unknowingly revealed something that spoke truth to her heart?

"Such wounds have not prevented me from hurting others," she said. "Hurting you, I believe."

He said nothing. This was no time for accusations, but he would not be dishonest either. It had been more than six years—six long years—that he had waited for her to return his feelings. Such a wait was painful, but looking at her now, he wondered if it weren't also necessary. He was a better man than he used to be, and she a woman more aware of her own heart and mind. He could not share his life with a woman less than that. Dare he hope that this change in her was forecasting a future for *them*?

"Do you think you can ever forgive me for being so cold to you, for treating your affections so lightly?"

"I have no need to forgive you, Miss Appleton."

"Fanny," she cut in. "You've stopped calling me that."

"You never gave me invitation," Henry said. "That I would take upon myself such familiarity is an example of my arrogance. In regards to you, I have always been impetuous in ways that my age and wisdom should have prevented."

"And I took it as poorly as a girl could," Fanny said. "But I am a grown woman now."

His awareness of such truth raised an ache that was not as familiar as it once was. He had made good progress in suppressing the physical attraction he felt toward her, but her confirmation of fact was more than he could hold back. "Yes, a beautiful woman."

Her cheeks colored again, but she did not look away. "Perhaps more handsome than beautiful."

Had her tone been anything other than teasing he would have been embarrassed to have the sentiment shared in *Hyperion* directed back at him. Perhaps he could dare to believe that, in rereading his words, her opinion of that book had changed.

"I am not as foolish as I once was," she said. "And I sincerely hope I have not frightened you away entirely."

Had Henry not thought she had done that very thing? Just yesterday when he'd thought of her, he had reminded himself that she was nothing but a source of aggravation. He had needed such protection; the heart could not bleed itself dry, after all.

"Am I to interpret this conversation between us as an invitation to renew my attention to you, Miss . . . Fanny? Properly this time?"

"I was a silly girl to chastise you the way I did when you have done nothing but compliment me with your regard. I can only hope that the benefit of my actions was to place me on a path that led me to greater understanding, though the journey has been a slow one. I do not believe I was ready then, Mr. Longfellow."

"But you are ready now?"

Her smile grew and she nodded.

A tremor of fear rushed through him. What had prompted such a change of heart? Was he a fool to trust it? Falling back to his better judgment, he took a step back and gave her hand a squeeze before releasing it and putting out his arm once more. He could not erase the smile from his face, and he did not want to, but neither did he want to act rashly. He needed to think on what had transpired between them, dissect and quantify the insight he had gained, before he allowed his heart to take flight.

"Perhaps I had best see you home," he said softly.

Thirty-Seven

Vain Regrets

Fanny looked into Mr. Longfellow's face, illuminated by the gaslights of the Commons, and wished she could read his thoughts. She couldn't blame him for being hesitant, after so many years of keeping him at a distance, but she hoped he could feel what she felt and know what she knew.

She had been nervous about seeing him again. He'd been back from Germany almost six months, and she had begun to wonder if the opportunity for them to talk would ever come. What if she still felt uneasy in his company? What if she could love him from afar but not up close? And yet, as soon as she'd made the decision to cross the room and talk with him, those fears had lifted. He was the same man who wrote poems of such depth, tenderness, and passion. The discomfort between them was gone, and the realization was invigorating—only she did not know how to make sure he understood the change. Short of seducing him into understanding, however, she did not know what might do the job. And she was not yet desperate enough to resort to feminine wiles.

"Perhaps you *should* see me home," she said in response to his suggestion. It would be good to have some time with her thoughts, to review this night and become comfortable with the changes in their relationship. Likely he would need that same time. She could only hope that once they parted company, he would not talk himself out of the good that had transpired between them.

How they would proceed was out of her hands, and she knew it. The entire time they had known one another could testify against her, but she hoped with all her heart that tonight would be enough to overcome the past. They turned toward Beacon Street and walked in silence.

The front door opened when they reached the steps, telling her that Mathews had been waiting for her return. Would Mr. Longfellow forgive her all the things she'd said and the thoughts she'd had about him not being good enough for her? Would he forget that she had once called him old and thrown his love for Mary Potter in his face? She wished she could convince him that her intent tonight was worthy of his trust. Her only hope was that the feeling she'd had so often that he could see through her, beyond her moods and her masks and her challenges, would help him see and feel her sincerity tonight.

"Good night, Miss Fanny," he said. He bent over her hand and kissed the back of it in such a way to ignite the very fire she both feared and longed for. Through reading Mr. Longfellow's poetry with new eyes and a fresh heart, she had come to understand his passion. She felt quite wicked to want to explore that passion further. He straightened and fixed her with a gaze that made her feel more wicked still.

"Good night, Mr. Longfellow."

"Henry," he said. "I would be very pleased if you would call me Henry."

"Well, then, good night, Henry."

His name was sweet on her lips. He released her hand, but he was still standing on the sidewalk when she reached the front door and glanced over her shoulder. She smiled before she entered the house, and Mathews closed the door.

The household was quiet—small children meant that the family did not entertain late anymore—and so she made her way carefully up the stairs where her maid awaited her. Fanny could not get the evening out of her mind and reviewed the events over and over again as her hair was unpinned and she readied herself for bed. Where could she have spoken better? What exactly did Mr. Long—*Henry*—say and how did he say it? She could not misconstrue that he was open to her change of heart, but her fears were not entirely satisfied either.

What will happen next? she wondered as she burrowed beneath the covers, grateful that her maid had set a water bottle there early enough to warm the sheets.

"What if I am too late?" she asked the dark and empty room. She wished Molly were there to talk to. It seemed so long ago that they had been able to take one another's presence for granted, and although Fanny had become used to the distance between them, tonight of all nights she longed for her sister's encouragement. Molly would feel Fanny was doing the right thing, wouldn't she? She could help Fanny believe that she was not too late.

Molly was not there to say such things, however, and Fanny was left with only her own company and seven years' worth of memories of pushing Henry away. Over and over again. She wondered now what she had been afraid of, why it had seemed so necessary to keep him at a distance. Why had she been so certain he could never make her happy?

"What if I have lost my chance entirely?"

Thirty-Eight

Personal Easter

Henry sat at his writing desk, looking over the field that seemed to dribble into the Charles River. The water looked inviting, and the day was quite fine for early May. Perhaps he could find a friend up for some rowing. It was not typical for sport to call to him, but he had been living on nervous energy ever since writing Fanny the letter. *The letter.* Just thinking of it prompted him to jump to his feet and pace the floor where perhaps General Washington had once paced. But Washington had Martha at his side; she'd come to him in this very house and attended him though he was leading an army. What a lucky man Washington was to have such a woman.

Could I . . . Would she . . . Henry did not know how to form his hopes into words, so he settled for images. He remembered the look on Fanny's face when she'd stood beside him that night at the Nortons' party. He remembered the warmth of her hand when she'd placed it on his cheek. The brilliance of her smile. The clarity of her eyes. All the supposed healing he thought he'd found in Germany slid aside to reveal the flame of hope that had never truly gone out but that now offered another kind of healing within its light. He'd accepted he could live without her, but now he was presented with a new future he'd dared not expect.

When Henry had exercised through his impatience, he returned to his writing desk and forced his mind to focus on the next line of the poem he was working on. The cadence was off. He needed a different word or phrase for "reprimand" and turned his attention to the stack of books beside the desk in hopes that work could envelop him, fold him in tight and keep him aware of only this ink on this paper.

Sometime later, a knock on his sitting room door caused him to look up from his paper, which had blessedly consumed his attention. He stood and crossed to the door. Miriam, standing almost as tall as he did, held out an envelope.

"Just came for you, Mr. Longfellow." He took the envelope, and she leaned forward to point at the return address printed in familiar hand. "Don't Miss Appleton live on Beacon Street?"

Henry felt the muscles of his face pulling into a grin, and for the first time in a while, he did not mind that everyone in Cambridge knew of his *tendré* for Miss Fanny Appleton. "That she does, Miriam," he said. "Let us hope it is good news."

He closed the door and crossed to his desk. For a moment he simply looked at the thing: the fine paper, the perfect letters. There was a chance that this letter would not bear the news he was hoping for. She could reject him. Again. And yet somehow he knew she would not. In the past, he had felt hopeful but desperate. Now, he simply felt the rightness of everything. The past, the present, and the future.

Without wasting another minute, Henry turned the envelope

over and broke the seal. He unfolded the letter, took a breath, and began to read.

With every word his heart grew lighter, the air was clearer, the sun moved higher in the sky. He finished reading and bowed his head as peace and calm washed over him like the waters of baptism. The afflictions of his soul had been swallowed up, and his heart began to pound with a new rhythm, as though forever changed by this moment—his personal Easter, where all was redeemed and salvation was nigh.

"Thank you," he said in tender prayer. He paused another moment before jumping from his seat and running for the door.

He took the front stairs—thinking of Mrs. Craigie and how she had not liked him to use those stairs—and sent a little smile heavenward to her. She would find this turn delightful. It was because of her that he had tried to forget Fanny, tried to move forward without her, and perhaps that was why Fanny's heart had finally come to him. As with Abraham and Isaac, he had been willing to give up, but in the end it had not been required of him to do so.

Henry grabbed his coat and hat from the rack by the door and was buttoning his coat when Miriam came into the foyer.

"Where are you going?" she asked, looking him over from head to toe.

Henry beamed at her. "I am going to Beacon Street."

"Shall I call a carriage?"

"I could not sit still if I wanted to," Henry said. "And I don't want to!"

He pulled open the door and fairly ran toward Cambridgeport, pressing his hat further onto his head during the walk he had taken so many times before. Across the river by the West Boston Bridge and along Charles Street until finally he turned the corner onto Beacon Street.

How many times had he walked the Commons hoping for a glimpse of his *Dark Ladye*? And now she had called him to her. Despite his awkwardness. Despite his missteps. Through some prism he was eager to understand—but did not yet know—she had come to feel just as he did. She loved him. She'd said so in her letter. Every dream of his heart was to become a reality.

Henry slowed his steps as he approached the grand house. He stood on the sidewalk a few moments longer, letting his eyes travel from the ground level to the rooftop. He thought back to that night at Craigie House after Fanny had rejected him the first time and how Miss Lowell had listened to his confusing account of it. "She does not love me," he had said. Because of that, Fanny could not move past the obstacles between them. He'd decided then—that day—to establish his writing career, to be patient, and to not give up hope. It had been five years since then. Five years! And yet here he was, in exactly the place he'd been the first time. But he was a better man now.

And she was ready.

He took the steps with reverence and removed his hat, smoothing his hair which was in need of a trim. At the front door he took a breath, said a prayer, and knocked.

He expected the butler to open the door—would she miss having a butler?—but instead Fanny herself stood there. She looked him in the face, a smile growing on her fine lips. "I had hoped it was you," she said, thrilling him to his very toes. "Won't you come in, Mr. Longfellow?" A maid approached as Henry entered the foyer. "Please bring tea to the drawing room," Fanny asked the maid. The young woman curtsied and headed for the kitchen.

Henry's mouth was suddenly dry. He turned the brim of his hat in his hands and looked around as though he'd never stood there before. Fanny faced him, her hands clasped in front and her head cocked to the side.

"Did you . . . walk?" Fanny asked, a laugh in her voice.

"I did." In two long strides he stood before her, close enough to raise his hand, tentatively at first, and touch her cheek. She swallowed at his touch while he relished the warmth spreading through his body. To be so near to her. To touch her soft skin and hear her gentle breath. "I could not contain the energy I felt upon receipt of your letter."

"I'm sorry it took me so long to respond to yours." She sounded nervous. "I wanted to be sure. I needed to be certain."

He held her eyes. "And you are certain now?"

She raised her own hand, pressing it against his hand cradling her face. She smiled and tears rose in her eyes. "To think you knew all along," she whispered. "And never turned away from me."

"I tried," he said, thinking of Germany and how certain he'd been that he was through pining for her. "My heart would not allow it."

"Bless your beautiful heart," she whispered. "Can it ever forgive me, Henry, for taking so long to recognize my own?"

Sweeter words had never sounded in his ears, and Henry could not resist the desire to seal such sentiment with the sweetness of a kiss. He lowered his face, and she stepped close enough that every one of his senses was filled with her. He wrapped his arms around her waist and pulled her close. Her cheeks colored, but not once did she look away from him. She clasped her hands behind his neck and touched the hair at the base of his neck. He lowered his face to hers.

Henry had imagined Fanny's kiss a thousand times, and yet the moment their lips met, he realized he could never have adequately imagined *this.* He had known, almost from when they first met, that his life would have no meaning without Fanny in it. She had healed him and haunted him and nearly driven him mad, and yet now she was in his arms, returning every beat of his heart with her own until he could scarcely believe there had ever been less than this wholeness between them.

She pulled back, a bit breathless, and looked at him with an expression of surprised satisfaction. "I thank God you did not give up on me."

The husky quality of her voice nearly undid him while the future—something that so often was heavy and guarded—began to blossom, unfurling possibilities and grandeur he could scarcely comprehend. "Some part of me must have known that holding you in my arms would feel exactly like this."

Their lips met again, at first with tenderness, then passion, and then promise.

The Past and Present here unite
Beneath Time's flowing tide,
Like footprints hidden by a brook,
But seen on either side.

—Henry Wadsworth Longfellow,
"A Gleam of Sunshine"

Chapter Notes

Henry and Fanny had six children—Charles, Ernest, Fanny, Alice, Edith, and Anne—though Little Fanny (their third child and first daughter) died at sixteen months of age from an unknown illness. Fanny herself made medical history when she gave birth to Edith while unconscious due to the use of ether after Henry had found a dentist willing to help her avoid the pain of childbirth. It had always distressed him how difficult childbirth was for women. Longfellow's posterity continued to live in "Craigie Castle" until 1950. In 1972, the Longfellow house became a national park.

In 1861, Fanny died following a tragic accident when her dress—a Victorian hoopskirt design—caught fire and could not be extinguished before she sustained fatal injuries. Henry attempted to put out the flames and was left with facial scars that became the reason he wore a beard for the rest of his life. Fanny succumbed to her injuries and was buried in the Mount Auburn cemetery on the couple's eighteenth wedding anniversary. Henry was not present as he was still recovering from his own injuries.

In a letter to Fanny's sister written a month following Fanny's death, Henry wrote: "I never looked at her without a thrill of pleasure;—she never came into a room where I was without my heart beating quicker, nor went out without my feeling that something of the light went with her." One could say that when she died, much of the light in Henry's life went with her as well.

Henry remained unmarried and became increasingly solitary for the rest of his life. Although he continued to write, and, in his later years, undertook the auspicious translation of Dante's *Divine Comedy*, he was never quite the same after Fanny's death. He was cared for by his daughter Alice and lived in Craigie House until his death in 1882 at the age of seventy-five. He passed away in the same bed where Fanny had died more than two decades earlier.

While it is impossible to separate the tragedy from the love story, the love Henry and Fanny shared, with each other and their children, was profound and moving. Through exploring their lives and the abiding love they shared, I can imagine that, if given the choice of eighteen years of love with a tragic end, or nothing at all, both Fanny and Henry would have chosen the years they had together. They truly brought out the best in one another, and they loved one another fully to the end of their days.

I tried to keep to the facts as much as possible in telling this story, but there were a lot of blanks in need of filling and motivations in need of understanding that necessitated some fictional license on my part. The following notes break down what I knew to be true and what I admit to being fictional.

Chapter One

A European Grand Tour was a popular journey through several European countries that, in the 1830s, was a new adventure for families—especially American families—to embark upon. Before then, it had been something that young men used as a tool of education, as Henry had done a decade earlier.

The Appletons left for their tour rather spontaneously, three weeks after Charlie's death and a year and a half after Fanny's mother, Theresa Maria Gold Appleton, had died. The assumption is that Nathan was overcome with grief at the loss of his son, who he believed would take over his business interests, and felt he had to get out of Boston and distract himself from all the loss that had happened in such a short time. Both Maria Gold and Charles died of consumption, also known as tuberculosis, which would not have a cure for another hundred years.

For the Appletons to have taken such a trip is evidence of the family's wealth, and they spared no expense. Halfway through the Appletons' Grand Tour, Henry Longfellow's own tour intersected theirs. Longfellow was seeking respite from a long, dark winter spent in Germany following the death of his first wife, Mary Potter. In June or July 20, 1836 (there are varying accounts, but I chose July for the sake of the story), Fanny recorded that Henry Wadsworth Longfellow had left a card for them in Thun. She expected a "veritable gentleman" and hoped he would not call on them, though she did record that she liked *Outré-Mer,* which had been published a few years earlier. Henry was traveling the other direction through Thun, toward Berne, and did not meet up with the family at this time.

It was not uncommon for people on tour to meet others from their own country or city, as a Grand Tour was all the rage among the upper classes in the 1830s. As Henry did not yet live in Cambridge, nor was of the same social class, the Appletons would not have known him beyond his writing.

Mary Appleton, Fanny's older sister by almost four years, is most commonly referred to as "Mary" in the resources I studied, however I found reference that the family's nickname for her was Molly, just as Frances was called Fanny. In an attempt to avoid confusion between Mary Appleton and Mary Potter Longfellow—Longfellow's first wife—as well as the smattering of other *Mary*s that appear in the book, I chose to reference her as Molly throughout the work, even from those people outside of her family who would likely not have addressed her so informally.

William Sullivan Appleton was the son of Nathan Appleton's cousin, William Appleton, making him a second cousin to Tom, Molly, and Fanny. "Willie" was very close to the family and invited on the tour even though he was known to have a sickly constitution. He had enjoyed the trip until he became ill in Italy, thus prompting the family to seek out the mountain airs of Switzerland in hopes it would revive his health. That he would have anticipated the turn of his illness enough to make arrangements for an early return from the start is of my own creation.

Nearly a year before meeting the Appleton family in Interlaken, another Appleton, John James Appleton, had assisted one of Mary Potter Longfellow's traveling companions, Mary Goddard, to return to Portland after her father had died unexpectedly. I used that connection as an excuse for Henry to have sought out the Appleton family, though I am unsure it was the case and do not know for certain if or how John James was related to Nathan Appleton.

The facts regarding Mary Potter's death are consistent with what I learned in my research, and though I found it surprising that Henry and Clara Crowninshield would continue the tour following Mary's death, I came to understand that such tours—especially for Americans—were a trip of a lifetime. Deposits were made in advance and a great deal of work went into making the arrangements. To leave early would lose the investment of both time and money. It was not unusual for those parties who experienced a death to continue forward as Henry did.

It was also reasonable for him to fear that he would not receive the position at Harvard if he did not have recent European credential, as faculty was often based on family connection, and Henry's was not equal to that of Harvard's expectations. Without the education of his trip to Europe, he had little recommendation.

In his journals following Mary's death, Henry wrote of experiencing a heavy depression. He wrote, "What a solitary, lonely being I am. Why do I travel? Every hour my heart aches with sadness."

Henry met up with the Appleton party in Interlaken on July 31, 1836. Fanny recorded in her journal that he was not an old man after all, unless perhaps he was the poet's son.

Outré Mer was first published anonymously in America in 1833. It was common at that time for unknown authors to leave their name off their works until and unless those works became popular, but the identity was often known through whisperings and speculation. The British publication took place after Henry had left for Europe, and he saw the first copies in London. An American editor working in Denmark criticized the book when Henry asked after it during a meeting, not realizing Henry was the author.

Chapters Three through Five

After meeting the Appleton family, Henry traveled with them for some time, another common aspect of the Grand Tour. He certainly spent time with Fanny, but he was especially attentive to William, and the friendship he established with Tom Appleton would last throughout his life. Though he did not specifically comment on it at the time, in later years he said that he first fell in love with Fanny during this time they spent together. For Fanny's part, she found much to admire in Henry but did not identify her feelings as love for another six years.

Chapter Six

Henry was progressive in his thoughts on equality and education but not particularly outspoken this early in his life. I combined several of his sentiments shared throughout his life to create the conversation he and Fanny have regarding his thoughts on education as a whole but, specifically, the education of women. I found no indication that Fanny would have been surprised by his feelings, but I chose for her to be so as to show how Henry's opinions differed from the prevailing belief of the time. Henry was always very complimentary toward Fanny's intellect; he often said it was what first attracted him to her.

Henry was quite frustrated throughout his career as a professor by the approach to teaching as a whole but especially to teaching foreign languages. Greater emphasis was put on classic languages rather than learning another modern language, which Henry saw as a portal to enlightenment and cultural education. The sentiments expressed here are based on commentary made throughout his life on the topic and condensed for emphasis.

By this time in his life Henry had documented his feelings against slavery but had not made them public. The topic would eventually rise up in his writing. Nathan Appleton had championed rights for Native Americans and slaves during his time in Congress, but he was not necessarily opposed to slavery, only the poor treatment of slaves. It seems logical that his reasons for not standing against the institution was due to the fact that his industry—textiles—was dependent on the southern plantations, but I did not uncover his specific thoughts.

In time, Henry would use his writing as a platform to share his views against slavery, and there were indications that Fanny agreed with him at the time those works were published. At the time of this fictionalized discussion (1836), the Slavery Abolition Act of 1833 had ended the practice of slavery in England and British Colonies. America was resistant to the change but less than thirty years away from their own Civil War.

Chapter Seven

Henry remained in the Appletons' company for approximately three weeks and regretted having to part ways with the family in Schaffhausen. However, he had received a note from Clara Crowninshield expressing her eagerness to return to America. On Henry's final day with the Appletons, he read Derby's sermons to William as a parting gift. Henry left for Heidelberg—where Clara had remained during his trip to Switzerland—only a week before William succumbed to tuberculosis. William was buried in Schaffhausen; I am guessing they chose that city for its Protestant roots, though the Appletons had transitioned into the Unitarian religion by the 1800s.

Fanny records that she missed Henry after he was gone, so her feelings for him were at the very least friendly if not a bit warm. We also know there was a great deal of literary discussion and translation taking place between them.

There is no evidence that Henry planned to journey to Germany with the Appletons as a guide, though I used it to contrast their different circumstances and to plant the seeds of one of Fanny's reasons for resisting his attentions.

Chapters Eight and Nine

Fanny recorded in her journal that, while in the salon of the Strasburg hotel, she saw Henry walking down the street with three women who she would later learn were Miss Crowninshield and Mrs. Bryant and her daughter. There is no record that anyone other than Fanny saw him from the window. Miss Bryant would have been very young, perhaps only twelve or thirteen. Her being old enough to spark Fanny's envy was mistakenly included in one of the resources I read, but I decided to include it as it helped explain why Fanny would become so cold toward Henry. The day after she saw him on the street, Henry and his companions had breakfast with the Appletons at their hotel. In her journal, Fanny simply said, "They leave."

In Heidelberg, Henry became acquainted with the family of William Cullen Bryant, poet and editor of the *New York Post.* Their friendship continued until Bryant's death in 1878, just four years before Henry's death.

Chapter Ten

The Appleton family were members of the Federal Street Church during the years that William Channing served as minister, making it one of the first Unitarian churches in the country. Religion was an important part of the Appleton family, and Fanny's journal reflected very deeply thought-out religious ideas and spiritual experiences throughout her life.

For reasons not well understood, the Appleton children referred to their Uncle Sam and Uncle William's wives as Aunt Sam and Aunt William. They were very close to their extended family, and Aunt Sam did indeed play an important part in the girls' lives, especially after their mother died.

Other than an offhand mention of "Many suitors," I found little about Fanny's or Molly's interactions with other men. There is also little explanation of why Fanny resisted Henry's attentions, though I feel the motivations I created for Fanny are in keeping with their situation. It is interesting to me that two such eligible young women were not married by the ages of twenty-four and twenty, respectively, but their reasons presented here are my own conjecture. John Peterton is a fictional character.

Emmeline Austin, Susan Benjamin, and Robert Apthorp were all people with whom Fanny corresponded regularly while in Europe, as well as other times in her life. Letters to and from them make up a fair amount of the correspondence that allowed biographers to piece together her life and attitudes. I have attempted to stay true to the reflections of their characters and connections to Fanny made through their correspondence.

Chapter Eleven

Henry was actually the one to call on the Appletons on Beacon Street after the family returned from Europe in 1837, but because of the vagueness of the records regarding what transpired between Henry and Fanny at that time, I restructured some of the details to create a more natural transition.

Henry and Tom certainly renewed their friendship after the Appletons return, and since that friendship served as a connection between Henry and Fanny for several years, it did not seem to be much of a stretch to include it in the novel. From all accounts, Tom was an easygoing, jovial man, quick to laugh, and who enjoyed the finer things in life. There is some ambiguity regarding his sexuality, but whatever the reason, he never married, and he spent most of his life traveling the world and indulging in the best company, food, wine, art, and culture. He would become known as a "Great Wit" and respected on both sides of the Atlantic. Tom and Henry were good friends throughout their lives, and Tom helped Henry with his children after Fanny's death.

Henry came to lodge at Craigie House—which he called Craigie Castle—following the 1836–37 term at Harvard. The history included is the actual history of the house, including the fact that Henry's rooms were the very rooms George Washington had used when he stayed there during the Siege of Boston—or so he was told. Perhaps Mrs. Craigie told all her lodgers the same.

Nathan Appleton later purchased Craigie House as a wedding gift for Henry and Fanny, along with the ten acres between Brattle Street and the Charles River so that no one would ever build something that would block their view of the river. Craigie House is now a historical park and museum for both the Washington and Longfellow connections.

The preservation of the Longfellow house is remarkable; nearly all the furniture and artifacts in the museum belonged to the Longfellow family and have been kept just as they were when the Longfellows lived there. Henry and Fanny also worked to preserve the history of General Washington's time in the house and purchased several pictures and mementos in keeping with that time period.

Chapter Twelve

The Appleton girls did study French when they were young, and they were reacquainted with Mr. Longfellow after their return to Boston, but that the Appleton women would have continued to learn French or that they would have presented it to Henry is conjecture.

Henry did visit with Fanny under the mistaken idea that she wanted to learn German—something he had written to her about while she was still in Europe—but we do not know the context of the offer on his part or the acceptance on hers. Fanny's journals, though quite prolific during certain times of her life, were rather sparse during this time.

Chapter Fifteen

Jared Sparks and Sarah Lowell were both tenants of Craigie House during the time that Henry lodged there, but they were probably not all tenants simultaneously, and I do not know for sure who lived in Craigie House with Henry in 1837. Sarah Lowell was the aunt of James Russell Lowell, who was a student of Henry's and who went on to become a member of the Dante Club and a great poet himself.

Sparks did not actually become the McLean professor until 1839.

Chapter Seventeen

In 1837, Fanny rejected Henry's first marriage proposal a few months after her family's return from Europe. It is not clear why she rejected him or how exactly he had pursued her other than his determination to teach her German. In December of that year, he wrote a letter to Molly expressing his brokenhearted regret, reflecting the close ties he shared with the entire Appleton family.

Chapter Eighteen

While Henry had a great many male friends, he also seemed to feel comfortable with women of his mother's—and Aunt Lucia's—generation. He often dined with Sarah Lowell or Mrs. Craigie. There is no indication that Sarah Lowell, or any one person or circumstance, served to motivate Henry toward writing and publishing again, but we do know that after *Outré Mer* he did not publish another book until 1839. We also know that he did not abandon his feelings for Fanny following his proposal, though her rejection was painful for him.

Chapter Nineteen

On January 9, 1839, Nathan Appleton married Harriett Coffin Sumner. We do not know the details of the wedding or Fanny's feelings toward it. In letters she expressed her discomfort with the age difference between Harriett and her father when they were courting; Harriet was twenty-two years younger than Nathan, and merely ten years older than Tom. Following the wedding, Fanny and Molly traveled together a great deal—perhaps to avoid being underfoot at Beacon Street. Nathan and Harriet went on to have three children together.

In 1841, Fanny wrote in her journal that she was becoming quite good at faking her enjoyment in life, indicating that she may have experienced her own bouts of depression.

Chapter Twenty

One constant in Henry's life was his close friends. He always seemed to be surrounded by good and supportive men and women who surely helped him through the dark times he experienced. Around the time that *Hyperion* was published, these particular five men were so often in each other's company they became known as the "Five of Clubs" around Boston and Cambridge. Cornelius Conway Felton would eventually become president of Harvard College. Charles Sumner would rise in the political ranks throughout his life. All of them remained good friends throughout their lives.

That the five of them would travel with Henry to pick up the first copies of *Hyperion* after it was published in New York is an aspect of my own imagination.

Chapter Twenty-One

What motivated Henry to send a Swiss cheese along with a copy of *Hyperion* to the Appleton family is unknown—but after meeting

Jewett in New York, that's exactly what he did. Fanny's response to the gift Jewett brought to Beacon Street was put in ink in a letter she sent to Emmeline Austin not long afterward where she expressed in razor sharp words what she thought of both Henry and the book, marking perhaps her very lowest regard for the man who was still in love with her. In regard to the book, she said it was "a thing of shreds and patches like the author's mind!"

Chapter Twenty-Two

Theresa Maria Gold Appleton had been raised in the Pittsville area of western Massachusetts, and Fanny and Molly often spent summers and holidays with their mother's family. In 1839, they were allowed to rent their own set of rooms and their own carriage for the first time, and they spent the next few months living more independently then they ever had before. They had many friends, in addition to their family, with whom they visited and explored the area.

That their visit to Massachusetts followed Fanny's discovery of herself within the pages of *Hyperion* and would have been a type of escape from the whispers is my own conjecture. That said, both her reflection in Mary Ashworth and her reaction to it was well-known following the book's publication. She would become rather infamous for it in years to come. It seems reasonable that even if the visit to Lenox was not because she was running from the unwelcome notoriety, the distance from Boston at that time certainly could have been a welcome relief.

Chapters Twenty-Three and Twenty-Four

Hyperion was Henry's second prose novel, and his first romance. All the details included in these chapters are true regarding its reception, the financial problems of the publisher, the accusations regarding

Mary Ashworth being a caricature of Fanny, and Fanny's irritation at the infamy that followed.

What is ambiguous is whether or not Longfellow meant to mimic Fanny in the work. Some accounts say he was surprised so many people made a connection between Mary and Fanny, while other accounts said he had written it as a kind of purging.

Regardless, after learning of Fanny's reaction, he seemed to accept that his love would forever be unrequited. However, he did not "fall out of love" with her despite the further distance the book created between them and instead claimed to have accepted that he would always live as though "maimed" not to have her love returned to him.

On December 26, 1839, Mary Appleton married Robert James Mackintosh at 39 Beacon Street. The ceremony was simple and the wedding party small, probably due to Harriet being eight month's pregnant. The ceremony was followed by a luncheon before the bride and groom left for their honeymoon.

The sentiments shared by Fanny in this chapter are reflective of her journal entries and letters written about the event. She was very happy for Molly, and would travel to Washington D.C. with her and Robert for a few months before they left for England, but she would always miss the connection the sisters had shared before Molly's marriage.

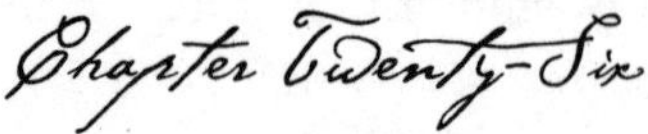

Ronald Mackintosh was very nearly a honeymoon baby and was born on his mother's twenty-seventh birthday, October 18, 1840. Fanny learned of her "Cockney Nephew's" birth a few weeks after it occurred.

Fanny's journals show increased study and reading during 1840, including her enjoyment of two lectures given by Richard Henry Dana Sr. that fall, which I assume would have been part of the lecture circuit Henry had been instrumental in developing. She likely did not attend the lecture with Jewett as her thoughts in this chapter were written in a letter to him. Henry's introduction of Mr. Dana is fictional.

Fanny had always been interested in literature, but it was at this time that she seemed to truly take on the cloak of a critic and expanded her reading to new places. Henry did not necessarily recommend she read Macaulay's lecture, but they did discuss Milton during their time in Europe and she did enjoy the essay first published in the Edinburgh Review that she had read during the summer of 1840.

Incidentally, Henry and Fanny's daughter Edith would eventually marry the grandson of Mr. Dana, Richard Henry Dana III, in 1878. Their son would be the last Longfellow to live in Craigie Castle prior to the house and its contents being donated to the National Park Service in 1972.

Chapter Twenty-Seven

Ronald Mackintosh's delivery was a difficult one, but the effects were not well understood until Tom and Fanny went to England. Though what Molly's diagnosis would be today is unknown, she had specific problems with her hips and, likely, an opium addiction as a result of trying to manage the pain. The effects of opiates were not well understood at that time.

That there would have been such a formal "counsel" between Fanny, Tom, and Robert as shown here is unknown, but we do know that Fanny and Tom were attentive to Molly's needs while still seeing the sights of England.

Tom and Fanny would have arrived in Liverpool and likely made their own way to London rather than being picked up by Robert.

Chapter Twenty-Eight

Mrs. Craigie's failing eyesight is a fictional detail, but Henry did sit with her as she became ill, and she enjoyed his work and his company during the years of their friendship. Upon the death of Elizabeth Craigie, John Worcester, the other boarder at Craigie House at the time, leased the property from the Craigie heirs and lived in his half with his new wife.

I'm unsure what legal agreements might have been entered into between Henry, Worchester, and Mrs. Craigie, but after Henry's marriage to Fanny, Nathan Appleton was able to purchase the house. Worcester and his wife continued to live there until the home they were having built was finished, at which time the Longfellows became the sole occupants of Craigie House, determined to preserve its legacy.

That Mrs. Craigie once told Henry that she feared seeing an old woman in bed would deter him from marriage seems a reflection of the level of friendship the two of them shared. The story of the canker worms is often shared to illustrate Mrs. Craigie's eccentric nature that increased as she aged.

Chapters Thirty and Thirty-One

Henry did not bring Fanny a cheese or a copy of *Ballads and Other Poems,* though she had read it by the time the New Year came along. The thoughts shared in this chapter by Emmeline are actually Fanny's thoughts from her letter regarding *Voices of Night,* which had been published in 1839, a few months after *Hyperion.*

I do not know where Fanny's heart was when Henry came to visit, but she recorded in her journal that it was a "heavy visit." I had the visit take place with only the two of them in order to give Henry and Fanny an exclusive conversation.

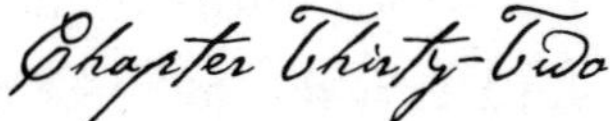

The relationship between Harriet and Fanny is not well communicated in letters and journals. Whether that was because it was unremarkable or because Fanny was attempting to be polite we do not know. We also don't know what type of mother Harriet was, but Fanny did love her half siblings, and when she became a mother, she was very involved in the daily lives of her own children. I would imagine that seeing Harriet—a woman not much older than Fanny—would have been a powerful example to Fanny, which I chose to reflect. However, it is speculation based on little more than impressions and hopes.

The Water Cure was based on the idea that impurities in the body could be "broken" with an induced "fever" and minimalistic approach to diet and activity. Henry arrived at the convent, which had been turned into a medical spa of sorts, in late May and resided there for four months, taking multiple baths in the waters every day, eating a very bland diet, and getting plenty of rest and relaxation.

Henry did not have a face-to-face meeting with Sumner before he left for Europe; instead, Sumner sent him a letter that expressed the depth of their friendship, which I tried to reflect here. Sumner struggled socially and may have had what we would call Asperger's as he functioned on a highly logical plain.

In their later years, after Sumner had risen in the ranks of the Republican party, a famous portrait was done of the two of them titled *The Politician and the Poet.* It shows the striking contrast between the two men even in their appearance: Sumner was big and broad and imposing, while Henry looked like . . . a poet.

They remained close friends until Sumner's death in 1874, an event that was difficult for Henry due to how close the men had been.

Chapter Thirty-Four

Though there may not have been medical merit to the Water Cure, it did seem to be effective for Henry, restoring his health and equilibrium of mind. He returned to Cambridge in the fall of 1842 believing that he had finally overcome the hold Fanny had on him as well as accepting that he was not just a writer but a poet. He was also able to deepen his friendship with Charles Dickens while in London, and he made a dear friend in Ferdinand Freiligrath, who had great influence on the works that followed. He was inspired at this time to write the sonnet "Mezzo Cammin," included in this chapter, but which Henry considered too personal to publish in his lifetime.

On the sea voyage back to Boston, he wrote his first antislavery poems, a daring prospect at the time and one that began to shape his future in numerous ways. It was published as a thin volume entitled *Poems on Slavery* in December of that year.

All in all, the Water Cure seemed to be a turning point for Henry, and he left his darkest days behind him, though he would never be completely free of his depressive episodes.

Chapter Thirty-Five

The scene of Fanny recreating "The Bridge" is fictional; there is no indication that particular poem had any special meaning to her. That she spent the year of 1842 rereading Henry's works and changing her heart is also of my creation.

We do know from her journals that 1842 was a year of spiritual awakening, and she seemed to mature a great deal. She was lonely without her siblings and friends around her, and she continued to read and study a great deal, which likely led her to a softened heart—especially in regard to Henry.

Chapters Thirty-Six and Thirty-Seven

On April 10, 1843, Henry and Fanny attended a party at the home of a mutual friend, Andrew Norton. We do not know the details of their interaction at this event other than Fanny was more attentive to Henry than she had been in the past, and Henry felt encouraged to renew his attentions toward her, which he did.

Chapter Thirty-Eight

On May 10, Fanny wrote a letter to Henry, in response to one of his own, where she confirmed her love for him and essentially accepted his proposal. Henry was so energized by her pronouncement that he walked from his house on Brattle Street in Cambridge to Beacon Hill—approximately a ninety-minute walk. His path led him over the West Boston Bridge, featured in his poem "The Bridge." It was rebuilt in 1906 and renamed "The Longfellow Bridge" in 1927, in commemoration of Henry's walk to Fanny Appleton.

For the rest of his life, Henry would reverence May 10 as his "Personal Easter"—a day in which redemption came in the form of the woman he loved giving him her heart. Finally.

Timeline

July 1836: Henry meets the Appleton family in Thun, Switzerland, and spends nearly three weeks with them.

Fall 1837: Henry begins his attempts to court Fanny, proposes marriage, and is refused.

January 1839: Mr. Appleton marries Harriet Coffin Sumner, a woman twenty-two years his junior.

Summer 1839: *Hyperion* is published.

December 1839: *Voices of Night* is published. Molly marries Robert Mackintosh on December 26.

1841: *Ballads and Other Poems* is published.

April–September 1842: Henry takes his third European tour, including the Water Cure in Germany.

December 1842: *Poems on Slavery* is published.

April 1843: Henry attends the Nortons' party and is received more warmly by Fanny.

May 10, 1843: Fanny sends Henry her letter requesting that he formally renew his attentions to her. Henry walks from Cambridge to accept the offer.

May 1843: *The Spanish Student* is published.

July 13, 1843: Henry and Fanny marry in the drawing room of 39 Beacon Street.

Fall/Winter 1843: Nathan Appleton purchases Craigie House and the acreage between it and the Charles River as a wedding present for Henry and Fanny.

June 9, 1844: Charles Appleton is born. *Poets and Poetry of England* is published.

1845: Ernest Wadsworth is born. *The Belfry of Brugs and Other Poems* is published. *Poems* is published.

1846: *The Waif* is published. *The Estray* is published.

1847: Frances is born. *Evangeline: A Tale of Acadie* is published.

1848: Frances dies.

1849: *The Seaside and the Fireside* is published.

1850: Alice Mary is born.

1851: *Kavanagh* is published. *The Golden Legend* is published.

1853: Edith is born with the help of ether for sedation.

1854: Henry retires from Harvard College, becomes America's first professional poet.

1855: Anne Allegra is born. *The Song of Hiawatha* is published.

1858: *The Courtship of Miles Standish and Other Poems* is published.

1860: *Paul Revere's Ride* is published in *The Atlantic* magazine.

July 9, 1861: Fanny's dress catches fire. She dies the next day as a result of her injuries.

July 13, 1861: Fanny is buried on the couple's eighteenth wedding anniversary.

July 14, 1861: Nathan Appleton, who was too ill to attend Fanny's funeral, dies at his home on Beacon Hill.

1863: Part one of *Tales of a Wayside Inn* is published. Henry writes "Christmas Bells" on Christmas Day.

1865: "The Dante Club" is formally organized to assist in Longfellow's ongoing translation of Dante's *Divine Comedy. Household Poems* is published. "Christmas Bells" is published in *Our Young Folks* magazine.

1866: *Poetical Works* is published.

1867: English translation of Dante's *Divine Comedy* is published, entitled *The Divine Comedy of Dante Alighieri.*

1868: *The New England Tragedies* is published. Henry takes his children, daughter-in-law, Tom Appleton, two of Henry's sisters, and former governess on an European tour.

1870: Part two of *Tales of a Wayside Inn* is published.

1871: *The Divine Tragedy* is published.

1872: *Three Books of Song* is published. John Baptiste Calkin first puts "Christmas Bells" to music, beginning the legacy of the now-popular Christmas carol "I Heard the Bells on Christmas Day."

1873: *Aftermath* is published. *The Complete Poetical Works of Henry Wadsworth Longfellow* is published.

1874: "The Hanging of the Crane" is sold to a New York magazine for $4,000, the highest amount ever paid for any poem to date.

1875: *The Masque of Pandora and Other Poems* is published.

1876: *Poems of Places* is published.

1878: *Keramos and Other Poems* is published.

1880: *Ultima Thule* is published.

1879: Henry writes *The Cross of Snow* in tribute to Fanny. It is not published until after his death.

1882: *In the Harbor* is published.

March 24, 1882: Henry dies at Craigie House in the same room and in the same bed where Fanny had died twenty-one years earlier.

March 26, 1882: Henry is buried at Mount Auburn cemetery alongside his two wives and his daughter, Fanny.

1883: *Michael Angelo: A Fragment* is published.

Bibliography

Calhoun, Charles C. *Longfellow.* Boston Massachusetts: Beacon Press, 2004.

Irmscher, Christoph. *Public Poet, Private Man; Henry Wadsworth Longfellow at 200.* Boston Massachusetts: University of Massachusetts Press in Cooperation with the Houghton Library, Harvard University, 2009.

Tharp, Louise Hall. *The Appletons of Beacon Hill.* Little Brown and Company—Boston-Toronto, 1973.

Wagenknecht, Edward, editor. *Mrs. Longfellow: Selected Letters and Journals of Fanny Appleton Longfellow 1817–1861.* London, England: Peter Owen Limited, 1959.

Discussion Questions

1. Prior to reading this book, were you familiar with Henry Wadsworth Longfellow, his poetry, or his courtship of Fanny Appleton? If so, were there things about their story that surprised you? If not, what elements of their story touched you the most?
2. Have you ever traveled to Boston or Cambridge? What are your impressions of those two locations? If you could travel to any European country, which one would it be and why?
3. How do you feel about Henry having sent the body of his first wife, Mary Potter, back to Boston unattended after her death? Should he have ended his Grand Tour early to tend to his family?
4. In America, many colleges and universities require two years of foreign language training. How does that factor into Henry's feelings regarding the teaching of language? Do you feel that learning another language is worthwhile? Do you speak a foreign language?
5. Do you enjoy poetry? What is your favorite poem or poet? Do you feel that poetry—as opposed to prose—is more successful in touching our hearts and minds?

6. Fanny undergoes a substantial change of heart regarding her feelings for Henry. Have you experienced or seen a similar change in modern relationships? What, in your opinion, might change someone's mind regarding how they feel about a person?
7. Henry and Fanny's seven-year courtship is certainly unusual by today's standards, where the average courtship lasts between two to three years. The Longfellows went on to have six children and enjoyed nearly twenty years of a very happy marriage. Do you think that a longer courtship can result in a happier union?
8. Fanny embarks upon a spiritual journey to find God's path for her. Have you had a time in your life when you have undertaken a similar pursuit? What motivated you to do so, and what was the result?
9. Was there a particular scene or sentiment expressed in this book that stood out to you? Why?
10. At the time this story takes place, men tended to form very deep friendships that in today's culture might almost seem romantic. Henry maintained many of these close friendships throughout his life. What do you think has changed in our culture regarding male friendship? Or has it?

Acknowledgments

In December 2014, Heidi Taylor and Lisa Mangum from Shadow Mountain asked if I would be willing to write a different kind of love story. They wanted a historical romance novel based on a real person—preferably a literary figure. It was an exciting prospect for me, and we talked about their expectations. I told them that my biggest concern was that I'm not a "literary" writer. I have read exactly one Jane Austen novel—though I watch the movies over and over—and I relied on CliffsNotes to get through my high school English classes. I doubted I could answer the $200 question in a "Literature" category on *Jeopardy*. Still, they were sure I was the right choice.

I spent weeks trying to find a person who was well-known and had a beautiful love story. It was a much harder prospect than I expected it would be, but then I discovered the amazing seven-year courtship story of Henry Longfellow and Fanny Appleton. The research was intimidating and trying to recreate these people authentically was overwhelming at times. Two things proved very helpful. First, I was able to visit Boston and Cambridge with my daughter, Madison, and my good friend Jennifer Moore—the trip made a huge difference. Second,

Henry was mindful of his legacy while he was alive and preserved a lot of information. By the end of this project I was absolutely in love with Henry and Fanny, and I am humbled to have had this chance to try to bring them to life.

Thank you to Heidi and Lisa, who gave me this invitation and then made the final version prettier than I could ever do on my own. Big thanks to Jennifer and Madison for traveling with me to Boston and letting me geek out over the history there. Jennifer also read through the finished manuscript on a very short timeline.

Thank you to my writing group: Nancy Allen (*My Fair Gentleman,* Shadow Mountain 2016), Becky Clayson, Jody Durfee (*Hadley Hadley Bensen,* Covenant 2013), and Ronda Hinrichsen (*Simply Anna,* Covenant 2015).

Big thanks for the readers who have followed me into a new genre—historical romance—and who have been so kind and encouraging.

This book also marked a change in our family dynamics: my husband, Lee, moved his office home so that I could write nearly full-time while he took on more responsibility at the home front. I don't know how I could have written this without being able to immerse myself into the project. I thank him with every breath in me for all the support and sacrifice he gives me. Thanks to my kids for their continued support as well, and for my Heavenly Father, who has put so many opportunities in my path.

About the Author

Josi is the author of twenty-five novels, one cookbook, and a participant in several co-authored projects and anthologies. She is a two-time Whitney award winner—*Sheep's Clothing* (2007) and *Wedding Cake* (2014)—and the Utah Best in State winner for fiction in 2012. She and her husband, Lee, are the parents of four children. You can find more information about Josi and her writing at josiskilpack.com.